SANCTUARY

Garry Disher has published over fifty titles across multiple genres. With a growing international reputation for his best-selling crime novels, he has won four German and three Australian awards for best crime novel of the year, and been longlisted twice for a British CWA Dagger award. In 2018 he received the Ned Kelly Lifetime Achievement Award.

garrydisher.com

SANCTUARY

GARRY DISHER

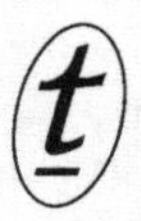

TEXT PUBLISHING MELBOURNE AUSTRALIA

The Text Publishing Company acknowledges the Traditional Owners of the country on which we work, the Wurundjeri people of the Kulin Nation, and pays respect to their Elders past and present.

textpublishing.com.au

The Text Publishing Company
Wurundjeri Country, Level 6, Royal Bank Chambers, 287 Collins Street,
Melbourne Victoria 3000, Australia

Published by The Text Publishing Company, 2024

Cover and page design by Text
Cover photo by W. H. Chong
Typeset in Garamond 13.25/18.25 by J&M Typesetting

Printed and bound in Australia by Griffin Press, a member of the Opus Group. The Opus Group is ISO/NZS 14001:2004 Environmental Management System certified.

ISBN: 9781922790620 (paperback)
ISBN: 9781922791696 (ebook)

A catalogue record for this book is available from the National Library of Australia

The paper this book is printed on is certified against the Forest Stewardship Council® Standards. Griffin Press – a member of the Opus Group holds chain of custody certification SCS-COC-001185. FSC® promotes environmentally responsible, socially beneficial and economically viable management of the world's forests.

for Barry Reynolds

1

IT'S A TUESDAY evening and you're watching *Caught Out* on YouTube. If not *Caught Out*, maybe *Born to Kill?* or *Killer Couples*, one of those. A murder that shocks a small town, the victim usually a young woman offed by her husband or boyfriend, although they like to drag out the reveal. But you know it's a close male connection because he's the only one they don't interview: he's locked up. Meanwhile, you get plenty of screen time with the mouth-breathing parents, rednecks who look too stupid to have had a child in the first place, the victim's shock-and-awe girlfriends, all lip fillers and smoky eye, and fat cops faking tears and gasping 'Sorry!' as if thirty years hadn't passed since they'd worked the case. Not much in the way of IQ or planning in these shows. Still, you're kind of hooked.

Hooked on the CSI-type shows, too. Finding a suspect's car in CCTV footage. Spraying luminol to show blood-spray patterns. Connecting a gun to a crime from firing-pin impressions and bullet lands and grooves, hair testing for poisons, cell-tower pinging used to trace a phone.

And the cock-ups. Some guy jailed for arson because an expert mis-read the charring patterns in a house fire, another for rape because the lab tech spent the whole day testing samples from other cases without changing her gloves. Cases that fell over when it came out that the forensics hero had lied about his qualifications for twenty years.

Caught Out specialises in CCTV. Solving murders where people's movements—victims, suspects, perpetrators—hold the key. It's a Canadian show that sometimes looks at cases from other countries. Tonight's is Australian, so you're maybe a little more interested than usual.

July 2022: a man walking his dog—what else?—stumbles upon the body of a young blonde in bushland near Tailem Bend, southeast of Adelaide. Alisha Kennedy, reported missing four days earlier. Raped and strangled, her car abandoned in a sports-centre carpark. And here's footage of the car: as the narrator points out, there are cameras everywhere these days. ATMs, dashcams, traffic lights, above shop windows, bristling on the corners of buildings, aimed down at cash registers and along department-store aisles.

It's easy to multitask when you're watching a show like *Caught Out*. Emails, Facebook, eBay, the dark web—see if anyone's bid on your lock of the Sydney granny killer's hair. Even sew on a button. Tonight you're polishing your netsuke pieces: a boxwood rabbit, a cherrywood lunar hare and an ivory wild boar. All authenticated, genuine Edo period, and valued by Christies at $250,000.

You look up. The big TV washes the sitting room with murky colours but the voiceover narrating the standard banal re-enactment is aiming for edgy tension. Not that easy to inject tension into a couple of 'detectives' with bad suits and worse hair looking up at a carpark CCTV camera, then checking out grainy footage on a tiny monitor. It's made on the cheap, this show. Dragged out, too: they could cover everything in ten minutes. You return to the little boar you're buffing with a lens-cleaning cloth.

Here's Alisha on her last day alive, locking her Kia and weaving through a field of parked cars. The time stamp reads 4.38 p.m. Winter. Grey, gloomy, getting dark outside. A cold light drawing in. And here she is again, entering a big hardware barn—a TradeWorks, judging by the logo—and heading straight for the paint section. Tins, brushes, rollers. Talking to a guy mixing paint for another customer. He points to a shelf behind her and she turns.

And here's the killer, lurking at the end of the aisle. An opportunistic killer in this case, a stranger.

As if to reinforce that, the show jumps to Alisha's boyfriend, then her father, her uncle and a handful of old boyfriends, none of them currently doing time. All with alibis, all choking up as they pour on the clichés: 'So much to live for.' 'Just a beautiful soul.'

Now here she is again, reading the label on a paint tin tilted in her hands. And here's her killer, watching from behind a stand of colour charts.

But this is a solved-by-CCTV show, and it's leaning hard on CCTV footage it doesn't have enough of. Let's go back forty-five minutes to Alisha leaving work—a primary school—and driving along a high street. She steers into the TradeWorks carpark again. Locks up and weaves through the cars again. Now a twelve-minute jump forward: the killer's black Dodge Ram pulls in. He hasn't followed her here. He's just randomly prowling at this stage.

See him sidle his way through the parked cars too. A stocky, bearded guy in jeans, a hoodie and a beanie. You couldn't pick him in a line-up, the camera's too far away.

Now he's on another camera as he enters the shop and pauses for a moment. A clearer shot now, and faintly comical because two other young women, potential prey, are just leaving, one passing each side of him. *You can almost see him thinking*, breathes the voiceover. *Have I left it too late?*

Cut to the 'detectives' still peering at the monitor, tracking his every move. Up and down aisles, fingering a shovel, a sander, a wheelbarrow. A counterfeit of casual browsing, except that a couple of times he goes very still. He's spotted a potential victim. *You can almost see his growing excitement.*

But these women are going to be lucky. One is joined by a kid in school uniform, another by her husband or boyfriend. The killer veers away.

Now he's wandered into a broad display space dotted with portable barbecues and outdoor furniture. We see a slender young woman testing a recliner, a deckchair, a garden bench. The killer lurks, one hand feeling the quality of a roll of sailcloth. He's only five metres from her. *With the scent in his nostrils, you can almost feel the cruel heat in him.*

Caught Out has no aversion to the bleeding obvious.

Uh, oh. The slender woman is hailing a male staff member who takes her around the corner to an aisle full of garden equipment. She pushes a hand mower experimentally to and fro. She nods, and the staff member delivers it to the cash register for her. *She doesn't know what a close call she just had.*

And so the beanie-clad killer swerves away again and resumes his prowling. Up one aisle, down another. Out to the gardening section—he hunches his shoulders against the chilly air—then back on the hunt indoors.

That's when he sees Alisha Kennedy in the paint section. *She has less than one hour to live.*

But you don't give a shit about Alisha Kennedy. She's not real. None of them are, these true-crime victims. You have no stake in who they were or what they went through.

Right now, you give a shit about the woman who bought the mower, not knowing how lucky she was. You lean forward with the remote and the boxwood rabbit topples gently from your lap to the carpet of your new apartment. You press rewind.

Watch her testing the garden furniture again. You quiver, a sudden jolt of adrenaline. Tears sting in your eyes.

Found the bitch.

2

SHE'D BEEN CALLING herself Grace for a while now. Too long, probably. She'd be safer using one of the other names, of which she had a few stashed away, culled from death notices and gravestones over the years. But she'd grown into Grace, somehow. It was a long way from Anita, her name in the orphanage in western Sydney.

'Neet', Galt had called her. Murmuring as his cruel, slender fingers roamed over her. Grace was happy to know she was a long way from him, too. About as far as you could get, really, since he was dead. He'd finally got himself into a situation where being a copper didn't make him untouchable—she'd left him bleeding out on a sandy lane behind some sand dunes and moved on.

Kept moving. A few weeks here, a few months there, in places where she'd stashed small caches of safety-net funds over the years. Trying to look like just another citizen wherever she went. Act like one. *Become* one. But every time, something happened. She might run out of money, or her old habits and muscle-memories would start to twitch.

Right now, a Thursday evening in June, Grace was in the conference room of a fancy Brisbane hotel for the opening of the biannual Brisbane Stamp Expo, a long weekend of trading and unscholarly conference papers. According to the name tag on her lanyard she was Sue Wilson—a name to slide off the mind; evaporate in the memory. And she looked as plain as her name. In this vast, elegant room of lounge suits and little black numbers, Sue Wilson was lost in a dowdy dress two sizes too big, with hair and glasses a few seasons out of date and huge, distracting hoop earrings. You'd think, if your gaze did hesitate, that she might be the harried personal assistant of a buyer from one of the big firms: Sotheby's or Prestige Philately, for example. You certainly wouldn't think to pause for a chat. You wouldn't imagine someone like her had anything interesting to say about the rationale behind the different areas of focus in rare stamp collecting or the deep appeal of printing flaws to some collectors. She was probably there to fetch and carry.

Certainly no one noticed her as she slipped through the crowd, a champagne flute in one hand, a spring roll and a dab of soy sauce on a paper plate in the other. Motion was important: wallflowers got noticed. People felt sympathetic, or perhaps contemptuous—they felt something, anyway.

She lingered sometimes, peering in at the treasures on display: an 1847 Blue Mauritius; an 1854 Western Australian inverted swan; a mint block of four £1 Brown and Blue Kangaroos. Her fingers itched. She liked stamps—for what they were worth and what they looked like, their beauty, exquisite or humble. And stamps were small. They didn't set off metal detectors and were less likely than gold ingots, jewellery or paintings to be on a register. But she wasn't stupid enough to try for one of tonight's treasures. They had cameras, sensors, alarms, unbreakable glass—the works. And guards, big Islanders in black suits and earpieces occupied every corner of the vast room. They were watching restlessly, and later they'd escort the display stamps to the hotel's main safe for overnight storage.

Grace made another pass through the Hinze Plaza's elegant function room, a place of dim lighting, a soft jazz quartet and cute little hors d'oeuvres. Tomorrow it would be transformed into a few aisles of booths, and the glossy men and women into just another bunch of swap-meet traders. That was going to be the best time to act. This evening she was looking for different opportunities, such as a drunken hook-up or a snatch of conversation related to a buy or sell rendezvous—some kind of inattention she could exploit. The edge of a room key card or an envelope of $100,000 stamps glimpsed in the corner of a handbag, for example. Her hunger and focus were intense but her eyes didn't betray it and her smile was thin and polite. Unreadable—if anyone had bothered to read it, which they didn't. Otherwise they might have blanched, seeing there an unreachable core and the sense of a mind clear, alert and sceptical. Grace knew the need to hide these things about herself. Knew also that she didn't always hide them well, behind that smile.

She listened to snatches of conversation. Now and then someone would call it a night, another would say, 'Me too,' and twice Grace accompanied these dribs and drabs of expo-ers into the lift and out along corridors, striding briskly as if to her own room. She never used the stairs when she did this: guests and hotel staff look at you twice if they see you emerging from a stairwell. She noticed room numbers, and she was on the lookout for carelessness. At a rare-banknote convention two years ago she'd watched a door fail to latch, waited until the pissed snoring began, then entered and found a briefcase beside the bed. An 1881 Bank of Van Diemen's Land £1 note, and a Second World War Hay Internment Camp two-shilling note with the words *We are here because we are here* concealed in the outer border. She hadn't risked selling them herself, but a fence had given her $3,000, a fraction of their worth.

No such luck this evening. She spent her remaining

time downstairs, watching and listening. She was prepared to attend each day of the expo: she'd forked out a $450 attendance fee for that privilege, offset by a room in a cheap hotel in Spring Hill. Travelling light, in case she had to make a quick exit without her belongings, and she'd be sure to wipe everything she'd touched before leaving each morning. She took all her rubbish with her. The soap wrapping, the soap itself, anything that might hold prints or DNA. Tomorrow, and again on the weekend, she'd hover in the Hinze Plaza's public spaces wearing a basic disguise of wig, glasses, lanyard, ugly pantsuit and iPad. The part she played was an efficient woman taking care of business—yet still not leaving a trace of herself on a glass or plate. And not wasting emotion, either. She might end up with a 1928 imperforate threepenny Kookaburra worth up to half a million dollars, or a packet of 1970s Queen Elizabeths worth $10—or nothing.

The room was looser now, everyone flushed and shouting. The heat in them: boasting, flirting, making deals. It was as if an optimum skin temperature had been reached and perfumes, deodorants and aftershave lotions were vaporising, spreading. It might go on for hours.

Then, around 11 p.m., the crowd began to thin until only the barflies remained, along with a few Brisbane locals claiming bags from the cloakroom and calling taxis. Grace didn't want to latch on to a drunk, all grunts and sour breath as she slid a hand into his pockets. There was a time, before Sergeant Galt, when she'd done that kind of street-brat thing: purses on Oxford Street, lifting iPods on Bondi Beach, trying car door handles and rolling bar drunks.

Poor takings. Simpler days, though. Fewer cameras back then, too.

That amazing year when she was sixteen and had worked the carousel at Sydney Airport arrivals, claiming suitcases as if they belonged to her. The cases themselves—the good ones, Samsonites and the occasional Louis Vuitton—she'd pawned or sold. The women's clothing she'd kept or sold. The men's clothing she'd let Adam pick over.

It was Adam who'd shown her that some suitcases rewarded closer attention. The good jewellery tucked into the hollow handle of a hairbrush. Cash, cards or drugs in secret lining pockets, memory sticks inside roll-on deodorants. And, once, a bearer bond folded into a BHP envelope marked *Your Prospectus*. She didn't even know what a bearer bond was, let alone a prospectus or the significance of BHP, and would have tossed that envelope aside if not for Adam. She let him fence the bond to some guy and was pleased to have the $500 he handed her later. She knew he'd ripped her off, but that was okay. She hadn't known what she had, or how to move it.

She knew now, of course: Galt had introduced her to the kinds of anonymous-shopfront men who handle bonds, paintings, stamps and coins.

Speaking of airports and luggage: everyone would be flying out on Sunday. If she had no luck here, maybe she could spot the most smug-looking stamp dealer at the airport and swipe his carry-on?

She was uneasy suddenly. Why had Adam Garrett popped into her mind? Adam, who'd been chased off by Galt? Adam, who'd never forgiven her? Adam, her foster brother from the last of her arid foster homes, on an arid street in Sydney's west?

Because he was here. She was abruptly aware of it. In this room, glimpsed just now through the dwindling expo delegates.

Grace pivoted neatly, stepped out of the hotel and out of her role, then ducked around the museum and into QEII Park. From there to Victoria Bridge. As she went—swiftly, seeking the shadows of the city—she removed and binned her wig, her dress, her snap-off heels. Until, if you didn't look too closely, she was just another lycra jogger under the city's streetlights.

3

GRACE RAN LIGHTLY in shoes not meant for running. Across the river, then left into George Street and right into Adelaide Street, the Brisbane nightlife patchy, teeming on one block and inexplicably quiet on the next. Reaching Edward Street, she turned right again, heading back towards the river, passing through a region of cheap eateries and trying to plan her next thirty minutes.

Know when to walk away from a job, Galt had said, and that's what she was doing—albeit in the guise of a jogger. Halfway down Edward Street, just before Charlotte, a taxi nosed into the intersection, the driver eyeing her before speeding away. Nothing to do with her on this strip of hard, grey buildings. But it was the fright needed to jolt her from woman with a striving heart to woman with a striving brain.

As she loped on, nearing the Mary Street intersection, she sorted through her impressions of the man she'd just seen at the expo. If it was Adam, he was in disguise too. His hair, for a start. Once upon a time—before it all went wrong for her—she'd loved running her fingers through it, a dense brown curtain that fell to his shoulders. Tonight it was darker, short, conservative—as if he meant to merge with the other young, on-the-make dealers in that crowd.

And his eyes...In her memory, warm, wry, pale blue. Concealed this evening behind chunky black frames that made his bony face rounder, softer.

Bony long legs and torso, too, bulked up tonight in a sharp lounge suit with a black silk shirt open at the throat.

A representative outfit. You looked at the clothes, not the man. Her gaze had probably passed over him a couple of times during the evening. Of course she had been wary of everyone in that room—alert for undercover police, Galt's old associates, or expo staff questioning her presence—but it hadn't occurred to her that Adam would be there. Yet he'd popped into her mind. As she hurried now, keeping close to the shadowy walls, she guessed that something about him must have registered subconsciously as she made one of her passes through the room. That louche stance of his: head cocked, chin tilted amusedly, one hand in his pocket, the other twirling a glass. Or his voice in the babble of voices. Something had set off a quiet charge deep in the pathways of her memory.

But had he seen her?

Reaching the partial cover of an Australia Post mailbox, she chanced a quick look back along Edward Street. A middle-aged couple heading home from a cinema. Two couples leaving a restaurant. Two jaywalking young women screeching on perilous heels, fighting down their thigh-length hems.

She turned and hurried again, sorting through various scenarios. Adam had recognised her. Adam had not recognised her. Adam's attendance was coincidental. Adam's attendance was not coincidental—he wanted her, and he knew how she operated. Or he was the pawn of others equally ill-intentioned: Galt's old crime-squad crew, even legitimate police. Find her and we'll give you ten grand. Find her or we'll kill you. Find her or we'll throw away the key.

Adam would be the perfect spotter, she thought as she ran. Didn't matter that she was a chameleon, he'd be as good as facial-recognition software at isolating her face in a sea of faces. And he knew the way her mind worked.

A car drew beside her and slowed, the driver leaning to the open passenger widow: 'You call an Uber?'

She started violently, then relaxed. The car was a Camry, fairly typical for Uber drivers, but this was a guy hoping she was drunk enough to pick off. Grace could disregard him, but he gave off a whiff of persistence. She said, 'Let me take a photo of you and your numberplate first,' fumbling in her purse, and he spurted away with a squeal of tyres.

She continued. She had no one to look out for her, only her wits and innate wariness. But there was a time when Adam had looked out for her, and she for him. In a sense, they'd grown up together, twelve and thirteen and placed by Children's Services in the same Bankstown house. Too many kids, too much noise, too many chores. Greedy, distracted foster parents Colin and Eileen. The predators who thought they'd 'just pop in' if Colin and Eileen were out. The sticks, stones and hurled abuse—on the street, at school, in the mall. Everyone knew the kids in that house were foster trash.

She and Adam, close in age and older than the other kids, gravitated to each other. Adam was dyslexic and could barely write, so she'd often done his homework for him—or transcribed it at his direction. He always knew the answers. And he kept the creeps away from her.

By their mid-teens they'd begun to roam at night, later falling in with a set of older kids. Car theft, B & E, shop-lifting. An older member of the gang—nineteen—taught them all the tricks. If you're out at night, it's better if you're wearing dark blue than black. Blue, you're out for a walk. Black, you're a thief. And: if you're carrying a prise bar, make it a little one and keep it in a bum bag under a loose fleece. Not a hoodie, cops hate hoodies. And: don't flash a light around inside a vacant house. Might get a neighbour putting his bins out, someone who knows the owner's not due back for another week.

And then she was arrested.

Detective Sergeant Galt said he'd been watching her; had developed quite an appreciation for her abilities, in fact. But now she had a decision to make: enter the New South Wales youth justice system or work for him. That was easy. He could put better jobs her way—based, she guessed, on real estate and security agent tipoffs—and it was certainly safer to have a cop in your corner.

As for her friendship with Adam? Galt told her that was finished. Adam, slow to get the message, had been beaten up one night. He'd retreated from her, badly hurt. Not just physically. She heard that he'd started gambling heavily. And, apart from tonight, she'd only seen him once since then.

What kind of reach did he have these days?

Grace couldn't really afford to take any chances. Tracing a long, meandering route through the Brisbane CBD to flush out possible tails, she finally caught a cab to a McDonald's on Musgrave Road. Here she sat at a window, nursing a burger and chips while she watched a multi-level parking garage on the other side of the street. She knew Adam might have people in there, staking out her car, but first she checked for street surveillance. She gave it twenty minutes. Seeing nothing that troubled her—feeling no twang in her bones—she binned the remains of the stone-cold burger and stepped out onto the street.

She headed a hundred metres down the block, crossed to the other side and entered the parking garage via a side street entrance then took the lift to the first level. She waited a while, watching, listening. No new vehicles arrived; none of the parked ones departed. And, behind her, the lift remained stationary.

She began to walk up the ramps, through the second, third and fourth levels and out onto the open roof. Her Hertz Hyundai was the only car there, just as it had been the only car there when she'd parked it at 6 p.m. There were plenty of vacant spots on the way up, but she'd wanted to flush out anyone else with an illogical desire to park under the stars.

Keeping well back, she watched the Hyundai for a few minutes. Nothing moved. She dropped to the greasy floor: no shapes under the chassis. Pressing the unlock button, seeing the parking lights flash, she crossed to the car with the ignition key between her knuckles. She checked the rear footwells, got behind the wheel and, with a succession of little tyre squeals, drove down and out onto Musgrave Road. Here she merged with the traffic and followed it for three kilometres before turning off and taking a long loop north and east to the rental-car precinct at Brisbane airport.

She left the Hyundai in a Hertz parking bay, dropped

off the key and made the long walk out along Southern Cross Way to the parking area behind a motel where she'd left her Golf earlier in the day. It was white, anonymous, reliable. She'd never owned anything flashier, even in windfall times. Remaining on edge, she drove to the M1. Down to Nerang, turning off on Highway 90. There was a constant flicker of headlights in her rear-view mirror as the vehicles behind her twitched left and right on the winding roads, but no one sped up, drew level or switched places in any noticeable way. Whenever the road levelled out, she sped up to just under the limit, locking it with cruise control. The adrenaline alone would have had her flooring it.

The evening and the highway unfolded. Little settlements slumbered behind looming trees, and two hours later Grace slowed for one of those forgettable towns. There was some life at the pub; a two-star bistro was closing. Otherwise the place was quiet, as it generally was. Cruising through to the other side, she pulled in to the kerb a hundred metres past the entrance to a caravan park and watched it for a while in the rear-view mirror. She checked for other observation posts on that street: parked cars; the windows of the houses opposite the caravan park; pedestrians who didn't belong.

Nothing.

She restarted the car, U-turned and entered the park, coasting past the front office and into a network of permanent and visiting vans. When she reached her slot, she didn't pull in. She drove past, checking this time for any alteration to the configuration of the curtains inside the windows of her rental van. For people or vehicles she didn't recognise, a dark shape suddenly moving in the back seat of a car.

Nothing obvious. This corner of the world was settling in for sleep, with here and there a bluish light flickering, night owls watching TV.

Grace prowled right the way around the park and finally pulled up next to her van. Locked the Golf. Stood with her ear to the van's metal skin for a while, then unlocked the door and stood on the step. Listening, adjusting to the darkness, nostrils flaring for smells that didn't belong: aftershave, perspiration, cigarette smoke caught in the weave of fabric. Finally, she knelt to gaze across the top of a little rug that she kept just inside the door. She'd vacuumed it before she left: no unwelcome visitor had trampled the fluffy raised pile.

Doing all of these things was completely routine, necessary and automatic. It was what kept her alive.

4

THE VAN WAS BENIGN, inhaling and exhaling like any structure in the coolness of evening as Grace stepped over the threshold. It took her only a few seconds to check the dark corners.

She almost packed everything and left, but was racked with tiredness and convinced herself that she could last until dawn. She didn't need food, only sleep. Someone might yet come for her in the night, so she should pack a bag, and she should get some shut-eye.

Clothing basics and toiletries first, stowed into two

small wheeled cases. Then her dwindling supply of cash, a gold bar and some alternative ID, including vehicle numberplates. Finally, her treasures: a Jaeger-LeCoultre watch, a religious icon and a small Paul Klee oil. The icon, *O All-Hymned Mother*, dated from the late 1700s in the Old Believers' workshop of Holui village on the Volga River. It showed mother and child posing in vivid colours, with a rich play in the folds of drapery and a tender melancholy in the Virgin's face. Decorated with gold leaf and a thin film of tempera, it glowed as if lit from within. The Klee painting, titled *Felsen in der Blumenbeet* and signed and dated 1932, showed pastelly grey-blue shapes choked by exuberant blue, yellow, red and green cones, triangles, crosses and rhomboids. It was similar in size to the icon, about 25cm x 30 cm. The watch, the icon and the painting went everywhere with her.

Then she prepared for sleep. First, a crude intruder alarm: a saucepan balanced on a chair leaned against the door. Then a Pilates mat to sleep on under the table. She checked that the knife was still taped to the underside of the table. Her old pistol would have been better, but she'd turfed it after shooting Galt. Anyway, this was supposed to be her new life.

Sleep was slow to come inside her meagre shelter, not helped by the knowledge that she'd been forced to move on yet again. She'd thought she might settle this time, putting out feelers for local jobs and babysitting for a couple of the single mums in the park. Feeling frustrated and nervy, she tried to assess the evening and her decisions. This kind of thinking always brought her back to the rules. Galt's and her own. Know when to walk away from a job was the big one, but you also needed to know *how*. What were the escape routes? Keep the job itself simple, quiet and unobtrusive—not that Galt had been above setting off smoke bombs or sirens to distract police and emergency services—and always have a plan B, which was a way of saying always plan for and expect the worst.

Like Adam Garrett showing up.

Adam…

Before Galt, they'd worked as a team. Shared the thinking, the burdens, the rewards. Then came Galt, who wasn't into sharing. These days Grace worked solo. No experts, no insiders. They might make her very rich, but she'd always be wondering about private agendas, or drugs or gambling or just plain inability to keep a secret.

Keep your cool: that went without saying. Galt the thief-catcher always poured scorn on the other burglars he arrested. The risk addicts, the dills who couldn't distinguish between hallmark and fake silver, the grab-everything merchants, the idiots who didn't move the gear straight away, the fuck-ups who needed meth for their nerves. 'You're not like that, Neet,' he'd say. But she had been like that. The times she'd needed a little bump before a job, or left behind the prize piece because it looked unassuming, or ditched everything when she ran into a Neighbourhood Watch patrol. She *had* been addicted to the rush.

And she'd hung on to her three treasures all this time, even knowing they could put her away for years.

Be honest: the watch had been *Adam's*, not hers…

It was one of Galt's jobs, put together from an insurance clerk's tip-off, and involved a 1952 Rolex—one of the few designs with a moon-phase calendar—that had been left for cleaning with a side-street watchmaker. The business had been there for three decades and was currently separated by a common side wall from New Age Crystals, which had been there for three months before folding, leaving behind bare shelves. No power, no alarm system.

She'd gone in through the empty shop's back door, up through the ceiling manhole, and then along dusty beams to a point above the watchmaker's little bathroom. Removing a couple of ceiling tiles, she had lowered herself onto the rim of the toilet bowl, then crept into the room facing the street. The watchmaker's external security was sound enough, alarms on the main windows and the front and rear doors, but there were no motion sensors and the display cabinets and drawers had not been secured. She opened the ancient safe first (Galt had taken her to one of his guys for a crash-course in safecracking), but it contained only property deeds. She found the Rolex in a drawer under the cash register.

A Rolex worth a hundred grand, according to Galt. If he couldn't fence or sell it, he was going to ransom it back to the owner, a stockbroker in Woollahra.

It was even possible Grace had burgled that stockbroker at some stage in her life. She wouldn't necessarily have remembered. People like that were not real to her in the way Children's Services bureaucrats, teachers, policemen and foster carers were real. Even the messes she found in some of those Woollahra houses, the frayed lives she glimpsed here and there, didn't persuade her that the rich were like her, except richer. They were utterly foreign. But there was no reason she couldn't own the sorts of things they owned, particularly the beautiful ones. In her hands, they would have true value, cleansed of the imprint of people who didn't deserve them.

Not that she *had* owned anything back then. Galt expected her to give him everything.

That night, in the watchmaker's, she'd just pocketed the Rolex when she spotted a pink and gold Jaeger-LeCoultre among the other watches left for cleaning. A rare bird, although she didn't know it then—only five hundred ever made. She knew beauty, though. The Jaeger took her breath away, and she'd hidden it in her hair, twisted into a knot beneath her beanie.

Two minutes later she'd collided with Adam in the alleyway that ran behind the watchmaker's.

They each took a step back, poised to fight or run. Stared at each other. She couldn't read him, but he was so dangerously beautiful, like an angel about to change sides, that her hand floated automatically across the gap that separated them and came to rest lightly on his upper arm.

He recovered first. Knocked her arm aside, shoved his upturned palm against her breastbone and hissed, 'If you came for the Jaeger, it's mine. My info.'

My info—a law of the streets where they came from. She didn't ask how he'd known about that particular watch. Like Galt, he would've had his own tipsters. Some insurance company or security firm clerk. She felt a kind of shame: he'd made his own life, he was independent, while she was owned by a middle-aged man, and did what he told her.

But then, to her greater shame, she fished the Rolex from her pocket. 'Jaeger? Don't know what that is. I came for this.'

She reached out to touch him again. He curled his lip and ducked away, huddled with his lockpicks at the door to the vacant shop. Again, she had a sense of his independent, parallel life. Unlike her, he'd arrived there knowing how he was going to get in. *Her* instructions had come from Galt.

'See you,' she said.

Nothing from him—not even a grunt.

Now, as she tossed and turned on the Pilates mat under the table, Grace found herself recalling his claim: 'The Jaeger—it's mine.'

Had he been at the expo because he expected her to be there? Because he knew how she operated? Because he still wanted the watch back—after all this time?

5

ADAM GARRETT WAS attending the Brisbane stamp expo to 'intercept' a Red King—Edward VIII in his naval uniform. Of the millions printed by the Postmaster-General in late 1936, all but a handful were destroyed when the King abdicated a few weeks later. A very valuable stamp now: one example had fetched $120,000 at Mossgreens as far back as 2017—not that Garrett expected to get anything like that kind of money for this one. He couldn't sell it himself. All he could expect for his trouble was a small percentage of the commission that Melodie, his boss, was getting.

Apparently an Adelaide collector named Casdorff wanted to sell his Red King, and had lined up half-a-dozen appointments with dealers and fellow collectors while he was in Brisbane. Garrett had followed the man up to Queensland—even booked the same flight—on the off-chance there'd be an opportunity to lift the stamp along the way. No such luck, but he was there at the Hinze Plaza on Thursday afternoon when Casdorff—sweaty, balding, wheezy—checked in and handed his briefcase to the receptionist for deposit in the hotel's main safe. The briefcase was a tan R. M. Williams, and Garrett had immediately left the hotel after completing his own check-in and bought an identical briefcase at Myer on Queen Street. On special—but $450 even so. This job was getting expensive. Then back to the hotel in time to change for the evening event. He planned to make his move on Friday or the weekend, when Casdorff was circulating or meeting prospective buyers. He wasn't sure how he'd do it: a briefcase switch would be ideal now that he was nearly five hundred bucks down. But if that didn't work, should he snatch and run? Pose as a buyer? Wait for the sale then do a snatch and run on the actual buyer?

Those questions had gone out the window when, two hours later, he clocked Anita across the room, and she clocked him, and they both bolted through different exits. Instinct. Then, as he was looking both ways along the alleyway behind the hotel, sense took over. He could understand why she'd run from him: guilt and fear. She'd dumped him for Galt; she'd stood by while Galt had him beaten up; she'd stolen his Jaeger-LeCoultre. He shouldn't be running *from* her, he should be running *at* her.

He returned to the function room, wondering where she'd go to ground. And why had she been at the expo? For him, to serve him up to someone he'd ripped off in the past? But how had she even known he'd be here? Years since they'd had anything to do with each other. He'd once heard a rumour that she'd shot Galt, but nothing else, and he'd been keeping his own activities way under the radar since those days.

He thought about that last time he'd seen her, behind the watchmaker's shop, when she'd lied about the watch. There'd been a glow on her that night, something radiant and hungry about her looks; probably cocaine. She didn't look like that now, but that wasn't the point—had she also come here for the Red King? Better fucking not have. The stamp was his. Or rather, his on behalf of Melodie the Malady, who'd make his life extremely difficult if he didn't fly back to Adelaide with it.

The celebrations were winding down. Seeing Casdorff stagger into a lift, shirt untucked, bowtie askew and comb-over fighting the stuff he used to paste it to his watermelon head, Garrett decided to call it a night, too. It was possible the Red King was in Casdorff's jacket pocket or room safe, but pickpocketing and hotel-room break-ins were risky in these high-end places. He'd stick with his original plan and improvise.

Before going to bed, he logged on to Telegram. He had a network of men and women who operated in the shadier corners of his world. Stamps, coins, art and antiques. Dealers and collectors who didn't operate through normal channels; art-theft detectives with debts or habits; conservators, forgers...Most just usernames, but he knew a handful of them. He skim-read for a bit then, using his own username—*bricabrac*—posted a be-on-the-lookout for Anita. Age, appearance, names she was known to use, how she operated, where and when she was last seen. He posted an old photo, too, stressing that although she customarily altered her hairstyle and clothing, her face had barely aged. Some chat members responded immediately with ticks and thumbs-ups. There was no chance that outsiders would see any of this: all posts were protected by end-to-end encryption and would later be deleted.

On Friday morning he dressed in a sports coat, chinos and plain brown shoes, feeling so square he thought his corners would chip, and took his briefcase down to breakfast. Sat where he could watch the room, and saw Casdorff come in late, looking bleary and badly shaven. Excellent: easier to steal from an inattentive mark. Even better, Casdorff had evidently retrieved his briefcase from the main hotel safe before entering the dining room. Garrett watched him tuck it under a window table then trudge like a zombie towards the coffee machine and peer at the touchscreen, hovering a baffled forefinger. Garrett sympathised: you'd need an engineering degree. He didn't follow through with this thought, however. Simply rose from his table and strolled to Casdorff's, knelt as if to retie a shoelace and switched briefcases, his fingers wrapped in a handkerchief.

Then up and out past a line of steaming bain maries to the foyer and the door to the men's room. Into a stall, where he found the Red King in a glassine bag inside a padded envelope. Not the best way to treat a delicate scrap of paper worth around $200,000, but that was another thought he didn't pursue. Instead, he observed a stillness in himself. Measured heart rate; mild adrenal tingle. Pocketing the stamp, he returned to the dining area where Casdorff was feeding slices of bread onto a moving toaster rack. Garrett switched briefcases again and went upstairs and showered, washing the product out of his hair and changing into his costume for the day, a sleeves-rolled black linen shirt over designer jeans and Camper shoes, blue-framed glasses and soft, flyaway hair.

Then downstairs and out into the park, where he sat for a while on a bench. After messaging Melodie that he had the Red King—*See you Monday*—he returned to the hotel, leaving his empty briefcase for anyone who wanted it. Then he passed the day at the expo: having stolen a valuable stamp, he didn't want to attract attention with a sudden departure. At one point he saw Casdorff in a panic on the other side of the room, hauling papers and catalogues out of his briefcase and shaking out the padded envelope. He managed to lip-read a little and imagined the rest: *I could have sworn...Has anyone seen...?*

Garrett stayed on for most of Sunday, too. By the afternoon Casdorff was looking frankly haggard. As far as Garrett could tell, the police hadn't yet been called—perhaps Casdorff continued to think he'd simply misplaced the stamp. Nevertheless, Garrett knew he ought to behave as if the police *might* turn up to question everyone, so he reinforced his bona fides by forking out $300 for a set of six 1963 pre-decimal Navigators—Captain Cook, Matthew Flinders, Abel Tasman and so on. Then, late afternoon, he took a cab to the airport. He logged on to Telegram as he waited for his flight to Adelaide. No news about Anita.

Next, he looked at flats to rent. At the moment he was stuck in a run-down two-storey boarding house in North Adelaide with a bunch of overseas students. It was cheap, and the landlord, Mr Saggio, was okay, but Garrett wanted a place of his own. Maybe with the fee from Melodie...? Unless she did what she usually did, paid him peanuts and told him the rest was interest on the money he still owed her.

Funny how that amount never decreased. He needed a big score of his own.

6

MELODIE PITHOUSE PARKED her BMW—old, but still a BMW, and she'd get around to changing the New South Wales plates one day—at the rear of Elite Investigations on Adelaide's Norwood Parade. Entered through the back door, then up to her office on the first floor, where she switched on lights and her desktop computer. Monday mornings were often busy, people thinking about a private detective because things had fallen apart over the weekend. There was Covid fallout too. People screwing around on their partners when they were ostensibly working from home; lack of oversight in offices and factories that had led to an increase in pilfering. Not that Pithouse bothered herself with the reasons. There was only so much speculating she was prepared to waste time on.

Her first client that Monday was a walk-in, a woman wanting to know if her boyfriend was, as he claimed, a troubleshooter for a secretive federal agency. For about one millisecond, Melodie thought: I'm being set up. Then she took a longer glance at the woman's dress (fuchsia, with an ill-advised flounce), another at lover boy's photo (a porky-looking bald guy in shorts resting a forearm on the roof of a Maserati) and thought, he's an accounts clerk for the railways with a wife and kids he hasn't told you about. Five minutes' work.

'No problem,' she told the woman. 'It'll take a few days but I'm confident we can get you the answers you need.'

The client, suddenly wincing in embarrassment, said diffidently, 'I, um, live near here, that's why I tried you first. But, you know, I, er, couldn't find much about you online, just some testimonials.'

Glowing ones, too. Colleen of Magill: *Elite's operatives spotted my warehouse pilferer in just a few hours, saving me thousands of dollars*. Name Supplied of Enfield: *Elite cleared all my doubts about the man my mother was engaged to and even refunded part of the fee!*

'As you can imagine,' Pithouse explained, 'the whole foundation of our business is discretion. We can't afford for our faces to become public.'

'I understand,' said the woman, 'Mrs...Ms...'

'Nor our real names.'

'I understand.'

'But you can call me Meghan,' Melodie Pithouse said.

'Meghan.'

Pithouse delivered a smile designed to let the dumpy little soul feel like she was in on the secrets of the private inquiry business. And, with any luck, stop her from digging further. Although she wouldn't find anyone named Meghan—or Melodie—in the register of business names. Elite Investigations was in Adam Garrett's name. Not that he knew that.

She drew up the paperwork, took an advance payment of $500 and rewarded herself with half an hour on her socials. Her main Instagram indulgence was the influencer Aimee Pollitt, who owned twenty-thousand-dollar breasts, views on ethnics and sons named Forest and Bear.

If Pithouse wasn't careful she could lose herself for hours down these rabbit holes, so she switched to a bit of online browsing, and was poring over a pair of Gucci women's loafers when her mobile chirped. Her niece in Sydney, saying she'd had a knock on the door, some collection-agency thug wanting three months' rent on a ground-floor office in Glebe.

'Auntie Mel, he thought I was you!'

'That's odd,' Melodie said.

'He showed me this lease document with my name on it!'

‘That’s very odd,’ Pithouse said. ‘I’ll get onto it straight away.’

There was a partly mollified pause. ‘Haven’t seen you for ages. Maybe we can have a coffee sometime?’

‘I’m interstate at the moment,’ Pithouse said. ‘We’ll catch up when I get back.’

‘Where are you living—’

‘You’re breaking up, sweetie,’ yelled Pithouse. ‘Speak soon!’

She’d been APlus Inquiries when she’d had that Glebe office. But a business can stumble, rent can fall due, all part of being a businessperson, which some people never seemed to understand. Or you can lose your licence through no fault of your own. A Turkish guy, owned a café in Glebe, had come to her: find my sister. Result, Melodie had found the sister with the help of a contact at Sydney police headquarters—except the Turk had gone around there and shot his sister dead. Honour killing. The sister had refused an arranged marriage and was in hiding. True, Melodie could maybe have done more homework at the time, but the regulators had seen it as all her fault. You pulled a long face and carried on—which meant you shut up shop under the cover of darkness and rebranded yourself somewhere else. Like Elite Investigations in Adelaide, in business for nine months now.

Why the fuck couldn’t the world leave her alone for once? Her heart thumped for a while. Nerves, and her dodgy cholesterol. She dealt with it by buying the Gucci shoes and doing more preparation for a couple of long cons she wanted to set up. She was never going to keep her head above water with pissy spousal surveillance work, and jobs like sending Adam to steal a stamp for Dav and Ivan Varga were few and far between. Not to mention overheads: a fair chunk of the commission Dav paid her would have to go to Adam, and she had debts of her own, including rent on the office and her house in Tusmore. She needed to think big, long term and strategically.

First, she tinkered with the mock-up of a website for a business she was calling Allied Retrievals. She didn't want to go live until the text and the images struck just the right note. If your kid's been spirited away overseas and you've had fuck-all help from local and federal police and Foreign Affairs, then you might approach a private retrieval agency. In which case, you wouldn't be impressed by wild claims, effusive language and glossiness, you'd be looking for sensitivity and solid common sense.

Some testimonials might be useful. Louise of Townsville: *Allied Retrievals operatives got my son and daughter out of Syria where my abusive ex-husband had taken them and returned them to me safe and sound.*

She checked the time: 11 a.m. Adam should be here with the stamp soon. He was good at that sort of thing, but would he be an asset in the retrieval business? Maybe. She pictured him standing wordlessly in an office corner, arms folded, channelling an ex-SAS vibe while she lied to prospective clients.

Pithouse looked at her watch again. She had a bad coffee craving, and, shrugging her shoulders into her overcoat and placing a *Back in 5* note on the front door, she walked down to Surly Barista and ordered a double-shot latte from the surly barista. Dawdling on the way back, she thought through the stages of her second main con. A very long con, and expensive. It was just as well she knew a good hacker and a good forger from her old days in Sydney.

First, forge a painting by a dead second-rung Australian painter. Not someone like Whiteley, Nolan or Cossington-Smith, and not an Indigenous artist—too well known, too much scrutiny. Someone like Clifton Pugh or Roy de Maistre.

Then forge a few letters from relatives and patrons—and even the artist—in which the painting is mentioned. Something like, 'I finished *Still Life with Quinces* today and I consider it one of my best.' Maybe get a photo of the artist in their studio and photoshop the forged painting into the background. Mention the painting in a handful of fake online reference articles and exhibition reviews. Finally, the hacker gets into the National Gallery archives to tinker with the records so that the painting's listed in the artist's catalogue raisonné.

Establish a thorough provenance, in other words—what spymasters called a 'legend,' able to withstand scrutiny.

Then sell the painting.

She was just thinking that she wouldn't need Adam for that particular scam when she saw him drive past in his stupid little lime-green Mazda. He parked, locked up and strolled down the footpath towards her, wearing a beanie and a hoodie, smilingly patting his breast pocket where, presumably, he'd secured the Varga brothers' rare postage stamp.

7

GRACE SPENT TWO months on the move. In Byron Bay early in the first week she swapped her Golf for a white Corolla so bland it was invisible. The second-hand car dealer, a fatherly grey-haired man, seemed almost troubled that she didn't nail him to a better deal: the Corolla and $1,500 cash? The Golf was worth a lot more in a private sale. Grace gave him a smile and a shrug. It is what it is. She told him she'd lost her seasonal job, Byron Bay rents had skyrocketed and she needed to get home to Melbourne to see her elderly parents. He pressed another $200 into her hands before she drove off in the Corolla.

The Golf had been owned by Kerry White—another name to slide off the page. Now Kerry White owned a boring white Corolla, but did not hang on to it for long. Two weeks later, in Shepparton, Kerry obtained a roadworthy certificate for her Corolla and sold it to a Grace Latimore.

Tempting fate? After all, the name 'Grace Latimore' was not quite as likely to slide off the page. But Grace had grown into her name, it fitted her. She might own it forever, in fact. Move on until she felt safe, then put down roots. Make friends. Live, unchallenged, as a useful member of a little community somewhere.

She'd know it when she found it.

And so Grace steered her little car in and out of valleys and along rural highways and slowly down the main streets of regional towns and cities. Sometimes she stayed a night, other times a few days, maybe a week, always in a caravan park's rental vans or cabins. Never motels, hotels or Airbnbs, since she didn't know who Adam was mixed up with these days or what his reach was. And in a handful of these towns she merely paused long enough to park in some back street and walk through to the branch of a bank where, years earlier, she'd stowed fake ID, a stolen diamond ring, a set of numberplates or two or three thousand dollars in a safe-deposit box.

Then on to the next town, and the next. But what if the day *did* come when something stirred in her bones, telling her she'd found a town she could call home? Who should she be there? How would she fit in? Grace knew she was no dummy, but she'd not had much formal education, either. A flirting bank teller had once said, 'I'm guessing primary school teacher,' to which Grace had replied, 'You got me.' She didn't know if she should feel complimented or insulted by the observation, but she did like the idea of teaching small children. She'd let her mind wander for a few moments—it would be easy to obtain paperwork proving she was qualified and registered to teach—but gave up on the idea about a minute later, realising how quickly she'd be unmasked.

She could probably sell real estate. Serve behind a shop counter. Help women try on shoes. Empty bedpans in a hospital or nursing home.

Which led her to an obvious question: what am I good at? And an obvious answer: thieving. But not breaking into houses on the off-chance a wallet had been left on the kitchen table. Those days were long behind her. Galt had laid the groundwork for more advanced skills, and she'd built on them since then. She knew to avoid streets with apartment blocks, where there was a greater chance of random strangers hanging around. Better to rob a house obscured by a hedge or undulating ground or a kink in the street than one with visible doors and windows. And always dress as though you belonged: Grace could walk unchallenged along any leafy street in Sydney's north shore by simply pulling on tennis whites and carrying a racquet (and her lockpicks) in a gym bag, high ponytail bobbing. And she'd learnt to be alert for the things that might scuttle her. A bicycle abandoned on a front lawn, for example, meant the possibility of a kid at home with chickenpox. A basketball hoop indicated a teenager—who might have wagged school. A closed garage door didn't mean there wasn't a car inside. If there was a for sale sign on the front lawn, be prepared for random visits by agents or buyers.

That was the *how* of her thieving life, and along the way she'd developed an appreciation of the dollar value of paintings, silverware, old coins and stamps and the various gemstones. More importantly, she'd discovered that she had a natural appreciation of the *intrinsic* value of any item: its history and cultural significance; its quality of beauty.

There'd been no one to teach her these things—certainly not Galt, a thug who knew the price of everything and the value of nothing—and so, in the years since then, she'd built on this gift: attended adult-education short courses and weekend workshops, visited exhibitions, used the internet, and picked the brains of her fences, dealers and steal-on-demand clients.

Now she had a pretty good grasp of the role and significance of makers' marks on most silver and porcelain pieces; could match timbers and carpentry joints to the furniture of certain periods and regions; and, with her eyes closed, distinguish an 1840 Staffordshire Captain Cook worth $1,500 from a five-dollar copy made five minutes ago. To handle, look at, understand or know the story behind a beautiful painting, stamp or brooch made her feel better about herself.

Which was why she'd never relinquish the icon, the Klee oil or the Jaeger-LeCoultre watch.

She'd also begun to read, follow the news and consciously work on her voice, posture and manner to soften the rough edges of her old life. But she was lonely, and sometimes the old Grace crept in—hard, suspicious, cynical, too fond of jam donuts—and there was still so much that she didn't know. She wished she had someone to teach her. Which led her to think: why not find work in the fields of paintings and antiques? Everyone has to start somewhere.

She began to work up a legend as she drove the back-roads of the eastern states. Her parents had owned an antiques business in...Better make it New Zealand. Same language, similar accent, but further away and harder to investigate. And it was in her parents' shop that she'd learnt all kinds of arcane and useful knowledge. Then her parents had been tragically killed—T-boned at an intersection in Christchurch. In sadness she had sold up and moved to Australia, still only in her late teens. Yes, she'd lost most of her accent, but occasionally found herself referring to a 'chilly bin' rather than an Esky. She'd completed a business studies course in Perth, and since then had been visiting various parts of the country, looking for a base from which to launch her own career in buying and selling antiques and collectibles.

Grace kept driving. In the mornings, the long quiet of the afternoons and sometimes through the blackest reaches of the night, criss-crossing New South Wales and the ACT and down into north-eastern Victoria. Under the sweep of the stars one evening, on the coast road approaching Lakes Entrance, she asked herself what she should look like now, if she were to take on the role of a poised young woman with a head for business and antiques.

Clearly she should become that woman *before* she arrived anywhere, so that no one ever saw her regular look: slightly scrappy, slightly careless. Not as timid and frumpish as the PR gopher she'd played at the Brisbane stamp expo. Not too glitzy or chic.

She envisaged a slim young woman with brown hair falling to her shoulders from a central part. She'd go for good quality but unmemorable tops, jackets, skirts, pants; occasionally a stylish dress. Understated earrings; glasses from time to time, fashionable but not outlandish.

She inventoried her wardrobe as she neared the coast. Because she'd generally been poor and transient, ready to run at a moment's notice with only the clothes on her back, she'd always shopped cheaply. Target, Sportsgirl, Cotton On.

That would have to change. She needed to remake not only herself, but her old habits and preferences. They could get her traced if someone was searching hard enough. So: wear better-quality clothing. No more takeaway ramen or sushi, no bright, dangly earrings or hanging around craft markets looking for the perfect scarf.

Adam knew all these things about her. She'd need to become a Grace who bore no resemblance to the old one.

Meanwhile, though, she was driving the back roads of south-eastern Australia, where art galleries and antiques businesses were thin on the ground. And her funds were running low; she'd need to pull a job before long. And why was she thinking about pulling another job when she was also trying to go straight? Was that her true nature somehow?

No. She didn't have to be like that. It was just old thoughts, old habits, creeping in again.

And so, as soon as she reached Bairnsdale, she had her hair cut and coloured. Drove on to Cranbourne, visited an optometrist and stayed in a caravan park until her prescription was filled. Skirting Melbourne, she drove first to Bendigo and then across to Ballarat and bought three outfits in each place.

She was seriously broke now. Had just enough to pay for petrol as she headed across to South Australia, through Murray Bridge and up into the hills behind Adelaide. She thought she'd stay a few days before heading further west, avoiding the city just as she'd avoided Melbourne. It was mid-August now, too early for spring grasses, but all of the trees were in full, glossy leaf as she drove through Bridgewater, Oakbank and Woodside and finally along a secondary road to the town of Battendorf. The hills were full of old German names, all Anglicised during the world wars then mostly changed back again. Battendorf had been Bristol for a while.

Her main interest in Battendorf was the $2,750 she'd once stowed in a safe-deposit box in the Commonwealth Bank in the main street. Passing a small retail estate at the edge of town—an Officeworks, a TradeWorks hardware, a JB HiFi—she continued uphill to the main part of the town and parked behind a supermarket. She walked through to the broad, quiet, tree-lined high street, home to half-a-dozen antique and bric-a-brac shops, and finally into the bank. Pocketing all but $250, she walked out again, intending to find a café.

All the while, she policed her senses. She'd rewired herself early in life to trust nothing and no-one, a form of internal security that had mostly kept her safe since then. She eyed the nearby pedestrians first, then the occupants of the vehicles, parked and moving. Finally, the vehicles themselves, looking for obscured numberplates, customised antennas, illegally tinted windows. That white van opposite the bank, for example: just a normal delivery van? The black SUV at one end of the little high street, and the silver SUV at the other...Boxing her in?

Grace began to saunter as if window-shopping, but checking reflections. Then, as she passed a bakery, the silver SUV pulled out. She tensed, ready to disappear into the nearest shop and out through its back door. Relaxed as a little kid in the passenger seat poked out his tongue at her.

Rattled, still wary, she crossed the road to give the white van a onceover. Onto the footpath…And it was just a guy in overalls fiddling with a toolbox. Scrolled paintwork on his sliding door announced that he was *Battendorf Electrics*. He'd propped an aluminium ladder against the wall of a shop—*Mandel's Collectibles*—and was probably responsible for the loose wires sprouting from the fascia above the shop window.

She glanced at the window again. At a sign.

Help Wanted
Apply Within

8

WITH A NOD to the man in the overalls, Grace entered the shop, setting off a little bell above the door. She was struck first by the clutter. Tables, dressers, chairs and chests of drawers big, small and in-between; silverware and pottery in glass-fronted cabinets; dismal hunting prints on the walls; vases chunky and slender and, on a hall table, a box of sheet music and another of pianola rolls. All of it was variously tired, exquisite, bulky, beautifully restored or unlikely to be bought by anyone in their right mind. All of it smelt faintly of furniture polish and faded aspirations.

On the other hand, little of it was junk. Grace peered at a few of the labels: the four painted vases on a shelf were Olive Atkinsons, the watercolour above them was a Janet Cumbrae-Stewart. An 1835 Tasmanian myrtle work table partly barred her access to the sales counter.

There was no sign of life. Shooting a quick glance at the door, the window, in case the man beyond the glass was part of some trap, Grace edged past the work table and leaned on the counter. This gave her a clear view along an aisle between the wall and a line of dressers and armoires to a doorway that, presumably, led to a storeroom, a toilet and the back door.

She heard a small scraping sound. Peered over the counter into a pale, bony face. A woman; a nervy look about her.

Grace smiled to disarm her. 'Sorry to startle you.'

Relief washed across the face, the knotted brow eased, and then the woman was scrambling to her feet, brushing at her knees and thighs. 'Sorry! Looking for a hairpin. Must've kicked it under the counter.'

That seemed doubtful. Grace had been in the shop for at least two minutes. 'Find it?'

'Found dust balls!'

Grace smiled again, her gaze drawn to the woman's mousy brown hair. Dyed a darker shade, she thought, glancing then at the pale forearm hairs. Her natural colour was reddish, maybe auburn?

'Can I help you?' the woman said, with a fragile, naked

look, some of the anxiety returning. She kept glancing past Grace's shoulder at the electrician.

Grace turned. All she could see of him now were his legs on the ladder. She turned back to the woman: the man made her nervous? Feeling that she was getting mired in some kind of gridlock, she stuck out her hand. 'I'm Grace. I've just arrived in the area and I saw the note in your window.'

'Erin,' the woman said, her hand a hot, meek little creature in Grace's grasp. 'Mandel,' she added. 'It's my shop.'

'It's lovely.'

Erin Mandel turned wry. 'Well, not exactly. Some nice things, but...too much unsuitable stuff inherited from the previous business, and it's getting on top of me.' She gazed around at the islands and shoals of knickknacks and old furniture. 'I need someone who can help me sort it all.'

She turned her attention to Grace again. 'Are you interested in the job?'

'Very,' Grace said.

'Can you work full-time?'

'Yes.'

'By yourself?' the shopkeeper asked, as if broaching a deal-breaking condition.

'I'm sure I can manage,' Grace said, sensing that Erin Mandel was leading up to a revelation.

'It's just...' Mandel said. 'It's just that I've become a bit agoraphobic in my old age.'

There was nothing old about her. Maybe early thirties?

'Okay...' Grace said, nodding.

'I like to work from home,' Mandel said. 'You know, searching websites and catalogues while someone minds the shop.'

'Fine by me, I have experience,' Grace said.

'Experience,' Mandel said repressively. 'I had a girl here for a few months earlier in the year but she didn't know what she was doing. I've interviewed a couple of people since...Mostly it's all been on my shoulders and it's getting out of hand.'

'I can't claim to know everything,' Grace said, and outlined her New Zealand story.

'That's more experience than most people,' Mandel said. She paused apologetically. 'Maybe a little test?'

'No problem.'

'Would you mind turning your back for a minute? Everything's labelled, with a description and a price, so I'm going to remove a few and see if you can tell me something about the relevant item.'

'Sure.'

Grace turned to the window. The man was still on his ladder. She heard Erin Mandel move about the shop: the swish of her loose-fitting clothing; the sound of a cabinet door opening and metal objects clinking.

'Ready!' Mandel said, as if starting a game.

Grace joined her at a gleaming dresser. 'Okay.'

'Not everything I sell is antique, of course. Is this piece

of furniture vintage or antique?'

Grace peered, knelt, tapped, opened a door and sniffed, checked the back. 'Antique.'

'What tells you that?'

'Mortise and tenon joints, wood pegs, hand-cut dovetails. There's also that patina of something older than vintage, the colour's not consistent and none of the woodwork's been machined. I mean, it's not cut-and-dried, but I'm confident this is an antique.'

Erin Mandel smiled. 'Okay, how about this? Anything at all.'

A heavy vase. Grace took it from Mandel's hands, held it to the light, tested its weight, pinged it with a fingernail. Checked the base and handed it back. 'It's American, from sometime in the 1800s. Not unusual to find chunky vases like this one back then, with this sort of thick, drippy glaze. It's unsigned, just the "USA" mark, so that makes it less desirable than a signed one, like a Fulper or a Van Briggle. And the clay...probably a bit chalky. It looks nice, but it's not a top-dollar item.'

'And no one's been interested in it in two years,' grumbled Mandel, setting the vase down on the antique dresser. 'Over here now.'

She took Grace to a glass-fronted cabinet stocked with silver trays, sugar bowls, candlestick holders, thimbles and cutlery. 'Some of these are valuable, others are just nice to look at. People watch *Antiques Roadshow* and come in asking me to value some silver heirloom or sell it for them on consignment. I usually have to give them the sad news that their thousand-dollar silver ladle is a hundred-dollar silver-*plated* ladle. Perhaps if you could select a few things at random and tell me what you think?'

Grace obliged, testing for weight, looking for hallmarks and stroking finishes until her fingers were smudged as she gave her reports. At the end of it, Mandel smiled. 'Almost flying colours. This'—she tapped a butter dish—'is actually quite valuable.'

Grace knew that. She'd been testing Erin Mandel.

The anxiety crept back into Mandel's voice. 'Can you start work straight away?'

'I'll need a few days. Maybe the end of the week?' Grace said. 'I'm looking for somewhere to rent. The housing market's a bit tight at the moment.'

Mandel frowned, weighing something up. Then she said in a rush, 'If you're interested, I have a granny flat behind my house. It's pretty humble, but it's not that old. Everything works, it's well-insulated, partly furnished. I just haven't got around to finding a tenant.'

A lot of Grace's life was hoping for luck; a much smaller part was encountering it. In her mind's eye she compared a granny flat tucked away behind a house—perhaps near a back gate or easily hurdled fence—to a less desirable alternative, such as a house or a flat in plain view on an open street, where Adam Garrett or some other enemy could watch her come and go.

'I'd be very interested,' she said.

This threw Erin Mandel into a spasm of indecision. 'Oh. Good. Yes. I'll shut the shop for an hour,' she said eventually. 'It won't affect what Mr Iredale's doing.'

'He's fitting a light above your window?' asked Grace politely.

Mandel shook her head. 'CCTV camera. As much for the other businesses in the street as mine. We're splitting the cost.'

Grace tensed. She gazed about the interior of the shop. 'Do you have that kind of security inside?'

'Not yet. It's quite expensive. Would you like to come with me, or meet me there?'

Until Grace knew more, she didn't want Mandel to know what car she was driving. 'I'll come with you.'

'I'm parked behind the shop.'

Mandel ushered her through to a short, narrow, one-way alley. Grace took a moment to scan for traps and escape routes, taking in dumpbins, parking spots for the shop-keepers, and an eclectic range of back doors. Facing each other at the entrance to the alley were a tiny weatherboard cottage with a sign saying *Battendorf Local History Museum* behind an untidy hedge, and a brutalist concrete cube marked *RSL*.

'Hop in.' Mandel's car was a white Subaru SUV about three years old, with a deep dent in the tailgate. Roomy enough for small collectibles, Grace noted. South Australian plates, but the sticker in the back window said

Collectorama Fair Sunshine Coast.

'You're originally from Queensland?'

'What makes you say that?' The innocent question seemed to rattle Erin Mandel.

Grace pointed. 'The sticker.'

'Oh,' Mandel said, unlocking the car. 'That's been there forever; I should get rid of it.'

Grace strapped herself into the passenger seat. 'Is it far to your place?'

Mandel started the car. 'No distance at all,' she said, peering down to the end of the alleyway as if expecting something to jump out from behind every dumpbin.

At the give-way sign she checked for traffic, then shot Grace a quick glance. 'I assume you can drive?'

'Yes.'

'Look I'm probably jumping the gun, typical, but if it all works out, I was wondering how you'd feel about the occasional country trip? Op-shops, weekly markets, auction rooms, clearing sales, things like that.'

'Sure,' Grace said, allowing some hope to creep in.

Mandel turned left and left again, out along Battendorf's short main street. Most of the old-style shopfronts and verandas were intact: no garish advertising; no neon, no Maccas. Just plain, modest signs denoting a baker, a greengrocer, a bistro, a greasy spoon, the post-office-cum-general store and the half-dozen shops selling antiques, antiquarian books and local pottery and paintings. At the edge of the town, a garage named Battendorf Motors, and then a semi-urban world of leafy gardens and old stone houses set back from the road, with here and there a 1970s tan brick place with a couple of his-and-hers SUVs in the driveway, a boat on a trailer, a trampoline, a basketball ring fastened to a veranda post. An old man mowing his nature strip lifted a hand as they passed. Erin waved back, and Grace relaxed a little more, forming a sense of unhurried small-town life.

'And this is Landau Street,' Mandel said. 'Less than five minutes out of town. An easy bike ride; you could actually walk it.'

The street continued to unfurl for another half-kilometre across a shallow, leafy slope. Finally, at number 22, Mandel steered into the driveway and pulled up next to the side wall of a small two-storey stone house; late nineteenth century, Grace thought. Mandel led her through a half-hectare of eucalypts and past a single massive liquidambar—beginning to bud—to a small weatherboard cottage hard against the back fence and virtually invisible from the road.

Inside the air was stale, the rooms small and, apart from a wardrobe, a bed base, an oven, a fridge and a washing machine, mostly bare. But it was all solid and clean, and there was a bathtub. 'Think you could live here?' Erin said doubtfully.

'Oh, I think so,' Grace said, sounding just a little pleased as she listened for dogs and scanned for trees with low branches and footholds on the fence.

9

IT WAS MID-AUGUST before Brodie Hendren found the time to look for his ex-wife via the episode of *Caught Out* he'd recorded. He did have a life to lead, business to attend to. He lived in Melbourne these days, after being more or less kicked out of Brisbane.

A top-floor flat on Sydney Road, north of Blyth Street. Four sizeable rooms and a balcony, with views over the traffic that sometimes kept him awake at night. If not trams and cop cars, it was Lebanese and other towelheads hooning around in their modded Imprezas. Little princes adored since birth—thought they could get away with anything. On the upside, they kept shooting each other; on the downside, they were too dumb to shoot straight, and tended to get carted away in a shrieking ambulance instead of a nice quiet hearse.

He had a living area with a kitchen at one end and a sofa facing a big LG screen at the other. Bathroom, bedroom and, at the epicentre, a second bedroom with four computer screens, a 3D printer, a laser printer, cables, speakers, and a wi-fi jammer still in the box. He'd been in IT before Karen walked out on him, and it was good to be drawing on those skills again. He started each day in here—after a session in the gym and a large glass of Header, the energy drink he'd invented and promoted online: Hendro's Header.

Thank God he wasn't strapped to a nine-to-five gig. Today he started with the Brie Haven monitor. He'd met Brie at a club in King Street and gone out with her for a while, until she dumped him out of the blue. No reason. Just a text saying she didn't think it was going to work out, then she blocked him. A fucking primary school teacher! A charity fuck at best.

He tapped in a command and her sitting room appeared. She lived in an old-style Kew apartment—leafy street, high airy ceilings. She wasn't on the sofa, so he switched cameras and found her still in bed. She'd been having sex with some random one time when he checked, which had got to him despite himself. Another time she was masturbating, and he felt like shouting at the screen. *I'm right here, bitch.*

Hendren wandered off to the kitchen, poured another Header, microwaved some leftover vegie noodles and took both back to his command centre. Checked if he had any new customers for the remote access trojan, his own design, he was selling for $99.95 through one of the dark-web hacking forums. It was called SharedDomain. Enabled you to control someone else's life, basically. Turn on their webcams and microphones; steal their details from their phones and laptops.

The mistake he'd made with version one, two years ago, was selling a prototype on the open market—$35 on eBay. Found himself in the Brisbane magistrates court charged with 'producing, supplying or obtaining data with criminal intent to commit a computer offence', blah, blah, and although the charge had been reduced in the end, he still had a dishonesty offence on his record and had to spend two hundred hours picking up freeway rubbish. The prosecutor had made a big deal of the fact that some of the buyers were under DV orders or on the sex-crimes register. Arsehole. Just because you sold a product didn't mean you had any control over who bought it or how they used it.

Now he saw he had two new sales: nice. He switched screens to the one that monitored Third Realm, his dark-web Nazi memorabilia auction site. A gas canister had sold for $55 but bidding on the Luftwaffe tunic was sluggish. The Bundeswehr edelweiss cloth patch remained unsold with a buy-it-now of $75.

He checked Brie Haven again. She was no longer in the bedroom; he found her in the hallway that led off the sitting room, thumb-testing the pressure in her bike tyres. Black cycling shorts, runners, and now she was adjusting the straps on her helmet. Not something you saw every day. Brie was more of an Uber girl.

But he'd missed seeing her shower and change.

He switched to one of his stored images, the one with the vibrator, and emailed it to the principal of her school from one of his burners. Maybe she'd get sacked and come to him for solace.

Next, Serial Treasures. Currently he was offering a lock of hair from John Wayne Glover, the Sydney granny killer, for $150, and Ivan Milat's primary school crayon drawing of his mother's house for $300. Last year he'd sold a postcard signed by Ted Bundy for $1,600. Admittedly it might have been anyone named Ted, but he'd run an image search and the scrawled 'Ted' looked enough like other Ted Bundy signatures. No bids today, just an email: someone asking if by any chance he could get a lock of Martin Bryant's hair. Bryant...Bryant...According to Google, Martin Bryant was a mass killer, not a serial killer. Crucial difference, fuckwit. But his reply was polite: you couldn't afford to insult the punters, even if they were fucking idiots.

Still thinking about Brie wanking, Hendren walked

around to his bedroom wall mirror, stripped to his budgie smugglers, mounted a video camera and watched himself ripple through a series of martial arts moves. He loved anything Japanese: the country itself, the food, the art—his precious netsukes and a big woodprint of a cresting wave. He finished with a short clip of himself glistening with sweat, fixing another Header and downing it in one.

He played back the footage, looking for a usable still, and grabbed one where you could practically see his sinews popping as he raised the glass. Posted it to Insta, stressing that the ingredients of Hendro's Header were all available from EnergyWarehouse, and waited as the likes started clicking over. He'd have been concerned if they hadn't: he had 65k followers and was one of EW's main influencers. With any luck he'd soon overtake Gabe Eltis.

He posted the same photo on Facebook. *Here at EnergyWarehouse we're not selling drinks stuffed with caffeine to students who want to party all night, we're selling purity—as in my own formula, Hendro's Header, which is free of chemical solvent extractions, fillers, colours or other harmful chemicals.*

And settled back to watch the likes coming in there, too.

He logged into Seb Verco's TikTok. Ideally, he'd go international like Verco. He admired the guy's business ethic, which was quite simple: most people failed to become rich because they were not driven to succeed. They did drugs, drank too much and sat around watching TV.

Weak minds in weak bodies. Get up early, Verco advised. Work hard, work out, set goals. Drive yourself. No matter how big the task, don't back down.

It had paid off for Verco—millions of followers worldwide. And the visuals: Verco with beautiful young women; wearing tailored suits and expensive sunnies; looking lean and tanned on a jet ski. Ferraris, Gucci luggage. Success and physical fitness—and the virtues, not the shortcomings, of masculinity.

Brodie Hendren paused for a moment, staring into space. He'd been dealt a fairly average hand genetically. A bit chubby—girls weren't interested—but he'd worked hard to turn that around and had gone a long way to achieving the body, and the drive, necessary to succeed. He didn't have the other stuff yet—cars, women—but he was getting there.

For the first time in weeks he allowed himself a couple of hours to watch *Caught Out* again. When he got back from his Bali trip—part business, part pleasure, couldn't be avoided—he wanted to be able to pinpoint exactly what TradeWorks store Karen had been in.

A complete run-through first, paying close attention to exterior footage—numberplates and signage, mainly—to confirm that the store was a TradeWorks, somewhere in South Australia. Astonishingly, the narrator avoided identifying the store: to protect it from loss of reputation? He googled news accounts of Alisha Kennedy's abduction and murder. Again, no mention of the store—probably because the girl had not been snatched at the TradeWorks, but from a carpark near netball courts in the town of Bridgewater. He checked: Bridgewater was in the Adelaide Hills.

After that initial viewing, he started again, concentrating on the interior footage. At first it didn't tell him much. Men and women and the occasional kid walking up and down the aisles, reading labels, arguing, asking advice. Most of them looked mildly stunned, as if they'd lost the ability to simply turn around and go home, and might wander the TradeWorks aisles for all eternity—unlike the tradies, with their in-and-out again style, clutching a drill, a plank, a box of screws.

The tradies...Hendren found himself pausing the tape every few minutes, examining caps, overalls, hi-vis jackets. There was one guy in Telstra overalls, but that was no help. BP...TNT Haulage. He needed something local.

He found it towards the end of the tape, when Alisha Kennedy was at the cash register paying for a packet of sandpaper strips, not knowing she'd soon be raped and strangled. Behind her was a guy carrying two cans of paint. Scrolled across the back of his overalls were the words, *Balhannah Brushstrokes.*

Hendren googled Balhannah. It was also in the Adelaide Hills. He googled *TradeWorks Adelaide Hills* and found that the closest outlets to Balhannah and Bridgewater were in Oakbank, Stirling and Battendorf. And, slightly further afield, in Echunga and Lobethal.

Hendren played the tape again, concentrating on the

footage of the streets the victim had travelled from her primary school to the TradeWorks where her killer targeted her. Her car had been caught by cameras mounted in a Commonwealth Bank ATM, at a set of traffic lights, and at a Shell service station. By the end of it, Hendren was fairly sure Karen had been shopping in either Oakbank or Battendorf.

He fast-forwarded through the footage a final time, pausing at thirty-seven minutes and sixteen seconds to watch her testing the sunlounge in the garden furniture section before buying the hand mower. What was she doing, setting up house? The footage dated from 2022 and she looked thin, her hair no longer auburn but mousy brown.

Fucking Karen. She'd not only packed her bags and walked out while he was doing a job interview at Sunshine Fitness in South Brisbane, the bitch had taken half their savings and the Forester, leaving him with their ten-year-old Yaris.

As Seb Verco liked to say, you can't let them get on top. Keep them at home and ensure they know their place; stay away from the older ones; they're used up, they've had too much dick and they get mouthy. Karen had fucked him around, and that couldn't go unchallenged. Soon as he found her again, he'd remind her of the calibre of man she was dealing with.

In a pretty fundamental way.

10

GRACE SPENT THAT first night, a Monday, in a caravan-park cabin some distance from the town where she'd found a job and a home. Tuesday morning, she studied maps of Battendorf and the wider area: roads in and out; nature reserves; the locations of police stations. Tuesday lunchtime, she went shopping, and late Tuesday afternoon—timing it to coincide with the delivery of a mattress, pillows and bedding—she moved into Erin Mandel's granny flat. Mandel hovered anxiously. *She wants me to feel comfortable*, Grace thought. *And she's wondering if she's done the* right thing allowing a stranger into her life.

Later, when Mandel had gone back across the yard to her house, Grace removed the panel that ran around the bathtub. Room enough for her valuables: the remaining cash, a gold bar, the watch, the Klee and the icon, and her two sets of numberplates and fake ID.

On Wednesday she added more furniture: a bedside table, a sofa and a mismatched armchair. On Thursday a desk, a standing lamp, a panel radiator and a small TV. She'd need a microwave soon, but that could wait until she had a bit of money under her belt.

Now it was Friday, her first work day.

7 a.m., a chill in the air. Full of first-day nerves, she ranged around each of her rooms, parting the curtains to scan the yard for anything that didn't belong. Only a wintry sun slanting in and a frosting of dew on the grass and the car windscreen.

Undisturbed dew.

She showered, dressed in a dark top and pants—anticipating a day of dust and grime—and downed muesli and a mug of coffee before locking up and heading for her car.

'Yoo-hoo.'

Grace paused. Erin Mandel. She must have been waiting by her back door. 'Hi.'

'Hi,' Mandel replied. Wearing grey tracksuit pants, pink rubber boots and a black hoodie, she crossed the grass, waggling a package wrapped in foil.

'Banana bread,' she said, thrusting it at Grace. She added worriedly, 'I hope you eat sweet things?'

'Sure do.'

'And remember to park your car behind the shop. There's only two-hour parking on the street.'

Grace had seen Erin Mandel several times since the start of the week, but still couldn't quite work her out. Shy, lonely, heart of gold, hiding from the world but would like to be friends? It also occurred to Grace that she and Mandel were of a physical type: slight build, average height, straight hair. Similar souls? That remained to be seen. But I do know we're women who've been under pressure at some point, she thought as she got behind the wheel of her Corolla and started the engine. And we're both starting anew.

She stopped for a moment before turning onto Landau Street, old habits kicking in. Were there any vehicles different from those she'd spotted here during the week? Pedestrians who didn't belong? The time was 8.05 a.m. Satisfied that the streetscape hadn't become a trap overnight, she emerged from the driveway and accelerated gently towards the main street of Battendorf.

By 8.12 she'd parked behind Mandel's Collectibles, let herself in the back door and loaded the till with a cash float. According to Erin, there wasn't much call for cash these days, but Grace should be ready for that customer who offered a ten-dollar note for a silver napkin ring or a yellowing lace antimacassar. The larger, costlier pieces were generally bought by credit card. And, wouldn't it be great, Erin had added, if Grace got lucky in her first few days and sold some hulking old chair or cupboard so some floor space could be freed up?

Grace glanced around now, with not much expectation of that. Some of the furniture had apparently been sitting on the shop floor ever since Erin had set up shop two years ago. A sideboard attributed to the convict cabinetmaker James Penman. The Tasmanian myrtle work table. An 1830 cedar what-not and a pair of 1840 cedar carver chairs. An Adelaide hotelier had told Erin he'd come back for the Olive Atkinson vases—'But that was back in March.'

Closing the till, pleased to be alone, Grace set out to explore. First the drawer under the cash register: crammed with unopened mail. Mostly junk, with a couple of out-of-date auction catalogues and letters addressed to the previous business, Timeless Treasures. Mandel warding off the world?

Then a closer look at everything on the shop floor, before checking the tea room, which doubled as a storeroom, the bathroom and the lock on the back door.

She returned to the showroom and made straight for a glass-fronted blackwood cabinet set against the back wall. 'Too banged-up to sell or even restore,' Mandel had said, when she'd showed Grace around during the week, 'but useful for storing anything we have duplicates of.' Grace had nodded obligingly, not really listening: what interested her was the cabinet's bottom drawer. When Mandel had pulled it out to reveal a stack of folded table linen, she noticed that the internal space was shallower than the facing board would have indicated.

She knelt now and removed the drawer in a musty waft of old linen. She tipped the contents onto the floor and tapped the base—a hollow sound. She lifted it out. Under it, more mustiness and a broad hollow about the size of a briefcase.

Grace sat on her heels and thought it through. If something happened and she was forced to run before she could get back to Landau Street, it would make sense to split her stash in two. Hide the icon, half the cash, a pair of numberplates, Adam's Jaeger watch and one set of ID here, in the shop. Leave the other items where they were, behind her bathtub panel.

She was putting everything back in place when the shop bell tinkled and an elderly woman entered. Her first customer. She said hello, stood smiling for a while behind the cash register, then thought, hang it, I'm a salesperson, and charmed the woman into parting with $65 for a vintage wicker sewing basket with an embroidered lid. She spent most of the day leaning on the counter staring into space after that, but at 1.40 she sold one of the carvers and, late afternoon, six matching napkin rings. Cheaper than expected, she explained to the suspicious buyer, because they were electro-plated and not all that scarce.

Then, at closing time, her first ever customer came

back and paid the asking price of $2,000 for the 1924 Lines Brothers Tudor doll's house. Grace hadn't even been aware that the old woman had been interested in it. Excited, she called to tell Erin.

'That's fantastic,' Mandel said. 'You're a godsend.'

You're the godsend, Erin, Grace thought.

So, the day had high points. But at every stage she'd felt eyes at her back. No one was watching her, it was just everyday hyper-awareness, yet there were eyes out there, taking aim at her from a great distance.

11

A MONDAY MORNING in mid-September, the Sydney office of Allied Retrievals. The client, a solid, nuggety man with wispy white hair, said, 'Fat lot of good it did me, approaching Foreign Affairs. They don't negotiate with terrorists, full stop.'

'I'm afraid that's correct, Mr Tolhurst.'

'Call me Craig,' Tolhurst said, before continuing in a voice laced with bitterness: 'My son could die for all they care.'

Again, Meghan Henneberry, the head of Allied

Retrievals said, 'That's correct,' this time glancing at the third person in the room, introduced to Tolhurst as Steve. He was leaning against the wall. Ex-military; tall, fit, stony-faced. Muscles bulging under a black T-shirt. Giving Tolhurst a solemn nod, he said, 'That's where we come in, Mr Tolhurst. We help family members negotiate.'

Tolhurst returned his attention to the woman who sat in a swivel chair behind a solid-looking desk. According to the Allied Retrievals website, Henneberry was ex-police and had been a private inquiry agent for many years. Now she advised on local and international child retrieval, kidnap negotiations and product-tampering extortion demands, among other things. She was in her fifties and had fluffy auburn hair. A bit powdery about the face and cleavage, with chunks of gold on her fingers and ears. 'Brassy,' Tolhurst's late wife would have called her. But not brassy in nature. There'd been no hard-sell so far, no smarm, just a kind of low-key professionalism that Tolhurst found reassuring.

She was successful, too, if the view was any gauge: a sweep of Sydney Harbour with the Opera House in the background. A plain office, though, no expensive frills, which was also reassuring. Tolhurst had driven all the way from Gosford to Brisbane a few months ago, an appointment with an outfit calling itself Safe Recovery, and they'd wanted $400,000 to get his son back—most of it upfront, probably so they could install more teak and marble, and park more Porsches in the forecourt of their building.

'How much do you charge?'

Meghan Henneberry curled her lip, but so minutely that Tolhurst almost missed it: he'd offended her. She took a breath and said, with a deep, kindly regret tinged with we-have-to-be-practical-about-these-things: 'A total of two hundred thousand dollars for a successful extraction. That's made up of a down-payment of one hundred thousand, which is partly refundable if you decide not to go ahead, and one hundred thousand on completion—which reduces to fifty thousand dollars if we have not been successful.'

'Mmm.' Tolhurst was non-committal. He gazed again at the filing cabinets and an array of photographs—Steve in a commando uniform, Meghan Henneberry with Tony Abbott—then at a corner niche of high-end monitors, radios and sat phones. The bookcase held mostly military studies and international politics, with some German and English legal tomes, a biography of General Monash and a history of the flintlock rifle. A couple of certificates, too—certifying what, he couldn't tell from this distance. Poked at his glasses, but that didn't help.

'Two hundred thousand dollars.'

'That's a round figure,' Henneberry said. 'The final figure depends on your specific requirements but is unlikely to be a great deal over or under that amount. There are various factors to take into account: larger than usual bribes, for example. Special equipment costs. Method of extraction: by air or by sea. And we might need to create a specific narrative to explain our presence. We once posed as a film crew to get into Yemen, complete with a script, cameras, a sound boom…'

Tolhurst was curious. 'What was the mission?'

The ex-soldier spoke again, fixing on Tolhurst as if taking aim. 'To retrieve twin boys. Australian mother, Yemeni father. She had custody, but the father abducted them and took them back to his family's enclave outside Aden.'

Here he stopped, still staring at Tolhurst, and Tolhurst saw mud walls, armed sentries, robed men with Arab faces, a speeding boat in the moonlight.

Gunfire, too.

Henneberry said, almost hastily, 'It's tricky when children are taken to places like Yemen—any country that's not a signatory to the Hague Convention governing the return of minors taken across borders. The poor mother in this case spent hundreds of thousands of dollars on lawyers and court actions before she came to us. Please consider carefully, Mr Tolhurst—Craig—but bear in mind that lawyers talk, we act.'

The soldier said, 'We do try peaceful means first.'

Meghan Henneberry flashed him a smile, then returned to Tolhurst. 'Yes, of course. You shouldn't think we go in with all guns blazing—or that we go in armed to begin with. We always try bribery and negotiation first—which in the case of your son is practically mandated because they're asking a ransom. We'll try to negotiate that down, and if that doesn't work, we'll try bribing people on the margins of the operation. Snatching your boy will be a last resort.'

Tolhurst visualised his son: the main photo on the sideboard at home. In boots, shorts, a safari-style photographer's jacket and cameras around his neck. A big guy, but emaciated by now, probably. He smiled sadly and said, 'Hardly a boy. My son's thirty-nine.'

The soldier returned the smile thinly. 'If we do an extraction, it won't be through an airport, where he'll be noticed.'

'We'll probably use a secluded beach or landing strip,' Meghan Henneberry said.

She tilted her head, a kind woman who knew just how emotionally charged the issue was for Tolhurst. 'I always take the custodial parent with me when a child is involved. It eases the process; it calms the child and the parent—usually the mother. That doesn't apply here, of course, but would you want to be part of the operation to get your son back?'

'Well,' smiled Tolhurst, tapping his right knee, 'I've got a gammy leg, so don't get me into a situation where I have to literally make a run for it.'

They all laughed. 'We'll keep you in the background,' Henneberry said. 'Seriously, it can help with the bribing process if the recipient—a local mayor, for example—meets the parent. The human touch is sometimes very important.'

She gave a nod at the thin briefcase beside Tolhurst's

chair. 'You brought all relevant records, affidavits, DFAT memos, that sort of thing? Just so we know you're on the up and up,'—a tight smile—'no offence.'

'It's all here,' Tolhurst said, leaning sideways awkwardly, his left leg outthrust so that he knocked the briefcase over. The movement seemed to release a hint of lemon from the carpet; he realised it had been cleaned recently.

'Leave it there,' Henneberry said. 'I just need to know you have the paperwork.' She looked away. 'It's just that once, early in my career, I almost returned a child to the man who'd been abusing her.'

They all winced.

'Now: tell us about Rohan,' she said. 'What kind of man he is, why he went to Somalia, what happened to him there, anything at all that might help us.'

The main thing Tolhurst wanted to say was that two whole years had passed since Rohan was abducted, and the experience had killed his wife. Two years of torment on top of long Covid.

What he said was: 'Rohan's a photographer who does a bit of freelance travel writing and foreign affairs journalism on the side. He was travelling through Africa for a series of travel articles when a London paper asked him to do a story on a Somali town that had been retaken by pro-government forces after being used as an Al Qaeda training base for years.'

'What kind of story?'

'Interview the people who'd lived there. What it had

been like for them, what it was like now, that kind of thing. Anyway, he flew into Mogadishu, hitched a ride north, and was abducted by a local militia gang. He planned to spend no longer than five days on the story; it's now been two years.'

His voice broke a little. Meghan Henneberry looked around her desk, then fished in her drawer for a packet of tissues and slid them across the desk to Tolhurst.

He took one to be polite. 'Thank you.'

'Two years,' Henneberry said, shaking her head. 'Long time to be a hostage.'

They all pondered that. Eventually the soldier remarked, as if professionally interested: 'Been wondering about your leg. You didn't hurt it trying your own extraction?'

Tolhurst laughed and said, 'No.'

'How…?'

Tolhurst smiled tiredly. 'I can't claim some noble cause. Too young for the Vietnam War, too old for anything else.' He tapped the leg. 'Accident. Unloading a ship.'

The soldier nodded distantly.

Meghan Henneberry leaned towards Tolhurst. 'Getting back to your son. How did you learn he'd been abducted?'

'A phone call. I answered because I recognised Rohan's number. But it wasn't him, it was someone calling himself Ahmad, and he asked, "Are you Rohan Tolhurst's father?" I said yes, and he said, "Your son is in good health but he is in my custody and I want three million dollars US for his safe return." I can't remember what I said but he said, "I will call you tomorrow to discuss."' Tolhurst shrugged. 'We didn't know what to do. We called the newspaper that commissioned the trip, but they didn't know anything. We called the police; they said call around all his friends, see if Rohan had contacted them.' He paused. 'I think their first thought was Rohan had gone off the rails or maybe even wanted to rip us off.'

Henneberry nodded. 'That has been known to happen.'

'Yes, well, this Ahmad character did call a few days later and we taped it and played it back for the police. They weren't totally convinced, as if Rohan might be working with him, but then we heard a Dutch aid worker was snatched at around the same time and we were sent a photo of her with Rohan. They looked scruffy and scared, sitting on the dirt floor of some hut.'

'The police believed you then?'

'Yes. They put us in touch with an expert who coached us on how to negotiate with Ahmad—I'm sure he wasn't the only one involved, but he was the one who made the calls. Anyway, the expert said we should make sure Ahmad saw Rohan as a person, not just as a means to make money. Use his name regularly, for example. Express our emotions as parents. Also, how to ask for more time, how to bargain the ransom down from three million, that kind of thing.'

'Did it work?'

Tolhurst shook his head in weariness. 'Hard to say. Days would go by without a word. My wife collapsed. She was hospitalised with stress.'

'Awful for you both,' Henneberry said. She paused. 'Did you ask for proof of life during all this?'

Tolhurst nodded. 'They let me talk to him sometimes. He sounded okay, trying to put a brave face on it.' Tolhurst reached for a tissue. 'I still haven't told him about his mother's death, though.'

'I'm so sorry.' Henneberry cleared her throat. 'What was Foreign Affairs doing during all this? What was their position?'

'Their position? I think their position was my son was an idiot to have gone there in the first place. And they made it clear they had no intention of paying the ransom or even helping us negotiate.'

Henneberry gave Tolhurst an infinitely sad smile. 'My people and I have come up against that very same attitude.'

Tolhurst barked a laugh. 'My son even converted to Islam. As you can imagine, that went over well...Anyway, the only advice Foreign Affairs could give me was to stop taking calls from Ahmad. Just hang up, and eventually it would wear him down.'

'Eventually it would kill your son,' Henneberry said.

'Exactly. Meanwhile the Dutch woman's family raised two million dollars and got her back. I can't raise that kind of money. I can only just manage the two hundred thousand you're asking for.'

'Are you still in contact with the police?'

'Not often. They say they're monitoring the situation.'

'Foreign Affairs?'

'They're monitoring things, too, or so they claim. Off the record, they did say I might consider contacting a firm like yours.'

Tolhurst ran his palms down each thigh, then through the wisps and tufts of the hair remaining on his head. 'If we go ahead with this, what approach will you take?'

Henneberry glanced at the soldier, then back at Tolhurst. 'As you can imagine, I can't give away trade secrets—so to speak—at this stage. You're not our client yet. You could take whatever I say to another, cheaper company.'

'I understand.'

'But Steve here is an ex-SAS commando, expert in many types of weapons and forms of martial arts, and in touch with a network of similarly experienced men and woman—if you get my drift.'

Tolhurst did. The drift was: camouflaged mercenaries, parachutes, guns, night-vision goggles, a deserted airstrip. When he'd half-jokingly approached Foreign Affairs with the possibility of a freelance armed raid, the reaction was supercilious: 'Whereupon everyone involved is charged under the *Crimes (Foreign Incursions and Recruitment) Act*, Mr Tolhurst.'

'…whereas my expertise is in the digital field,' Henneberry was saying. 'IT. Hacking, intercepting—not only the communication systems of hostiles, but also their money flow, that kind of thing.'

Tolhurst nodded.

'And of course, there is bribery and negotiation, which is always our first line of attack.'

Money up front, in other words.

12

WHEN MELODIE PITHOUSE returned from escorting Craig Tolhurst to the lifts, she found her colleague packing the books and certificates into a plastic crate. 'Fuck's sake, Adam, put them back.'

'Huh? Why?'

The response was trademark, a whiplash snarl: 'In case he has second thoughts. Why do you think?'

Adam didn't always think, that was the problem. A pretty good thief—he'd brought back the Red King—and skilled at shadowing unfaithful spouses without being spotted. And he'd been fairly convincing as an ex-commando just now: unimaginative, serious, dedicated, sympathetic. But he wasn't a strategist. Which explained why he'd owed so much to a loan shark she was friends with. She'd acquired his debt, effectively buying him, and every now and then she knocked off a few hundred, a few thousand—like she would for his performance today. But if she didn't keep an eye on him, there was every chance he'd fuck up.

She glanced uneasily at the door in case Tolhurst did have second thoughts, either because he suspected something or wanted further reassurances that his hundred grand—transferred but not yet cleared—was on the right track to getting his son released from rebel hands.

She saw Adam slump into the client chair, which had cost her $15 from Savers. 'How long do we sit here for?'

Melodie assumed an expression at the extreme edge of patience. 'An hour should do it.'

'I have to tell you,' he said, 'this whole thing feels a bit grubby to me.'

'Grubby, how?'

'You said stand around and look like an ex-soldier. I didn't know you were going to rip off someone like him.'

'Like who?'

'In pain,' Garrett said. 'And for a lot of money.'

'It's not as if you don't benefit, too.'

'Did you even do any research on him?'

'Like what?'

'He was a wharfie. He's not soft. He probably knows people.'

'Look, if he's back here within the hour, wanting a refund, I'll return it. Meanwhile, sit tight and then we can fly home and he'll never find us.'

Adam was sulking, she thought. She gazed out at Sydney Harbour without really seeing the dramatic play of shoreline, water and criss-crossing ferries. Not for the first time was she struck by the ability of some individuals to be weak, stupid or annoying; often all three at once. Unless you nipped that kind of thing in the bud straight away, other people's needs could take up all the space you needed for your own.

And so an uncomfortable hour passed in the office with the million-dollar view, Melodie tense, Adam staring moodily at the floor. When she tired of this, she tried distraction. Mothering wasn't something that came easily to her, but she gave it a go. 'I've had an idea for a blackmail bug.'

Nothing for a long moment, then Adam gave her a look. 'What kind of blackmail bug?'

'In an ordinary desk calculator or stapler. Send it with real-estate letterhead as a free gift to a society doctor, sexual health specialist. You know, debutantes with herpes, trans footballers, shock jocks who can't get it up…'

'And blackmail them. Another dog act.'

'Might I remind you that you still owe me close to twenty grand?'

'Yeah, funny that—it never seems to get any less. Who's going to monitor this bug? Hours of listening with not much reward if you ask me.'

'We could share it.'

Adam grunted. But she must have stirred his criminal mind. 'How's Alarm Code panning out?'

She shrugged. 'Still waiting for someone to bite.'

Alarm Code had potential. If a factory, shop or business responded to its glowing testimonials and money-back guarantees re the installation of security systems and upgrades, Melodie would turn up in a skirt, cardigan and librarian glasses, and take a walk around the premises armed with a clipboard and concealed camera. Then she'd supply an inflated quote. It would be rejected, she'd be forgotten, and after a decent interval Adam would break in, using her secret photos as intel.

Then they ran out of things to say. At the sixty-minute mark, Melodie sighed, gave her hands a little clap, and said, 'I think we're clear. Might as well head home.'

It was almost festive, the way Adam leapt to it. While he boxed everything up, she bleached their prints and DNA from every surface, then vacuumed. As they left the building she peeled an Allied Retrievals sticker off the door, and another from the tenants' slot in the lobby.

Then to the airport, in separate Ubers. Separate flights home to Adelaide, too, Melodie in business class, Adam jammed in somewhere at the back.

13

A MONDAY IN late September, several weeks into her new life, and Grace was halfway up an incline on her way to work when the Corolla seemed to hesitate. A buzz and hum, a shake and grind, as it changed down a gear. A yellow warning light came on, and then she was over the rise and down the other side. Her car seemed to fix itself again as she coasted into town, but this had been happening for a couple of weeks now. She feared it was the gearbox, but she hadn't saved enough from her new job to take it in to Battendorf Motors. She crossed her fingers as she parked in the alleyway behind the shop and tried to put it out of her mind.

Her daily ritual before opening for business: reach her fingers into the hiding place at the base of the old display cabinet and touch her stash. A kind of benediction—ID, numberplates, cash, the icon and the Jaeger watch that always reminded her of Adam Garrett.

After that, she swept, dusted, turned the sign on the door to open and waited for the first customer to enter. A slow morning passed: two sales, one to an online client wanting the Royal Doulton Cotswold Shepherd quatrefoil, and one to a walk-in, who walked out again with a child's bentwood rocking chair. A very tidy total of $975.

Between customers she flicked through flyers and catalogues in anticipation of Erin's visit to the shop for their weekly strategy discussion. Pricing, customer wish-lists, upcoming sales and auctions. That morning there were three matters: a furniture and bric-a-brac auction in Woodside next Friday, a clearance of furniture and collectibles at Runacre Hall in the Barossa Valley in October, and informing Mrs Gellibrand, one of Erin's regulars, that she'd sourced a Vassilieff—of children playing in Collingwood—to Bridget Mack's Gallery in Melbourne.

Grace appreciated these sessions—not that Erin stayed for long. She'd get twitchy after about an hour and start glancing towards the street as though something hostile was out there waiting for her. 'But,' she explained one day, 'I do own this business, and I need to put in an appearance now and again, never mind the agoraphobia.'

It was 11.30 a.m. now and Grace, glancing out of the main window, saw Erin pulling up. The choreography never altered. The nervy parallel-parking, the rapid exit, the way she pressed her door shut, never slamming it, as she checked both ways along the street; the final scuttle inside. Our phobias, thought Grace, giving her boss and landlady, now her friend, a quick hug and telling her about the rocking chair.

'Oh, thank God. It's been sitting there for a year.'

After an early lunch of salads from the deli and a call to Mrs Gellibrand, they flicked through the Woodside auction catalogue, which listed the contents of a deceased estate. Erin's thin, pale forefinger tapped a page. 'Great minds.'

Grace had ticked a pair of 1899 jarrah ladder-back library chairs and an etching by Brett Whiteley. She shrugged. 'I'll see how I go. And there's this, in the Barossa next month.'

'Runacre Hall,' Erin said, peering down at the cover, which depicted the hall itself, a Georgian pile built for a Barossa Valley wool broker in 1912.

'I did a bit of research,' Grace said. 'The current owner's under investigation for sexual harassment and aged-care-centre fraud.'

Erin laughed. 'Hence he's selling up.' She began to flip through the glossy pages. 'I see it's in two stages...'

Grace nodded. 'Ordinary clearing sale on the Saturday

and an auction of the better stuff on the Sunday.'

Erin paused. 'Great minds again,' she said, touching a margin tick that Grace had placed against a four-door sideboard photographed in the Hall's main dining room. 'French walnut? If you could get this for the shop, I'd be over the moon.'

She continued to leaf through the pages, discussing the other items Grace had ticked: furniture, glass- and silverware, a little Blamire Young watercolour of rainy hills, an 1840s cedar chiffonier. Then she looked at Grace, troubled. 'I'd love it if you could go, but you'd have to stay a night or two. It's a long way.'

Not a long way, a bit over an hour. But Grace had come to understand that, for Erin, the world had shrunk to the dimensions of her house, her yard and her little shop. 'Happy to do it,' she assured her.

'Perhaps a motel? An Airbnb?'

'Leave it to me.'

The afternoon was also subdued. Grace sold a napkin ring, wrapped and posted a Royal Doulton cup and saucer, and pointed a middle-aged woman who was after a set of Mee's *Children's Encyclopaedia* to the antiquarian bookseller down the street.

Otherwise, she people-watched through the shop window. In the passing of the weeks, she'd become less afraid that she'd been tracked to the town, but she did need to take its measure from time to time. She watched people enter and leave the nearby shops, get in and out of cars, pause to chat to each other. At one point a toddler tripped over his feet and skinned his knees. His father immediately crouched, brushed off the dirt, kissed and soothed. To Grace's mind, that simple act illustrated what separated her, and people like her, from the world: the only comfort she'd ever been offered when she was little was grin and bear it.

At 4.20 an elderly man came in wanting her to appraise a Hecworth Art Deco trumpet vase. 'Bought by my mother in the 1940s,' he said. 'Solid silver.'

'It's lovely,' Grace said, turning it over, 'but it's silver-plated, not solid silver. If we were selling it, we'd probably ask between a hundred and a hundred and fifty dollars.'

He gave a little twist of his mouth. 'Are you the owner of this business?'

As if she looked too young or inexperienced to appraise a silver vase. 'I am the main buyer and valuer,' she said. She smiled: 'Would you like us to sell it for you on consignment?'

'How much?'

'Let's say, ten per cent on an asking price of one hundred and fifty.'

He looked at the vase and shrugged. 'Memories,' he said, and walked back out with it.

Grace, thinking of her own treasures, understood what he meant.

14

FRIDAY, AUCTION DAY. As Grace drove to work, her old Toyota clanked, shook, whined and stuttered—the music of her days. She parked in the alley, entered the shop, touched her treasures, and worked through the morning. At 1 p.m. she placed a *closed* sign in the window, changed into a pale-yellow summer dress and took a takeaway salad to a park bench beside the leisure centre. The sun was high, the light dappling under the gums and pines. Kids on the swings, mothers nattering, two old blokes with dogs.

The auction was at 2 p.m. and by 1.55 she'd parked

at the rear of Woodside Auctions. A good crowd, at least fifty men and women of various ages and appearances, and she scanned them all, looking for anyone more interested in her than the bidding, but they all wore the barely contained intensity of hopeful greed, so she settled back to watch and wait.

The pair of jarrah library chairs came on at 3.45. She lost the bidding to a gross old man with damp armpits and a breathless wheeze. She clocked his vehicle later: a Mercedes van with *Norwood Olde Wares* scrolled across the side. Then the Whiteley etching came up, *The Back of the Asylum, St Rémy*—framed, signed, number 22 of 100 printed. But it was flawed slightly, with dark smudges in each corner of the white border, and no one was much interested. Bang: sold to the young lady in the yellow dress.

She called Erin before driving home. 'No luck with the library chairs, but I did get the Whiteley.' Describing the flaws, she added, 'Maybe get it cleaned before we sell it?'

'Hang on,' Erin said, coming back a moment later with a name, address and phone number. 'Gaynor Bernard, lives in Mount Lofty. I've never used her but she does a lot of conservation work for galleries in the city.'

'I'll give her a call.'

The woman who answered was brusque, with a low, rasping voice, and Grace sensed impatience as she described the Whiteley's stained corners.

'What kind of stains?'

'I don't know.'

Bernard, humming and hawing a little, said, 'I'll be out a fair bit of next week. Can you bring it in tomorrow afternoon, around four?'

'Sure.'

'I live at the top of a steep driveway. It would be best if you parked at the bottom and walked up.'

'See you then,' Grace said.

She was accelerating away from the auction house carpark when she noticed that her engine was screaming, stuck in first gear. Then a scorched smell, and an almighty shudder and clunk, so she pulled hard alongside the kerb and switched off.

Forty-five minutes later, she'd become a member of the RAA and the roadside emergency mechanic was saying, 'You need a new gearbox.'

'Is that expensive?' asked Grace, standing beside her car and looking in at him behind the wheel. She knew the answer, but was playing a clueless female driver so that she wouldn't be remembered.

''Fraid so,' the mechanic said, looking up at her. He was a young man, tall and lanky with dark eyes. 'You have to ask yourself if it's worth it,' he added with a sympathetic grin.

He made a not-quite-graceful swivel to get out of the car, brushing lightly against Grace as he closed the door. It was accidental and fleeting but also strangely intimate, leaving Grace with a powerful sense of the man's body beneath the overalls. The unsettling physicality meshed in a confused way with the sense of panic that had been growing since she'd called for help. She needed a car: the likelihood of having to flee was ever-present. And she's getting distracted by some man?

She gave a little cough. 'You mean, worth repairing, given the age and mileage?'

He nodded. 'Could cost you a few thousand.'

Grace gazed at the car forlornly. 'In other words, not really worth it.'

'I know a wrecker?' the RAA man said.

He made a few calls, chatted shyly for a few minutes and drove off in his yellow van, one lean hand waving from his window. When he was gone, Grace removed the Victorian numberplates and stowed them in her bag. The registration was legitimate, but the address was false. She didn't want anyone following up out of curiosity. Then, checking the boot and the glovebox for anything of value—finding only a packet of tissues—she settled in to wait.

Half an hour later, a truck from Woodside Wreckers pulled up and a burly mass of overalls and tattoos stepped out. 'You the lady with the Corolla?'

She was the only lady anywhere in the vicinity, with or without a Corolla, but she smiled and said brightly, 'That's me.'

'The boss said two hundred?'

Grace nodded. 'Two hundred.'

Then, poorer by one old Toyota sedan, richer by two hundred dollars, Grace stood waiting for an Uber to take her home to Landau Street. Friday afternoon traffic whizzed by; drivers looked at her with mild curiosity. According to the app, Omar was still three minutes away, so she walked up an inclined nature strip to where an old red Volvo station wagon was parked: *$5,500* in spidery writing on a cardboard carton flap behind the windscreen.

A toot: Omar had arrived. She walked to his car despondently. She couldn't even afford to buy a clapped-out old Volvo. What would the old Grace do? She'd think about doing over Norwood Olde Wares for the sheer satisfaction of aggravating the owner. She'd also think about old winery families—old winery money—in the Barossa Valley.

15

SATURDAY AFTERNOON, 3.30, Grace at the wheel of Erin Mandel's Subaru for the first time, adjusting the seat and the rear-view mirror. Erin standing beside the car, twitching. 'It's all straightforward.'

Yes it is, Grace thought. It's just a car. She also thought: is this one going to pack up on me too? She turned the key. A pinging sound, and the words *service due* flashed on the display.

'Sorry about that,' Erin said. 'I've been using a mobile mechanic, but he retired and I haven't...'

She tailed off. Grace understood. Everything Erin did was designed to limit how often she left the house. If she could no longer use her mobile mechanic she'd have to find another or take her car to a garage, and it was all just beyond her at the moment. 'How about I book it in for a service at Battendorf Motors?'

Erin's relief was excruciating. 'Would you?'

'Sure,' Grace said, thinking: such a strangely domestic, mundane, *lawful* task, booking a car in for a service. Yet yesterday afternoon she'd been the Grace who thought of a car only as a means of escape. 'I'd better get going.'

'Hope it goes well with the conservator,' Erin said, stepping back, giving a little wave.

Grace returned the wave and drove out onto Landau Street, listening as Google Maps took her through the little hills towns to Mount Lofty and then onto a series of winding back roads. At the words, 'Your destination is on the right,' she saw a wire gate and patch of dirt large enough for a couple of cars. Above the trees ranged up and across the hill, she glimpsed a red corrugated-iron roof. She pulled over, locked the Subaru and laboured up the driveway with the Whiteley print wrapped in brown paper under her arm.

The house was old, stone, with a steeply pitched roof and deep verandas on all sides. Shrubs, tidy lawns, a rain-water tank, a small SUV in a car shed. No children's bicycles, no clutter of tools, ladders, ride-on mowers or chainsaws that Grace could see.

She knocked and the woman who answered stared intently for a moment. She was tall, mid-forties, her greying hair escaping from a ponytail. A little frown, as if she'd forgotten Grace was coming.

'Ms Bernard?'

The woman's face relaxed into an almost-smile. 'Call me Gaynor,' she said. 'Follow me. Forgive the rush, I have to go out in half an hour.'

She took Grace around the house to a long, low weatherboard building set among peppertrees at the rear. The interior consisted of one large, cool room fitted with workbenches, with pots, tins, brushes, rags and unfamiliar tools on open shelves. Temperature controlled, she realised, with dim artificial lighting, and smelling pleasantly of the chemicals Bernard probably used.

'Let me see.'

Grace unwrapped and proffered the Whiteley. 'In each corner,' she said, touching one of the stains.

Bernard nodded pensively, peered closely, tilted the etching this way and that, and glanced briefly at the back. Turning the frame over again, she said, 'At a guess, some idiot had it Blu Tacked to a wall at some stage.'

'Are you able to clean it?'

Bernard said, 'Yep,' emphatically, her manner suggesting that she always proved her worth to her own exacting standards, not her clients'. 'I'll try to bleach it out, probably. Two hundred and fifty dollars? Should be ready by next Friday. Give me a call Thursday. Or I can call you?'

'It might be best if I call you,' Grace said. 'I travel a bit for work and can't always get a good signal.'

She headed back to Battendorf wondering what the conservator had made of her. She'd tried to be low-key and unremarkable, but she'd picked up the woman's slight wariness.

She began to feel tension in her neck and shoulders. She should've anticipated a degree of suspicion on Bernard's part; she would have come across art thieves in her line of work. I should've said something like, 'I bought this at auction. I work for Mandel's Collectibles, in Battendorf.'

The old life bleeding into the new again: say nothing, trust no-one. Even though I have a legitimate job now, for a legitimate employer.

Oh, bullshit. There was nothing legitimate about her.

A sense of dissatisfaction rode with Grace as she drove back through the hills, tossed the Corolla's numberplates into a quiet stretch of the Onkaparinga River and went shopping in Oakbank. No luck buying a microwave, the whitegoods shop had closed for the day, but Cycle World was still open. Twenty minutes later she was stowing a second-hand road bike in the rear of the Subaru. Until she had the dosh for a car, a bike was a pretty nimble escape vehicle. And it was affordable. And she could ride it to work, stream through the springtime warmth like a normal person.

—

Late afternoon now and she was reclining in the backyard, letting the sun work on her in its brief journey between the lowest branches of the liquidambar and the top of the side fence. Bees were busy, and the yard grasses were lush, ripe for a pass with the lawnmower—which was a cheap TradeWorks own-brand push mower, and why Erin hadn't bought a powered model was beyond Grace. She glanced at the old garden shed, thinking stupidly that she should find somewhere else to park her new bike where that fuck-ugly lawnmower wouldn't be next to it.

But right now...She stretched her legs along the sunlounge, losing a sandal. Shaded her eyes, reached absently for the gin and tonic on the slatted outdoor table beside her, took a sip, subsided again.

The movement seemed to wake Erin, who was also lounging, eyes closed, bony thighs shockingly white under her bunched skirt. 'Maybe we should finalise the plans for your trip to the Barossa?'

The last thing Grace wanted to do. 'Sure.'

'I'll be right back,' Erin said, swishing across the grass to her back door.

Grace drained her gin and tonic, swung her legs around to sit on the edge of her sunlounge, and waited. Then Erin was returning with the catalogue, the gin bottle and a jug of ice cubes in tonic water.

'More sustenance.'

'More sustenance,' agreed Erin, pouring, then clearing

table space. 'We'll draw up a wish list and work out a budget.'

She said *we*, Grace thought. 'Okay.'

Erin turned her thin face to Grace. There was doubt in her voice. 'I was thinking...twenty thousand?'

She wants my approval? 'Okay,' said Grace again.

A defensive note now, as if Erin were arguing with herself. 'We've had a good couple of months.'

That *we* again. 'We have.'

'All down to you,' Erin said. She took a breath, gathered herself. 'But maybe spread the twenty thousand around? It would be better if you bought a few things that *totalled* twenty thousand rather than a twenty-thousand-dollar folly we can't sell.'

'Good idea.'

'Furniture, silverware, porcelain...' Erin said. She tapped a photograph. 'I keep coming back to this chiffonier.' Flipped over a page. 'And this Blamire Young. I love his watercolours.'

'Do my best,' Grace said, the realisation settling deeply in her. *She trusts me.*

''Thank you. You're a good friend.'

Grace shifted uncomfortably. She wished she understood what friendship was. No one but Adam had ever wanted to be her friend. She smiled at Erin, hoping her caution wasn't apparent, hoping she wouldn't be seen as an imposter. Hoping she wouldn't have to *be* an imposter. She liked it here; didn't want to start running again.

Friend...Her mind ran on that track until it got to the RAA mechanic yesterday. His shy interest. A man who was single, attractive, not an idiot. Maybe it was drinking gin and tonic in the sun, but Grace thought she'd like to be in love, or at least have a lover. A long time since she'd even had sex, let alone made love. Either way, there was intimacy involved, meaning she'd have to lie to her lover and remember the lies. Lying was all she did, sometimes. Her life was one big lie.

And what if she slipped—revealed too much or contradicted herself? She had no difficulty in playing a young mum jogging past a house she wanted to burgle, a PA at a stamp expo, an assistant antiques dealer. But could she convince as a lover? Too much to go wrong; too much to juggle.

This was doing her head in. 'You're okay with me being away in your car for two days?'

Erin lifted a languid hand. 'Of course. It's a work trip.'

'Thanks.'

'In fact,' Erin said, 'I think you should consider the car yours for the time being. I can always get an Uber if there's an emergency. And I don't really need to come into the shop on Mondays, we can just as easily discuss strategies here, after work.'

'We'll see.'

'You should enjoy yourself in the Barossa. Visit some wineries.'

'We'll see,' said Grace again.

They lapsed into silence after that, letting the dregs of sunlight paint their limbs, until the last shadows hurried in and they went to their separate dwelling places.

Evening, and the warmth of connection remained with Grace. She'd been accustomed to solitude for too long. But she was confused by the clash of the new chances that had come her way with the old longings and habits that had always sustained her. Life had become…well, peaceful. But should she trust it? She liked her friendship with Erin. It was low-key and undemanding; they didn't live in each other's pockets; they'd only sat together in the garden once before, had lunch in the Battendorf café twice.

You could overthink things. Grace sprawled on her sofa with a novel; last night she'd listened to music. Both activities extended her, made her feel better about herself. She was learning how to discriminate. She liked the blues but not soul, enjoyed reading the classics and loathed fantasy. In this small new world, books and music took her roaming and woke her up.

Not tonight, though—that old itch building in her since yesterday's bad luck with the car. She tingled, her blood singing, wanting.

The Barossa Valley trip. Grace Latimer, moving about unseen in the treacherous dark.

16

THAT SATURDAY, ADAM Garrett had been called in to the office. Melodie wanted him to 'sit and look useful' while she conferred with a client who needed his nephew tailed.

The client, introduced as Ivan, was wearing a suit. On a Saturday? The fabric looked expensive, the shirt crisp, the shoes highly polished, but the hands, resting on solid thighs, were the hacked-about slabs of a labourer, and a smudged, blue-black serpent's head emerged from the top of one sock when he crossed his legs.

Garrett, sitting in the associate's chair next to Melodie's

desk, watched and listened, his face and eyes blank. A prison tatt? He couldn't tell for sure. Mel had said the guy was a developer, so maybe he'd started his adult life as a brickie. And maybe he was meeting clients later in the day. Or maybe he intended to harm the nephew, and thought he'd disarm them by wearing a suit. If so, it was a misfire. The outfit didn't go with the hands, the face—which was long, narrow, dark, the nose hooked like a raptor's—or the cold, close-set eyes.

He thought he'd try a little light needling. 'We don't often get in-laws requesting this kind of thing. It's usually the parents. Where do they figure in all this?'

It worked. Ivan gave him a prison-yard stare. But it was there and gone again, replaced by a sharkish smile and a shovelling-gravel voice: 'It's only Leigh and his mum—my sister. Been like that for years. She's worried about her boy, so I'm stepping in.'

'By having him followed,' Garrett said flatly.

You could read his tone as doubt, and he felt the force of Melodie's irritation as she leaned forward to cut across him: 'What my associate means to say, is, we need to be careful about bona fides. We need to be sure this lad's going to be okay.'

The lad, Leigh Calnan, was sixteen years old and had been acting out, according to the man named Ivan. Secretive, a bit mouthy, struggling at school and staying out until the early hours.

Ivan shrugged. 'If you're worried, call my sister.'

'That won't be necessary,' Melodie said, casting Garrett a side glance.

She turned to Ivan again. 'How many days did you have in mind?'

'A week? Including a weekend, to get the best idea of his routine.'

'We can start straight away,' Melodie said. 'This afternoon, in fact,' she added, looking to Garrett for confirmation.

He nodded. 'What's he usually do on Saturdays?'

Ivan seemed to search for inspiration. 'Football. Goes out with his mates later. Movies, Maccas...Look, for all I know he plays snooker. Smokes dope. *Deals* dope.'

Snooker? thought Garrett. 'Has your sister tried talking to him?'

Ivan shrugged. 'You know what teenagers are like.'

'Well, have you considered that he's been in contact with his father?'

Garrett saw Ivan think furiously again and eventually say, 'The cunt's gone back to Europe.' Pause. 'To the...to England.'

Giving Garrett another look, Melodie said, 'So basically you'd like to know who your nephew sees and what he does when he's not at home or at school.'

'Yep.'

'Photos?'

'That would be good.'

Garrett said, 'Have you tried following him yourself?'

Ivan practically snarled, 'How do you suggest I do that? The kid knows me.'

'Okay,' Melodie said briskly. 'If you could give us all the relevant information? Where he lives, his school, where he plays sport...Do you have a recent photo?'

'It's all here,' Ivan said, excavating an envelope from an inside pocket and tossing it onto the desk.

Garrett found himself trying to spot a handgun holstered under the suitcoat. 'Would you like regular progress reports as well?'

Ivan was vague. 'Er, that would be good.'

'I'll give you a call every afternoon,' Melodie said with another glare in Garrett's direction.

Then the man named Ivan was on his way out the door and Garrett was feigning a dodgy stomach, muttering about the men's room.

Melodie flipped her hand at him, a twist of distaste on her face, and busied herself with paperwork.

Once he was out in the corridor, Garrett held back. He could hear Ivan trudging down the stairs, and then there was the unmistakeable squeak of the door to the street. He waited for it to close, then raced to the bottom in time to see Ivan trot across the street and into the passenger seat of a black Range Rover. Garrett snapped the rear plates with his phone, then killed a couple of minutes before returning to the office.

Melodie was eyeing her watch impatiently. 'You need

to get going before this kid disappears on you.'

'Sure,' Garrett said, adding, 'Do you know that guy?'

'What guy?'

'The client. Ivan.'

'Of course I don't know him. What are you on about?'

Garrett shrugged. 'Nothing. Just wondered.'

An hour later dusk was settling in. Adam Garrett parked his Mazda half a block from a 1930s Californian bungalow on Galway Street in Toorak Gardens, waiting for Leigh Calnan to leave. Or his friends to arrive. Waiting, in fact, for anything at all to happen. And maybe nothing would, maybe the kid's mother was playing hardball and he'd been grounded for acting out.

Time passed. He fired up his phone and did some light research. There was only Leigh and his mother. She was divorced; her ex lived in Perth now, hadn't been on the scene for years.

Interesting. Tossing his phone onto the passenger seat, Garrett contemplated the client meeting. The dynamics between Melodie and the man she called Ivan. The body language, the undercurrents. She knows him, he thought. She always knows people—like the guy who sold her my debt, so now I'm doing her shit-work instead of his.

So why the play-acting? Maybe because she knows I didn't like what we did to the Tolhurst guy. Maybe she thought I'd arc up if I knew the real reason for tailing this kid.

What was the real reason? Garrett didn't have a clue how he'd find that out. His stomach rumbled. He should have stopped at a drive-through. And sitting for hours always gave him a back ache. He listened to music for a while, then his phone pinged.

Username *elbow-grease*, one of his Telegram contacts, had just encountered Anita. *Except she's calling herself Grace now.*

Adam Garrett felt a tingle of excitement. He started his engine, switched on the headlights, turned the car towards Portrush Road.

If not for one of Melodie's assignments earlier in the year, he might never have learnt that *elbow-grease* was a conservator named Gaynor Bernard. The client, a merchant banker embroiled in a bitter property dispute, had been ordered by the court to return a valuable John Peter Russell oil painting, *Morning Sea, Morestil*, to his ex-wife. Perhaps Melodie could arrange for someone to paint him a perfect copy so he could keep the original? Melodie had given the assignment to one of her many contacts, who did a beautiful job but was worried that it lacked the patina of age. Cue Gaynor Bernard, who'd joked to Garrett that usually she *removed* the patina of age.

Taking Portrush Road to the M1, he began winding up into the hills. At Crafers he turned onto a series of side roads, eventually reaching the conservator's house. He parked, got out, peered up the slope. Darkness. He was about to open the gate when nesting birds stirred in the nearby trees and a voice said, 'I'm here.'

He stiffened. It was Bernard, stepping away from a mess of moon shadows. Even so, he looked both ways along the little-used road, a ghostly ribbon curving around the hillside, and his hand reached automatically for his jacket pocket, which was empty. Habit.

'Settle down,' Bernard said. 'Sorry to startle you.'

'You didn't.'

'Anyway, not much I can tell you. She turned up with an etching in need of a clean, and I recognised her from the photos you posted.'

'Car?'

'Didn't see it. She would've parked down here and walked up the driveway.'

'She say anything? Where she lives, things like that?'

Bernard shook her head. 'No. Nothing.'

'Did you get the impression she lives nearby?'

'I have no idea.'

'And she called herself Grace?'

'Correct.'

'Last name?'

'She didn't give it.'

'Describe her.'

Bernard's description matched the stamp-expo version of Anita: low-key, modest and conservative. Except that her hair was light brown now.

'When's she picking up the picture?'

'I should have it done by this Friday.'

'When you know for sure, text me. A couple of hours' notice if you can.'

'Sure,' Bernard said.

Garrett saw curiosity in her face. But they were colleagues—albeit of the online kind—so she didn't ask questions, and he didn't expect her to. It was risky enough knowing each other's names.

He headed back to the Toorak Gardens house. Parked outside it until 11.30, when an Uber pulled up. A teenage boy tumbled out, lanky and awkward, with shaggy hair. Garrett, watching him wave and yell goodbye to his mates in the car, then stroll to his front door, wrote: *11.30 p.m., subject arrived home from seeing a film with two friends his age.*

Then he started his car and headed home to his miserable boarding house in North Adelaide.

17

BRODIE HENDREN COCKED his head as a flight was called. Not his 11.50 Jetstar to Melbourne—that would be too much to hope for. Removed from his reverie, he scanned the Bali Airport waiting area. Full of Australians flying home. Unfit. Unhealthy. Overweight. Look at them stuffing their faces.

He shifted to ease a nagging ache between his shoulder blades, checked the graze on his forearm and touched his bruised face gingerly. Fucking clapped-out rental moped. It was a miracle he hadn't come off till the last day.

He realised some fat kid was staring at him; gave her a death stare and she didn't even blink, the little cow.

He glanced around the airport uneasily. At least he was leaving the fucking country with a few bucks in tax write-offs—being a content creator, he'd posted from cafés and clothing boutiques in Ubud and Kuta Beach, and attracted some Insta and TikTok likes. Otherwise the whole thing had been a bit of a fizzle.

He propped his iPad on the rickety cane table and logged on, checking his socials. Insta first, then Snapchat with some trepidation: yesterday he'd suggested in a private feed that Gabe Eltis, the other EnergyWarehouse ambassador, was packing an extra kilo or so. And he was, yet he had twice as many followers. All the guy did was flog EnergyWarehouse products. It wasn't like he'd actually *created* something from them, like Hendro's Header.

Then the bottom dropped out of Hendren's world.

The Snapchat post had gone viral.

Someone must have leaked it. Who? Hardly anyone was meant to see it. No matter, the fallout was already massive, dozens of clients threatening to boycott EnergyWarehouse. Accusing him of body-shaming. *Very much high school vibes*, someone had posted. *Gross fatphobic attitude*, said another, and *Body conscious guys don't speak to each other like this!*

To which EnergyWarehouse had responded: *Brodie Hendren is no longer an affiliate with this brand.*

The walls closed in. He swallowed; his heart thumped.

Veins pulsing in his temples, tears in his eyes, Hendren checked what Gabe Eltis was saying and doing. And there he was with his pumped-up pecs, his stomach looking, yeah, fat, as he posed with a sports drink *he* had created, the rip-off bastard. Big E Energy.

Faintly, Hendren registered a final boarding call. He grabbed his carry-on and tore down the corridor towards his gate. He was the last passenger to board amid careful blank looks from everyone—none of these limp-dicks even had the guts to scowl—then found himself seated between two fat cunts who hogged the armrests, while the kid behind him kicked his seatback all the way to Melbourne.

He waited at least ten minutes for a bus to the long-term carpark, then forgot what section his Clubman was parked in and when he eventually found it, there was a new dent in the driver's door. Fucking shitbox. The Mini was the right fit style-wise but it had done over 160,000 km and things were starting to go wrong with it.

He calmed a little on the freeway: the smooth flow of the traffic, and the soothing voice narrating one of his favourite health and wellness podcasts. 'How to lead a healthier, happier life in a way that works for the *you* in you,' was how Tansy Marsh introduced each segment of 'Take Care Now'. She had 2.1 million followers, and, in addition to the podcast, she'd produced an app and a book of recipes that worked on building mind and body. Body image was a big thing for Hendren—for too long he'd had an unhealthy relationship with food and exercise—and he listened carefully as Tansy explained that *connection* was vital in obtaining a healthy mind and body. Connect to yourself, connect to others. Don't let bitterness towards successful people consume you. Cry when you need to—in fact, why not block out time on your calendar for a good cry?

Yeah, well. Brodie Hendren didn't have to timetable it: he was blinking away angry tears as he took the Brunswick Road exit. Those arseholes at EnergyWarehouse. Was he consumed by bitterness towards successful people? Fuck no. Consumed by bitterness towards fucktards was more like it.

Traffic was heavy. The Golf station wagon ahead of him had a bumper sticker in the rear window. *Little Miss on Board*. Jesus wept. Five minutes later a Hyundai cut him off suddenly and forced him to brake. It had a bumper sticker too: *It's okay not to be okay*.

He followed it into a supermarket carpark, waited until he was unobserved and knifed both passenger-side tyres.

The next morning he realised he had to take himself in hand. What would Seb Verco do? Move on, not look back.

First, recoup the costs of the Bali trip. Taking a few closeups of his moped injuries, he set up a crowdfunding site in the name of Amber, sister of Jason who'd been mugged at Kuta by guys with knives. Cleared him out of everything—return ticket, phone, cash—and left him with a hefty hospital bill.

Then he did a bit of work designing a medical certificate. If you were in breach of a community corrections order or something, a medical certificate could help you get off re-sentencing or jail time. He'd been thinking for a while now that he could start supplying whole new IDs for people. Credit cards, driver's licence, Medicare card…It had all started when the girlfriend of a Rebels enforcer lost her licence for drug-driving and asked him how she could get it back. Short of hacking the DMV and backdating her record, Hendren wasn't sure what he could do for her. He didn't have the equipment to fake a new licence, so he'd done a social-work letter for her that said she was the sole carer of her mother, who needed to be driven to her cancer specialists' appointments.

Finally, he sketched some ideas for Your Memoirs. In Bali he'd met three women in their sixties who said they were writing their life stories for their kids. Memories. His eyes had glazed over. What memories? Getting old and fat and then retiring and dying? Two of them were struggling to put words together, the other one had written something like three hundred thousand words on a life you could sum up in five. It would be better for old dears like them to seek help from a professional. He tried a few teasers: *Turn your priceless life stories into beautiful biographical hardcover books to be enjoyed by generations to come.* And: *From the initial interview to the final, professionally bound product that will grace your coffee table, Your Memoirs will be there to lend a guiding hand.*

Get the money up front, then delay, delay, delay…

After that, he checked his memorabilia sites: he'd made another $545 in the past week.

Slow money, though. Slow.

Late morning, he checked his mailbox in the foyer: four credit cards, in addition to the two that had arrived the previous month. They were genuine replacements, ordered using card numbers supplied by donors to a charity called Toddler Trust, helping kiddies with terrible illnesses. Photos of big, soulful eyes and wan cheeks.

Time to test one of them, so he walked down the street and bought a salad. Success. If the transaction had failed, no big deal, no need for embarrassment, everyone has the occasional credit-card glitch. He simply would've paid cash or used his own card.

He returned to the flat, red onion sharp on his tongue.

He thought back to his life two-and-a-half years ago. Karen leaving him, then his arrest for selling the remote-access trojan. Three months' jailtime—suspended—plus a fine and 200 hours of community work. Amusingly, Ipswich police had sent him a letter through the Recidivist Offenders Program a month later, urging him to have second thoughts if he was ever tempted to go back to his old ways. 'Consider redirecting your life,' the letter said. Well, that's exactly what he was doing.

Not in Queensland, though. Using the credit card that he'd used to buy lunch, he booked three flights: Melbourne to Hobart return, and Melbourne to Adelaide. He'd book his flight home from Adelaide once he'd found—and finished with—his bitch ex-wife.

18

MONDAY WAS SO mild and still that Grace cycled to work in the yellow glory of the sun. But the chain came off on the outskirts of Battendorf, making her late, so rather than linger over her customary soy latte in the main street café, she asked for a takeaway and drank it as she googled Barossa Valley motels on the shop's old laptop. There were five close to Runacre Hall. She rejected four as too modern or too exposed. The fifth, The Vigneron on the outskirts of Angaston, was cheap, which would please Erin, but Grace knew damn well why she was choosing it: judging from the website, it was a bit decrepit—so hardly any CCTV—and its two arms of ten rooms each extending from either side of the office were tucked behind veranda trellises choked with vines.

She called and booked an end room.

'It's the one closest to the road,' the reservation clerk said. 'We do have a quieter one.'

'The end one's fine,' Grace said. Farthest from the office. Along with her old itch, old habits of survival had also returned.

Which was probably why she glanced down at her coffee cup, discarded in the bin, and plucked it out. She opened the front windows and back door of Mandel's Collectibles for a cross breeze, then burned the cup. Stupid, really: anyone keen to get her could always obtain her prints or DNA by other means, but this was habit, and habit had so far kept her safe.

The air was still faintly acrid and smoky as she touched her stash for luck and reassurance, then opened for business.

The morning passed quietly, only three minor sales. Between customers, Grace called the proprietor of Battendorf Motors, learned that he was 'snowed under', and booked Erin's Subaru for a service early the following week.

At lunchtime she pulled on a baseball cap, Levi's jacket and chunky sunglasses, placed a sign in the window, *Back in one hour*, and cycled to a small branch library in a town five kilometres away. Two staff members; shelved books;

a beanbag section for kids; six unoccupied computers. Choosing a monitor that couldn't be easily observed by anyone, she clicked on a search engine. The home page loaded with breaking news and ads posing as news. She wasted five minutes on 'Most Memorable Movie Catchphrases' then, irritable with herself for wasting time, logged into her Dropbox account and clicked on the folder she'd labelled 'My Dream Homes'.

It consisted of notes, floor plans, photographs. A *Home Digest* article on the sprawling Sandy Bay house built for a Hobart scrap-metal merchant. A young dot-com millionaire's specially designed wet dream in *Architectural Monthly*. It wasn't the houses that interested her but the contents: a Sevres or a Helena Wolfsohn vase photographed on a hall table; a set of Paul Revere silver spoons in a glass cabinet; a small Hans Heysen above a fireplace. She'd saved details on twenty such places scattered around the country, and scrolled down to three located in the Barossa Valley. Immediately discounting Runacre Hall—the security would be too tight now—she familiarised herself with a winery residence and the home of a regional home-loan CEO named Jason Britton.

Pleased to see that neither place had close neighbours, she went to the next stage of her whittling-down process: studying the owners' habits and movements via social media. She didn't want to break into a house that was hosting a twenty-first birthday party on the weekend of the Runacre Hall clearance, for example. And sure enough:

the winemaker's place was doing duty as a stopover for an around-Australia classic car rally that weekend.

That left the home-loan CEO's modern eyesore, set on a hillslope several kilometres from Rowland Flat. According to Facebook, Britton was currently holidaying in Thailand. Sea-cave canoeing. Visiting the Phuket elephant sanctuary and Karen hill tribe villages. She checked older posts: six years ago he'd stopped mentioning his wife and children. Divorce? Nowadays all Britton did was work, attend conferences and holiday in Thailand, the Philippines and Cambodia once or twice a year. She went back to her original notes, including photos she'd uploaded from a *Home Beautiful* article. Britton seemed to own a bit of everything: antique silverware, a little Chagall, a collection of colonial-era coins and banknotes, another of unopened first-gen iPhones. Apparently, Jason was pretty proud of these. Grace liked it that they were small, easy to transport.

Next, she checked Google Earth in case local conditions had changed since her original research. Roads in and out—sealed and dirt. Fences. Dams and culverts—she'd been forced to hide in both, in the past. Bridges. Neighbouring houses. Distances.

Then—a kind of superstition—Grace made a deep dive into Jason Britton himself. How much did he deserve to be robbed? She had found, over the years, that this made a difference to her.

Google listed hundreds of Jason Brittons. She scrolled down until she found the right one. Britton setting up The

Cog, his home-loan firm. Britton shaking hands with Tony Abbott. Britton handing a poster-sized cheque for $100,000 to a local hospital…And there he was in a *Guardian* article about corporate bastardry. Last Christmas Eve he'd sacked a hundred workers by email.

A voice in her head: You're better than him?

She swallowed and straightened her spine. One last job. Be a better person later.

19

DESMOND LIDDINGTON HAD developed a passion for red wines in his many years serving in the Barossa Valley, first as a detective constable and now, dizzyingly, on the eve of his retirement, detective senior constable, in the Kapunda, Nuriootpa and Angaston police stations. Weekends, when he wasn't on duty investigating a stolen mower or a shop-lifting, he liked to take Josie on a little wine-tasting tour. Or rather, she took him—not a good look for a police member to fail a breath test. And she didn't mind. She liked driving around the countryside in their old red Saab, liked a drop of whatever they'd bought when they got home, and, apparently, still liked him. With the nature of his job, she said, out or away all hours, when else were they going to spend quality time together?

In the early years they'd visited all of the big cellar-door joints—Yalumba, Wolf Blass, Jacob's Creek and so on—but now Liddington preferred to hunt down what he liked to call 'overlooked, underappreciated and deceptive reds' in tasting rooms off the beaten track. Plenty of these in the Barossa. Hidden gems, lovely new releases, uncommon grapes and interesting blends. Expensive, yeah, but he could afford to buy one good bottle a week: it wasn't as if he was outlaying tens of thousands on mid-life-crisis Harleys or boats. On the other hand, with retirement coming up next month, he might need to stick to the good-value end of the scale, especially if he and Josie followed their dream of touring the European wine regions—Bordeaux, Mosel, Chianti, places like that. Maybe tour every couple of years, if their savings lasted the distance. Unless a new Covid strain hit, and the world shut down again, and airfares went up again.

Meanwhile there were always the wine regions closer to home. Margaret River, McLaren Vale, Coonawarra, the Hunter Valley.

Thus Des Liddington's daydreams one afternoon as he and Detective Constable Gabi Richter headed out in one of Angaston's unmarked Kia Sorentos. The Kia wasn't going to break any speed records. It wasn't going to break any records for style, either, especially with him at the wheel. Liddington knew he probably came across as an old grandpa to the young woman beside him: his hands correctly positioned, speed a constant 5 km/h below the limit, every turn signalled well in advance.

Grandpa. He was unlikely to achieve that status any time soon. He and Josie had one son, Andy, thirty-three, divorced and living with them again. Not a no-hoper; a young man whose hopes, dreams, marriage and career were cut short when he'd got long Covid on top of his existing autoimmune conditions. It broke Liddington's heart to see him so frail and tired. Good company otherwise, though. Never complained. Always tried to help around the house when he felt up to it.

At that moment, Gabi, checking Google Maps, said, 'Next turn left.'

Liddington blinked awake, slowed, signalled and eased the wallowing Kia onto a dirt road before slowly accelerating into undulating country, lush vines on either side. Had he been up this road before? Unlikely, he thought a moment later, spotting a sign that read *Dog-Leg Fence Vineyard and Cellar Door.* You saw it more often these days, wineries with folksy names like Dog-Leg Fence, Shut the Gate, Ten Minutes by Tractor. Was it a way of saying wine shouldn't be elitist? Anyway, he made a mental note to visit soon. Maybe he'd find the quintessential overlooked, underappreciated and deceptive red.

As he'd once complained to Josie, those very terms

could well be applied to him. They'd been in the Saab at the time, and she'd patted his comfortable thigh with her free hand as she steered up yet another winery driveway. She didn't say anything, but he took the pat to mean that she agreed with him, that she had his back. Forty-two years in the job and his colleagues and bosses barely knew he existed. There was going to be a little retirement ceremony next Saturday, at which Liddington and a couple of others would get up in their dress uniforms and the local superintendent would hand them a medal and a fountain pen. Nothing else to mark their careers.

He glanced at Gabi Richter, intent on her phone. Mid-twenties; arts-law degree; sublimely capable and also ambitious. Policing's new face, he supposed. Four years into the job and she'd already made more arrests than he had in his whole career. No overlooking or underappreciating Detective Constable G. Richter, that was for sure. Nothing deceptive about her, either: you could read her astuteness and drive. Liddington shrugged. Surely not everyone had to be a high-flyer? There was room for steady, decent, reliable, get-the-job-done coppers who played by the book.

Sensing his gaze, she said warningly: 'Des…'

Seeing that he was headed for the ditch, he gave a little cough, corrected and drove on sedately, eyes on the road ahead. He felt leaden there behind the wheel; felt the contrast with her youth and energy. I like my reds too much, he thought.

She said, 'Next right.'

Another dirt road, narrower, but the verges were cropped and tidy—an indication, Liddington thought, of money and influence: boutique wineries ahead. He cut his speed, hating to raise a dust cloud in a place like this.

'Not far now, hundred metres down on your right,' Gabi said.

Liddington saw that her energy had ramped up: she was practically humming. And then it made sense when she said, 'Can't believe I get to meet Pete Patmore.'

Liddington kept on ambling down the road. 'Uh huh.'

She couldn't stand it. Her body urged him to get a move on. 'He was like a hero in our house when I was growing up.'

These days you were a hero if you knew how to tie your shoelaces, but Liddington supposed Patmore was considered a hero because he'd won silver in weightlifting at the Beijing Olympics; gold, silver and bronze at various other games. Gabi would have been about ten. And if she was any kind of detective, she'd have known that some of the gloss had worn off Peter Patmore.

'Oh?'

She explained: 'My dad trained with him at one stage. Wasn't quite good enough to get picked for the Olympics, though.'

So she probably won't be interested to learn that I was bowled for a duck by Dennis Lillee in a 1995 charity match, Des thought. 'Wow.'

She seemed to think his reaction was adequate and

they continued along the road, Gabi apparently in a kind of reverie. Liddington had heard she was a runner, netballer. A bit of a gym rat.

But to see her so innocently expectant made her more appealing. He hadn't the heart to tell her anything about Patmore—or the sons.

They came to a sign, *Patmore & Sons Irrigation*, and Gabi said, 'Here,' unnecessarily, and Liddington rumbled the Kia over a buckled stock ramp and up an eroded driveway choked on each side by agapanthus. He slowed for a broad, dusty yard fringed on three sides by a house and several sheds and vehicles.

Irrigation. Generally more money—and more reliable money—to be made from irrigating, hauling, pruning and spraying grapes than in growing or fermenting them. Plus, you didn't have to tart up your place of business and build a fancy tasting room overlooking an ornamental lake. Pete Patmore and his wife—who, from the size of her, had also lifted weights in her time—lived in a sprawling 1970s triple-fronted brick veneer with low ceilings and aluminium-framed doors and windows. There was a parched lawn with stubby roses in the shade cast by a couple of massive green plastic water tanks.

Liddington pulled in several metres short of a small Isuzu truck, ignored by the two men working there, one hooking metal ramps to the rear of the tray, the other waiting at the wheel of a Bobcat fitted with a bucket. 'That's Pete on the machine,' he said, 'Scott helping.'

Gabi, peering through the glass, said, 'Not Scott. I think it's Drew.' As if she had their photos pinned to her bedroom wall.

'Drew,' Liddington said. 'You could be right. They do look alike.'

They watched Pete Patmore drive the Bobcat up onto the tray of the Isuzu and secure it, then flip like a gymnast to the ground—a slab of a man full of physical grace. Pity about his inner qualities. Now, with both Patmores finally deigning to notice their visitors, he and Gabi Richter got out and approached them across the dirt. 'Gentlemen,' he said.

The Patmore men watched. Waited. Then the older man said, 'Might've known it'd be you, Desmond.'

'Peter, Drew,' Liddington said, 'this is Detective Constable Richter.'

Gabi, glee splitting her face, stepped right up to father and son with her hand out. 'Lovely to meet you, Mr Patmore. You knew my father, I think: Col, Colin Richter? 2010 Commonwealth Games?'

'Col Richter. I remember,' Patmore said. 'I won't shake your hand.'

He held his palms out in explanation: both were stained a dirty orange, as if he'd sluiced them in rusty water. He loomed over her, wearing a big gut in a torn khaki work shirt, greasy boots and jeans holed at the knee. More blubber than muscle these days, but still shaped like a weightlifter, with massive thighs, shoulders and upper arms. A beard, earring, forearm tatts and cropped hair. A big old bandit with flinty little eyes in a fleshy face. His tone betrayed no interest in Gabi or recollections of her father.

He was interested in Liddington, though. 'Thought you'd retired,' he said sourly.

'It's my last couple of weeks,' Liddington said.

Drew, the son, had been standing to one side. He stepped closer, chin out. 'You here about the utes?' he demanded, swinging his gaze from Richter to Liddington and back again.

He was smaller than his father. Neater, less piratical, with an eye for Gabi Richter's looks. She smiled. 'We are.'

Peter Patmore said, 'We reported it by phone. All the information you needed. All we want is an incident number for the insurance.'

Surely he didn't think it could all be done by phone? 'A major theft, Pete, we can't not investigate,' Liddington said. 'We'd like to see where the utes were kept, for a start.'

Patmore gestured at an open implement shed. Drums of fuel and stacks of PVC piping at one end, a small grey tractor in the middle, nothing at the other end. 'There you go. General absence of Toyota utes.'

'Locked?'

'Always.'

'The keys weren't on a hook somewhere?'

'Nope.'

'So where were the keys?'

'In the house, and they're still there. We always lock up when we go to bed. No one broke or sneaked in and got the keys, if that's what you're thinking.'

Gabi Richter was nodding soberly. 'Hotwired them.'

Patmore ignored her. Waited for Liddington, who said, 'Spare keys?'

'Lost long ago.'

Convenient, Liddington thought. 'Who discovered the utes were missing?'

'Me.' Patmore gestured at a blue heeler in a kennel. 'When I got up to feed the dog.'

'Hear anything during the night?'

'Nup.'

'Your wife hear anything?'

'She's been in town the last few days. Our daughter's expecting.'

'Town?'

Patmore eyed Liddington as if he were slow. 'Adelaide.'

'You checked if anything else was missing?'

'I did.'

Liddington gestured at the remaining sheds; their doors padlocked. 'What do you keep over there?'

'What do you *think* we keep there? Stolen utes?' His tone said *moron*. 'Valuable machinery, all right? Things like pumps that are easily portable. Maybe you'd like to check?'

Liddington was about to respond when he sensed the force of Gabi Richter's disapproval: why was he being such a prick? She said hastily, 'That won't be necessary, Mr Patmore.'

—

Liddington drove again, waves of displeasure rising from Gabi Richter in the passenger seat. He compounded that by turning left out of the driveway instead of heading back to the police station.

'Where are we going? This isn't the way.'

'Something I need to check.'

They rode in silence until she said, 'We actually had this lecture at the academy. To do with the kinds of cultures that can breed in the police, like old-style coppers who do things their own way. Cut corners, never share, never explain.'

'I'll share in a minute.'

'Exactly. I'm not important enough for you to share with right now.'

Silence again and Liddington steered them through rolling vineyard country for twenty minutes, to one of the valley's little back-road towns and out the other side to another dirt road, poorly maintained this time, and they were a hundred metres short of a driveway when a long, top-heavy truck lurched out, a tarpaulin flapping over its boxy load. Liddington braked sharply, dust roiling, small stones pinging against the Kia.

'That was close. He didn't even give way,' Gabi said, a hand over her heart.

'Yeah, well, he wouldn't,' Liddington said. He gestured at the dust cloud and his smile was tired and old and barely there. 'That was Lance Heinrich, Pete's brother-in-law. Pete must've warned him to move the utes.'

Gabi stared at the dust, and Liddington saw her begin a slow, sad readjustment.

20

ADAM GARRETT CHECKED Telegram before bed on Thursday night, saw Gaynor Bernard's message—*noon tomorrow*—and by 10 a.m. Friday was heading for the Adelaide Hills, allowing himself time to get into place before Anita—Grace—picked up her picture. He had no qualms about abandoning the Leigh Calnan surveillance: he'd seen the kid's mother drop him off at school. He had until 3 p.m. at least.

Except that he was barely at Crafers when his mobile rang. Melodie. She had another job for him. 'Just until mid-afternoon, then I want you back on the Calnan kid.'

'Wish you'd make up your mind.'

'Sorry? Did I say this was up for negotiation?'

Garrett waited, counting and breathing slowly, until he had a grip. Not for the first time, he wondered what she'd do if he just cleared out. But didn't carry the thought very far. She knew people. 'What's the job?'

'Good boy,' she said—then paused. Her voice, when it came again, was layered in suspicion: 'Are you in your car?'

'School excursion,' Garrett said. 'I'm following the bus.'

'Forget that. What's the kid going to do on an excursion? Rush job, I need you to tail someone for a while today. I've just emailed you the details.'

She proceeded to outline the case anyway. The clients were accountants whose nineteen-year-old daughter had dropped out of her Flinders University arts course, moved in with her dodgy boyfriend and stopped seeing family and friends. Had been seen tootling around town in a red BMW coupe and partying at the casino on North Terrace. Was she on drugs? Were she and the boyfriend dealing?

'How come we get these kinds of jobs?' Garrett said. 'How come we can't bring down some paedophile or white-collar mastermind now and then?'

'Shut up. I want you on this straight away. The address is in the stuff I sent you.'

Garrett was pretty certain that a partying nineteen-year-old would still be in bed by the time he'd bugged Anita's car and headed back down to the city. 'Will do.'

'Photos, times and places. The usual.'

'Yeah, yeah,' Garrett said, and by 11.20 he'd parked at tennis courts half a kilometre short of his destination and walked to a clump of black wattles overlooking Gaynor Bernard's driveway. He knew Anita would be twitchy, looking for cars and pedestrians. She might even arrive early and scout around for half an hour.

Screened by the wattles, he settled in to watch. He wore dark glasses, a towelling hat, a long-sleeved shirt and cargo pants, with a daypack on his back and binoculars around his neck. A birdwatcher, maybe, if someone did spot him amid the heavy foliage and dappled light, except that few twitchers used any of the hi-tech gadgets he had in his backpack.

He saw a Subaru SUV drive past a couple of times, then pull into the parking area at the base of the conservator's driveway. A woman got out; he raised the binoculars for a closer look and saw her scan the area warily.

Anita.

No mistaking her litheness and strength, the economy of her movements. She was dressed simply, as if not wanting to stand out, and the face that he remembered so well was alive and focused. Never a cold face, but never entirely sympathetic, either. She lived in places he'd never reached; and she'd detached herself from him with minimal effort when Galt entered her life.

Or was he recasting her in this way because she'd hurt

him? There had been good times. They'd relied on each other. They'd been a team.

He shook off the memories. Who was she now? Was she on a job?

At the moment she aimed her key fob to lock the Subaru, Garrett activated the signal jammer, then watched her hike up the steep driveway. When she was out of sight, he waited for a couple of minutes, then left his tree shelter and ran at a crouch across the road and slid under the Subaru. He fastened a GPS tracker to the chassis, got to his feet and checked the driver's door. It was unlocked; the jammer had worked. He leaned in and plugged a second tracker into the on-board diagnostics port, which was under the dash and out of sight.

Then he trotted across country to his own car and settled in to wait.

21

THAT SAME FRIDAY lunchtime, Brodie Hendren flew down to Hobart to buy a gun. Tasmania seemed weaker on gun laws and enforcement than the mainland states, and he knew that Toni Bleasdale had a floor safe full of revolvers and pistols. He'd dealt with her before: she'd bought an SS songbook from him, and he'd bought Field Marshall Rommel's binoculars and three Panzerarmee Afrika uniforms from her.

He stopped in South Hobart to pick up his Airbnb key before going on to Bleasdale's restored whaler's cottage in

Sandy Bay. Knocked on the solid door and it was opened by a skinny seventy-year-old witch. 'You're late.'

Ten minutes late. 'Sorry about that.'

Bleasdale led him through to a back room. Desk, filing cabinets, carpet, curtains and icy chill, that's all. The whole house was like that. Minimalist. Suited to a witch.

She said, 'Take a seat. What kind of handgun? Pistol? Revolver? Be clear.'

'An automatic,' Hendren said. 'A Glock, if you have one.'

'Cost you five thousand.'

Their past deals should count for something, Hendren thought. 'Four.'

'Five,' Toni said, sticking out her bony jaw and neck wattles.

Hendren sighed, counting out $5,000 in hundred-dollar notes. She scooped it up, then, with a ghastly rictus that seemed to be meant as a kindly smile, gave him back $100 and slid the balance into the top drawer of her desk. Locked it and pocketed the key. 'Wait here.'

She slid out from behind her desk in a tidal wave of Chanel No. 5 and disappeared into another back room. Came back a minute later with a Glock pistol in an oilcloth. 'The clip's full, no extra cost.'

'Thanks.'

Thanks for nothing. Hendren got up to go. She said, 'I've got von Stauffenberg's watch, if you're interested.'

First, he doubted she had the real thing. Second, von

Stauffenberg was a traitorous pig. 'No thanks.'

'Got standards, have we?' she said, watching him stuff the pistol into a daypack and leave the house.

Wanting to drown the old cow, Hendren walked until the feeling ebbed. Long, fast strides through Sandy Bay to the steps down to Salamanca Place and then, skirting a section of Hobart's wharf area, up into South Hobart and his Airbnb, stopping to buy some small padded envelopes on the way.

Seated at the kitchen bench, he fieldstripped the Glock, first removing the loaded clip before operating the takedown lever, nudging the slide forward and removing the recoil spring and barrel. Next he packaged the separate items and addressed them to himself at various rental mailboxes in Adelaide.

By 3.30 he was back at the airport, flashing his fake frequent flyer gold card at the entrance to the Virgin lounge and settling into an armchair with his laptop. His flight wasn't due to leave for seventy-five minutes, time enough for one of the online catch-ups he ran throughout each day. Not much action anywhere. But people had rallied to his crowdfunding story of being mugged and hospitalised in Bali. $13,560 and rising.

22

ADAM GARRETT SAT in his car and waited, glued to the refurbished iPhone in the dash cradle, switching between the app for the simple under-chassis tracker and the app for the tracker in the OBD port. The latter was more sophisticated: long range, two-week battery life, good in weak signal areas, Google street-view format. Nothing yet. He pictured Anita settling the bill and walking down to her Subaru, the restored etching under one arm. She pauses at the driver's door. Checks both ways along the road. Even casts a long, unnerving look at the copse of trees before checking the rear footwell and driving off.

Then, spookily, he saw from the OBD tracker app that she really was on the move. He began to follow but stayed well back. There was no need to stick to her tail—the screen would tell him where she was—but nor did he want to be many minutes behind her. Not that he intended to accost her yet, or even in the near future. He wanted to know more about her first. If she was meeting someone, he'd like to eyeball them. If she was staying in a motel or an Airbnb, he wanted to know whether or not she was alone. If she lived and worked in the area, he wanted to know where and who she spent time with. What she did if she didn't work. Was she working on another heist, for example. If so, here or further afield? Was there a man in her life who would get in his way when he did act?

Suddenly, the winking cursor stopped moving. The Subaru was halfway along the main street of a town named Oakbank. He pulled over and waited for a couple of minutes. Anita—Grace—would be wary of every vehicle that entered the town soon after she did.

Checking that the signal was still stationary, he pulled out again and into the town and spotted the Subaru parked outside a shop with whitegoods in the window. He cruised past, his elbow on the windowsill and his hand to the side of his face, until he found a parking spot between a bike shop and a cafe fifty metres further down. He considered watching the Subaru by manipulating the side and rear-view mirrors, but Anita would look twice at anyone sitting in a car for any length of time.

Why the fuck had he bought a lime-green Mazda?

And so he locked up. Still in his birdwatching gear and towelling hat, he affected a limp as he crossed into the cafe. Bought a cappuccino, took it out to one of the footpath tables. Good cover: a trio of elderly women sat at one table, a man in a suit at another, two women with oversized prams at a third. With his back to the Subaru, still parked fifty metres behind him, he sipped his coffee, now and then checking his phone. Emails, both tracking apps, the news feed. Trump this, the prime minister that...

And Jesus Christ, a story about Craig Tolhurst. His son Rohan had been murdered execution-style in a Somali village.

Garrett found himself hyperventilating. He drained his coffee; that didn't help. Breathed in, breathed out, keeping it deep, slow, even...Eventually his pulse slowed. But he felt shithouse. Guilt. Shock. Dismay. Should he tell the Malady?

Well, no. At that moment she texted him wanting to know what the uni student was doing. He replied: *Still in bed I think.*

He was here to see what Neet was up to, nothing more. Play-acting a yawn and a stretch, he glanced back along the street. And there she was, staggering to her car with a cardboard carton. A microwave, maybe?

He got up, coffee unfinished, head bowed to his phone, and started walking towards his Mazda. He heard a distant thump as she closed the Subaru's hatch.

And then a dark shape blotted the sun, hands shoved him, he fell between two parked cars as though off the dark rim of the world.

Time passed, and when he blinked into consciousness, he was flat on his back and in pain. A timid voice was asking, 'Are you all right?'

Of course he wasn't fucking all right. Some arsehole on a skateboard had snatched his phone. He'd heard of it happening in Europe, ninety thousand cases in London alone last year. Apple picking, they called it, the stolen phones being whisked off to the Continent overnight, then reprogrammed and sold on to places in Asia.

One of the elderly women asked again, 'Are you all right?'

He groaned, turned onto one hip and creaked upright—then immediately hunched his shoulders and brushed at his knees: the Subaru was pulling out. His back to the road, his shape still altered, he said, 'Fine, thanks. Did you see where he went?'

'Where who went?'

'The man who grabbed my phone.'

'He grabbed your phone?'

Pointless. He was down $550 for that phone, bought especially for tracking Anita. Now all he had was guesswork: she probably lived in the area. She'd used a local rather than a city-based conservator, and she'd bought what might have been a microwave. She was setting up house?

But the Adelaide Hills was pretty big. Could take him weeks to find her, and she might spot him first and disappear again. Meanwhile she had a huge head start. Even so, he tumbled into his car, pulled out and shot down the street. Stopping at the first crossroads, he checked left, right and straight ahead. Not a single vehicle in any direction.

Then his phone pinged again, an angry text from Melodie. The uni drop-out's parents had called: their darling daughter had just tried to hit up her maternal grandmother for $1,000.

Where the fuck are you?

On it, he told her.

He headed back to the city. He was on Portrush Road when Melodie contacted him yet again—a call this time. Not wanting her to hear the rush of traffic, he pulled into a side street and switched off before answering. 'Mel?'

One of her trademark snarls. 'We're off the case.'

Garrett tried to sound as if he was on top of it. 'Really?'

'The parents are ropeable. They'd like to know—and so would I—why the fuck you didn't do something when you saw the daughter turn around and *go back* into grandma's house.'

'Didn't have time. She—'

'She put the old bag in hospital. Now they want their deposit back, and I'll have to let them have it. Jesus, Adam.'

'Think about it,' he responded hotly. 'Do either of us want the cops involved in anything we do? That's what would've happened if I'd tried to intervene.'

That didn't quite shut her up. 'Yeah, well, don't fuck up the Calnan surveillance. Be there when he gets back from his excursion.'

Cow.

Garrett stopped for sushi on Portrush Road and was parked outside the high school as the last bell sounded. He expected everyone to head home but some kids stayed on for sports practice, the girls streaming to the netball courts, the boys to the football oval—Leigh Calnan among them. Garrett moved his car further along the street and settled in to wait, occasionally training his binoculars on instances of head trauma in the making, sixteen-year-old boys flattening each other.

When they paused for a breather, he texted Gaynor Bernard. *Didn't quite pan out. Let me know if she contacts you again.*

Then, at 5 p.m., training ended. Kids straggled into the change rooms and eventually out again, heading home, lumping gym bags, some on foot or by bike, others by car. Calnan's mother drove a Peugeot. No Peugeot yet.

By 5.20 only one kid remained: Leigh Calnan. Garrett watched him walk to a wooden bench at the railing around the oval and bend over his phone, occasionally glancing towards a side street. Nothing happened for several minutes, and then the kid stiffened, stood, and hurried towards the side street, where a teenage girl had appeared. Jeans, a hoodie, a ponytail. This was new, a change in routine. Garrett expected them to hug or kiss, but the girl simply handed over an envelope, turned abruptly and headed back the way she'd come.

Follow her? No. Garrett swung his binoculars back to the boy, who was sitting again, hunched, tense, as he tore open the envelope. One sheet of paper. He read it intently, as if he wanted to meld with it; as if it might save his life.

Then, looking stunned and dreamy, he got to his feet and crossed to a rubbish bin at the side of the changerooms, where he tore the page into small pieces and fluttered them into the bin. He stood for a moment, shoulders slumped, before trudging to a bicycle chained to a railing. Unlocked it, strapped on his gym bag and cycled slowly away. Then his feet were pedalling madly—fear, elation or just an excess of youthful energy? Maybe, Garrett thought, it was a good-news letter after all.

Wearing gloves, he retrieved the paper scraps from the bin and twenty minutes later was at the wobbly desk in his room at the boarding house, matching torn edges with strips of sticky tape.

It was a densely typed love letter, the words passionate and heartfelt but also discreet, as though the writer—who'd signed it 'Kat,' with a row of kisses—knew that it would be handled and possibly read by an intermediary.

Kat missed Leigh, thought about him every day. It broke her heart that they'd been torn apart, all because of her stupid father. Why should she and Mum have to suffer? She wished she could just run away, but they watched her like a hawk 24/7 and they were all crammed together in a couple of crappy motel rooms so she had hardly any privacy and she wished she could message him direct and not through Carla. Wished she had her own phone instead of using the motel handyman's when his back was turned. She was still trying to work out where they were—somewhere in New South Wales, going by the numberplates in the carpark.

Maybe when I know where, you could come? I could sneak out and say I was going for a run or something. Or maybe I can catch a train or a bus to you. Or hitch. I'll be careful. The police will probably find me again but it'd be worth it just to spend five minutes with you.

And he shouldn't worry about Dav or Ivan's goons catching her, she knew all the psychos on the Vargas' payroll.

Sorry I was so depressed last time. Mum keeps saying be positive, but it's really hard and you can see it's getting to her, too, she's really pissed off with Dad, they argue all the time and I can't stand it.

Then the typed signature and the line of hugs and kisses. Garrett used his gloved forefinger to slide the patchwork letter away from him before opening Google on his phone. The names 'Dav,' 'Ivan,' 'Kat', 'Leigh Calnan' and 'Norwood High School' took him down many rabbit holes until he found the name, 'Davorin Varga'. Varga, with his parents and older brother, Ivan, had been charged with defrauding the National Disability Insurance Scheme to the tune of $5 million.

Earlier news reports had also mentioned the arrest of an associate, Louis Horvat. Horvat had a daughter, Katarina.

Kat.

23

AFTER COLLECTING THE restored Whiteley, setting up her new microwave and checking in with Erin, Grace packed for the Barossa Valley: clothes, burglary tools and the two sets of numberplates.

It was good to hit the road finally. The week had worked on her nerves, a hard-to-pinpoint dissatisfaction that seemed to stem from losing her car, and the feeling that she was waiting for something to happen was a large part of it. Waiting for luck. Waiting for money. Waiting for an easy pattern of life, rather than wariness and uncertainty. Waiting for the habits and expectations of her new, straight life to become a part of her, and wondering if they ever would. Maybe she'd been waiting for some kind of dramatic disaster ever since spotting Adam at the stamp expo? In any event, she engaged in some diversionary driving as she left Battendorf—speeding, ambling, sudden U-turns, unnecessary detours.

No one tailed her out of the hills or to the Barossa and the grounds of the Vigneron Motel. Her room overlooked the motel's carpark and the main road beyond. It was clean, cheap, cheerless and too scented, with a photograph of Chateau Tanunda above the drum-tight bedspread and a clumsy oil painting of a hillslope of vines above a chipped table. The bathroom was small and functional, with tiny squeeze-tubes of shampoo and conditioner and a bar of dolls-house soap. She didn't care about any of that. What she cared about—a touch of luck—was the bathroom window. It was an old single-hung type, frosted glass, set high in the wall above the toilet. Not painted shut, and it opened wide enough for her to slip in and out.

She returned to the main room and unpacked only the clothes she would wear on Saturday—clothes she could abandon if she had to run before then—and took her weekender case back out to the car.

Then she prepared the room. First, she opened the curtains slightly, leaving a two-centimetre gap, and dampened the largest towel before dumping it in the bathroom doorway, positioned so that an unwanted visitor to her room might be tempted to boot it aside. Finally, using her phone, she photographed the curtains, the towel, her unpacked clothes, the arrangement of shampoo, conditioner, soap and bodywash samples, and slipped out of the bathroom window.

The stop for the Gawler bus was two hundred metres from the motel. When the 3.30 arrived she settled on a back seat and spent the trip googling Jason Britton again and checking if the Barossa Valley had cropped up in any recent news stories. Only one mention: the Runacre Hall clearing sale in relation to the owner's legal woes. One other item intrigued her, a videoed interview with a man named Tolhurst, whose son had been kidnapped and later executed by Somali rebels. Tolhurst was bleakly sad—his voice and the contours of his face—but his eyes were fixed hard on something only he could see. He wasn't in the mood to suffer fools either. He practically bit off the head of the reporter who asked him how it felt to lose a son in such a way.

By 4.45 Grace was in the office of Off-Road Paradise, near the railway station in Gawler, using fake papers to rent a black Triton dual-cab ute fitted with a slightly dented bull bar. She'd called during the week. They were expecting her. She was headed for the Flinders Ranges, she said, and wanted a decent set of wheels to poke about in. What she didn't tell them was, she wanted a vehicle with some grunt for bush-bashing, something that would take her through creeks, fences, ploughed paddocks and saplings if she ran into a police patrol now or tomorrow night.

She drove the Triton back to the Barossa Valley with one diversion, onto a dirt side road a few kilometres before Rowland Flat, where, using a pair of vice grips to undo the tamper-proof screws, she swapped the white South Australian plates for a yellow New South Wales set. She had about sixty minutes of daylight left, enough to find Jason Britton's house and form a better sense of the lie of the land than she'd got from Google Earth. She had only one shot at this: in a perfect world she'd reconnoitre for several days, at different times each day, to see who belonged in the area, who visited, what they did, when they did it.

And who shouldn't be there.

Ten minutes later she was rattling over the corrugations on Schiller Lane, a gravel road that curved up into a low range of hills covered in vines and threaded by tree-lined creeks and intersecting roads. Britton's house was an architecturally challenged cube of glass, local stone, black metal and stained wood panels, set on a broad lawn dotted with gum trees and other natives. A simple post-and-wire fence ran around the property, hard against a cypress hedge, and twin gates secured the driveway. The nearest neighbour was half a kilometre away, the nearest police station ten kilometres. She idled outside the gates for a few minutes, watching the house with binoculars. The place looked mute and grim with no human presence to enliven it. The curtains were partly drawn on most of the windows, and, with evening dimness drawing in, she could see two lights burning. Then one light went off, followed a couple of minutes later by the other. Both came on again. They were on timers.

Lights in her rear-view. A spike of anxiety that didn't ease until the car passed, splattering her with tiny pebbles. The driver, a woman with a child in the passenger seat, paid her no attention. But Grace didn't linger; she had the place fixed in her head now.

Driving on for a few hundred metres, she passed an open farm gate near a haystack and an old shed in a paddock left to lie fallow. Useful to know. Then, U-turning, she headed back across country to Angaston, parked her rented ute at a twenty-four-hour service station in the town and returned to her motel on foot. Slipping back through the bathroom window, she paused to listen and sniff the air before entering the main room. No one had opened the curtains to admit further light. No one had kicked the pesky towel out of the way. No one had rifled through her clothing.

But they wouldn't—not if they were good.

24

MEANWHILE ADAM GARRETT was working up a few entries for the surveillance log: *6 p.m. subject arrived home from footy training*, and *7.30 p.m. Domino Pizza delivery, subject paid at the door,* and *10 p.m. lights out, no further movement from subject or his mother* and emailed them to Melodie. Then he walked down to O'Connell Street for fish and chips, wandered back to the boarding house, watched TV for a while and went to bed.

He couldn't sleep. His body ached from being mugged; he'd lost Anita; he still owed the Malady a heap of money.

And he was really fucking lonely.

He tended to get philosophical when he couldn't sleep: who he was and what he'd done; what he thought about doing. The notion of good and bad crimes. Was a crime bad if no one was harmed? What if the harm was minimal? You couldn't call Casdorff, whose stamp he'd stolen, a victim. Casdorff had no concept of abstract worth, let alone beauty, anyway. Only of money, and he would've had insurance. Insurance companies are loaded. What about crimes that brought about the greater good of society? That Wikileaks guy releasing secret government files, for example—if you could even call a government a victim.

So, what was a bad crime? One that harmed a person, or society in general. Or harmed *him*, obviously. Maybe the Casdorff robbery *was* a bad crime—since he, Adam Garrett, had been no more than a servant doing someone else's bidding. It didn't matter that Melodie had knocked three thousand dollars off his debt, or that he'd actually done a pretty amazing job.

And the Craig Tolhurst thing. No pride in that.

Garrett ranged further back through the things he'd done, the things he should have done, the things he shouldn't have done.

And the shitty things done to him, like Anita blowing him off when Galt came along. Pretending she didn't have the Jaeger watch that time in the alley. It occurred to him then that he didn't really know what he'd do to her if, when, he found her—except punish her in some way. Take from her something she held dear? Hurt her physically? He still had scars from when her cop boyfriend had him beaten up.

His legs tangled the sheets. He stripped off his sweaty T-shirt. Staggered downstairs to the kitchen at 3 a.m. and drained two glasses of water. Then back upstairs to his sofa, not his bed. Watched a few minutes of a shopping channel on mute…Woke, stunned, shivering, racked by aches, pains and the dregs of a dream at 5 a.m.

He'd seen a man with a gun enter a series of rooms. He'd tried to stop the man, but, too late, each door was slammed in his face and he didn't know what the man was doing on the other side. His feet stuck in a slough of mud. His car wouldn't start. He got lost. It was all a jumble, but Garrett knew this much: it was a bad crime to tail a teenage boy in order to find a teenage girl, and therefore her father, so that the man could be silenced. He guessed that Katerina Horvat and her family were in witness protection and sooner or later the Vargas would find them—probably through Katerina.

She'd been careful, presumably texting love letters which the schoolfriend had duly printed out and delivered to the Calnan kid. And he'd duly read and destroyed them. But these three kids wouldn't get away with it for long. Someone would spot Katerina using a mobile, the schoolfriend would let the secret slip, or Leigh would try to find her. Or she'd try to find him, and the Varga family's heavies would grab her.

—

At six-thirty Garrett showered, dressed, downed a coffee and took Payneham Road out to Tea Tree Gully in the foothills, where he bought a phone at a 7-Eleven. Then, after placing brief calls to state and federal police, the *Advertiser* and Sophie Calnan, Leigh's mother, he destroyed the phone and snapped the sim card and tossed the pieces into several shopping-centre bins. Thwarting young love, he thought, but maybe saving a life.

He was halfway home when Melodie called. 'I'm on my way to the Calnan kid's,' he told her, to explain the traffic noise.

'Okay. Keep me posted. Saturday—he'll be out and about.'

She rang off and Garrett took Portrush Road to Toorak Gardens. He was tired of being in the area, and wondered gloomily what a kid from a well-heeled family did on a Saturday. He realised he had no idea. When he was a kid his Saturdays and Sundays were like every other day. Fight the other kids for enough to eat. Beg in a doorway. Pick a pocket. Run from the cops.

As he drove, he ran the Tea Tree Gully phone calls through his mind. It was possible they'd amount to nothing, that everyone had thought the caller was a nutjob. But the woman on the *Advertiser*'s news desk had seemed interested. And Sophie Calnan's voice had moved from early-morning bleariness to full-on alarm.

Using a shopping-centre men's room to change into

shorts, T-shirt and trainers, he returned to his car and parked it two streets away from the Calnan place. The sun, still low, directed a cool, benign light through the area's plane trees, dappling his legs as he began to run. At first, he was the only jogger, then a couple more flashed by in the distance. An elderly woman collected her dew-soaked newspaper in her dressing gown. An unshaven balding guy watering his roses yawned and gave Garrett a nod: 'Sooner you than me, pal.' Cyclists now, and a woman bundling a pair of netballers into the back of her station wagon. A suburb waking up.

Garrett didn't enter Galway Street at first but simply made two broad loops around it, chancing quick glances down it as he crossed the intersection at each end. There were signs of life but none at the Calnan house. No panicky Peugeot accelerating away; no sirens; no unmarked cars angled at the kerb outside the front gate.

But then, at 8.15, a police car shot past him on Dulwich Avenue. Lights; no siren. Garrett ran on, and when he crossed the intersection closest to the Calnan house, he saw the cop car pulled up outside it, joining an unmarked Toyota Kluger. He continued around the block and this time entered Galway Street, loping down it casually on the opposite footpath, his cap low over his face as he cast a curious glance at the drama—the way anyone might. Two uniforms stood at the front gate. One of them gave him a hard stare. And on the porch, obstructing his view of the open front door, were a man and a woman in plain clothes.

A moment later they stood aside and Leigh Calnan and his mother emerged, toting overnight bags. Not altering his pace, Garrett reached the next side street and turned right. Now he charged like a maniac to his car, just in case that uniformed cop decided to follow up. He turned the ignition key, pulled out and shot down to Fullarton Road and eventually across to his North Adelaide boarding house. He imagined the doorstep conversation as he drove.

'We received a phone call, Mrs Calnan.'

'So did I. Should I take it seriously?'

'That's why we're here. You should each pack a bag and we'll take you somewhere.'

Or whatever. Didn't matter, the kid was safe now.

Garrett made one pass along his own street, checking cars, and then pulled against the kerb and took out his phone. He called Melodie's mobile, then the office landline. He wanted to say, 'Hey, Mel, something strange is going on at the Calnan house, I had to get out of there,' but she didn't answer.

25

AROUND THE SAME time, Grace was driving past the twenty-four-hour petrol station, checking that her rented ute was still parked beside the side wall. She continued on to Runacre Hall, five kilometres outside Angaston, then up a manicured driveway, following arrows that directed her to a broad stretch of mowed grass bordered by golden cypresses at the rear, where a parking marshal indicated a slot between an old Kombi van and a Jaguar SUV. All kinds here today, she thought, watching as other cars arrived. She looked up: a grey day, with high, silent winds tearing the clouds into ribbons and driving them across the sky. Yet curiously calm here on the ground, the air scented by tyre-crushed grass.

She set out across an expanse of lawn in comfortable flat shoes. She'd be on her feet for the next few hours, wandering about the Hall, buying, appraising. Even talking—she recognised a couple of dealers who'd come into the shop one day. Were they her tribe? She was not in disguise just now. Didn't need to be. Didn't need a story, a wig, oversized glasses or layers of clothing to bulk up her shape. She was who she wanted to be: Erin Mandel's assistant, an unremarkable young woman faintly excited by the prospect of a day spent looking, touching and buying. If anyone looked more closely, and saw the alert spring in her step, maybe they'd put it down to jogging and swimming.

A voice behind her: 'Hello there, gorgeous.'

Grace tensed, turned. It was Robert Stuart, a bric-a-brac dealer from Oakbank. Tall, skeletal, a bundle of bones stitched together under a once-classy woollen suit now too big for him, he was leaning heavily on a walking stick. Smiling a greeting, she waited for him to catch up, then they strolled together.

Stuart touched her forearm, slowing her. 'Not as young as I was.'

'Take your time.'

Another round of wheezing. 'Do an old man a favour, dear?'

'Glad to, Robert.'

'There's a Matchbox set...'

'I saw it in the catalogue.'

'Couldn't run on ahead and snap it up for me, could you?'

'Sure,' Grace said.

'I'll pay, of course, soon as I find you. But if you could at least save it from a couple of other old reprobates who are likely to be interested...'

'See you soon,' Grace said.

And she hurried off, slipping through the idlers massing on the paved area leading to the main entrance. A shuffling queue had formed inside the broad doorway, and then she was at a desk where she picked up a name card and a list of the items on sale. Then into a grand main room with small valuables and collectibles displayed on trestle tables. Visible inside a roped-off side room were the next day's auction items: cabinets, sideboards, chairs and other antiques. And at the end, also roped off, a broad staircase leading to the top floor.

Grace took a moment to take stock of doorways, obstacles and people, and felt uneasy. Too crowded, too few exits, too many security types wandering around or standing in corners. A couple at the top of the stairs, too.

She shook off the feeling: habit, and unnecessary today. Spotting a woman wearing an *Ask Me!* badge, she said, 'Excuse me.'

'Yes?'

Grace tapped the catalogue. 'These Matchbox cars. Where can I find them?'

The woman indicated a table beside a piano—and just in time, for two men of Robert's vintage were peering at the Matchbox set, thirty 1980s cars, trucks and vans in a wooden display case—asking price $800—next to a box of gramophone records and a set of Bean's history of the First World War.

Grace hurried. Sidled in so winningly that the old men apologised for blocking her. That changed when she called to a woman wearing a Sotheby's T-shirt: 'I wish to buy the Matchbox set.' One man said to the other, 'Talk about pushy,' and they walked off muttering.

Robert puffed into view a moment later. Abruptly thanking her, and just as brusquely dismissing her, he began to bargain with the Sotheby's agent.

Grace shrugged and turned away into the other rooms, touching, scrutinising, googling, buying. By 4 p.m. she had spent almost $10,000: $1,850 for the 1916 Blamire Young watercolour, *Rain over the Range*; $975 for a signed first edition of Patrick White's *The Twyborn Affair*; $6,500 for a pair of nineteenth-century Meissen porcelain oriels. Leaving just over $10,000 to spend tomorrow, when the furniture would be auctioned.

At 4.30 she took everything out to Erin's Forester and locked them into a strongbox. The Blamire Young would need a clean: there were age spots in the grey wash of rainy sky. Another job for Gaynor Bernard.

She was on the approach road to her motel when Erin called, the bluetooth connection routing her voice through the car's audio system.

'How…today?'

'You're breaking up a bit,' Grace said, 'but pretty good.'

She listed what she'd bought and spent, and Erin responded, her voice surging and scratching: 'I didn't quite…that last bit?'

Grace found herself shouting idiotically: 'I said I'll have just over ten thousand to spend at auction tomorrow.'

Static, then: 'Hope you…sideboard and the…'

Exasperated, Grace stopped the car, reached for her phone and tapped an SMS: *Reception not great, call you tomorrow.*

The reply came: a tick and a thumbs-up.

26

FIVE O'CLOCK NOW. Grace set an aftermarket alarm on the car, undressed and climbed into bed. She slept until 8 p.m., then showered. No soap or shampoo, just water. She wanted to slip unregistered through the darkness of Jason Britton's house: not be smelled, heard or seen. If anything, she wanted to be no more than a trick of the light.

She pulled on underwear, black leggings, a charcoal T-shirt and a dark-grey hooded top. All new; all had been rinsed in plain water. Then black running shoes. She was hungry and thirsty, but if she ate or drank now, her body might betray her later, when she most needed speed and nerve.

A last check of her backpack toolkit. A tiny torch. A radio frequency jammer. Pliers with a good wire-cutting capability, a screwdriver, a Swiss Army knife, duct tape, a thin steel pry bar, a spray can of insulation foam. Matches, in case she had to light a diversionary fire. And a bucket hat, overalls and a skirt and top—partly to stifle the noise of the items in the pack moving against each other, partly for a quick outfit change.

Finally, she checked Jason Britton's Facebook posts, just in case he'd flown home early. No: he was sitting in a kayak with a tropical flower tucked behind one ear. She ran through the news feed quickly, in case there was anything else to worry about—a major police action in the Barossa, for example. Again, nothing.

Slipping out through her bathroom window, then avoiding streetlights where possible, she jogged to the service station. Checked the Triton's footwells, then drove out of town and across the valley to the network of minor roads that would take her to Britton's house. And suddenly she was struck by the stark contrast between her intentions now and the ordinary events of the day just passed. Taking risks. Being stupid.

She gave herself a firm shake. Not a good time for doubts.

Twenty minutes later, she was on Schiller Lane, giving

Britton's house a quick glance as she passed. Nothing had altered since the previous evening. Heading on past the cypress hedge, the haystack and the run-down implement shed, she stopped to get out and eye the grass. No recent tyre impressions, so she drove into the paddock, then back along the fence line to the shed. It was open-sided, half the space taken up with fuel drums and an auger. Plenty of room for her ute. She reversed in and got out, leaving it unlocked.

Then she waited a while, listening. The wind gusted; iron flapped loosely on the shed. Cloudy starlight and a scrap of moon. The world felt empty but not safe. She should go home. Taking a few deep, slow breaths, she set out, walking to the cypress hedge and slipping through the fence wires, barely twanging them. She then waited again, wondering what she'd do to save herself if everything caved in. All she wanted was a quick in and out—and for the rented Triton not to let her down, trees not to have fallen across her exit roads, nails not to pierce her tyres or police cars to box her in.

The sound of a vehicle. Flattening herself on the grass, she listened, daring to poke her head up. Soon the sound dwindled. It had been out on the cross road, not Schiller Lane.

She got to her feet and ran at a crouch to a stand of banksias, casuarinas and other small native trees twenty metres from the house. She trod carefully now, the ground cover a noisy mix of fallen twigs, leaves and bark, threatening to bring her undone. Four steps, stop and listen; four steps, stop and listen. It was swift enough, and let her listen for the sounds that didn't belong. A dog. A cop. Britton himself.

At one point she smacked into a wheelbarrow. An almost soundless impact, but she waited before moving again. Anyone nearby would listen for the sound to be repeated.

Reaching the side wall of the house, she turned on the RF jammer. It looked like an oversized TV remote with four stubby antennas and could jam pretty much any device within a twenty-metre range—phones, garage remotes, home-security alarms, motion sensors, CCTV cameras, and anything using bluetooth or wi-fi.

It didn't necessarily open locks, though. More jittery now, Grace went right around the house, pushing experimentally on windows, testing door handles. She didn't like to break glass: the noise, the mess, the forensic risks of glass chips in her hair or her clothing, a blood trace left behind.

The back door. It looked sturdy, but was fitted with a thin plywood insert. Gouging a starter-hole in one corner, she used the serrated blade on her pocketknife to saw around the perimeter. Tossed the insert aside. Crawled through the gap, careful not to catch her skin or clothing on the splinters, and found herself in a mudroom. Coats and hats on hooks, rubber boots and gardening shoes lined up beneath a wooden bench. A door on the left led to the laundry. The door at the end led to the kitchen.

With frequent stops to listen for vehicles and watch the windows for a wash of headlights, she progressed through the house, pausing a while in the doorway of each room, reading the shadows within. A sofa parked right where she might need to run. A vacuum cleaner abandoned mid-chore. A ceiling mobile fitted with tinkly bells.

She checked wardrobes, cupboards, chests of drawers. No women's clothing, and the two children's bedrooms looked faintly stale, under-used. No partners since the divorce, she thought. And his kids barely stay here.

But the main thing was, nothing much of value remained in the house. No little Chagall above the main fireplace. No high-end TVs, computers, printers or electronic games, just cables snaking across the floor. Only inexpensive silverware left in the display cabinets. Someone had got here first? But that Rolex Chronograph she'd just spotted in a bowl of receipts, pegs, spare sunglasses and a lens-cleaning cloth on a kitchen bench: a thief would have swiped it, despite the cracked glass. Britton hasn't been burgled, she thought: he's put the good stuff in storage.

She found a wall safe behind a large, framed poster of native birds between two bookcases in his study. People often wrote passwords and codes on the backs of desk drawers or disguised them as phone numbers in desk diaries. Finding nothing like that, she returned to the kitchen and examined the slips of paper under the fridge magnets. All she found were business cards: a plumber, a wood yard, a medical centre—and a wi-fi password. Was it a password? She tried various combinations of the numbers and letters but the safe remained stubbornly locked.

Fifteen minutes. Too long—it was time she got out. But her attention was snagged by the printer beside Britton's desk, a bulky laser with scanning and copying capabilities. It looked dusty in the thin beam of her torchlight. She lifted the lid. Nothing on the glass. But the bottom contained a sheaf of copy paper. She fanned it: a scribbled-on envelope fell out. Passwords, phone numbers and email addresses. And the code for the safe.

A moment later, she had it open and her hands were on the little Chagall. Rocking back on her heels, she drew it into her lap and gazed for a moment, her heart beating. Lovers under a tree hung with birds and leaves; a friendly goat; the head of a horse. Gentle, calm, yet pulsing with vibrant reds and yellows. Sliding it carefully into her backpack, she reached in again and began to remove the other contents. A laptop, a tablet, the iPhone collection, plastic sleeves of stamps and coins—one or two of them worth a bit of money—and an envelope of banded $100 notes to the value of $30,500.

A little of her tension drained away: buy a decent car and return to her new life, with cash left over.

Finally, two envelopes containing photos and contact sheets, one labelled *Maria: Manila 2023* and the other *Jolene: Cebu City 2022*. Little girls. Six years old? Eight? Like Britton, they were naked. He probably had digital copies on the laptop or the tablet for sale or exchange; these were for his personal pleasure. Grace saw him sitting in his study in the dark hours, poring over them. She left the safe open, the photos in plain view, and stowed everything else with the Chagall—how did such a man get to own such a painting? She collected the RF jammer from the back door as she left the house.

She'd planned a circuitous route back to Angaston. It took her through Lyndoch, Rowland Flat and Tanunda, then across country on a series of back roads. It wasn't until twenty minutes later, when she was far from the house, that she relaxed a fraction and was able to turn her mind to what she'd seen in Britton's safe. She couldn't call triple zero from her mobile or hotel landline, or risk being captured on CCTV using a public phone—assuming it was still possible to find such a thing. She drove on through the dark, still night, on roads that seemed to run high above the world. Galt's voice was there in her head again: 'Without me you'd be nothing. Have nothing.' Why did she still believe there was some truth in that?

She didn't get to finish the thought. She came over a rise and down into a hollow, and now the dark night, pricked by the stars and washed by the ghostly moon, was suddenly busy. A church, a crossroads—where, in the bisecting headlight beams of an old Saab and a bulky off-road Jeep, something bad was playing out.

27

THE THINGS DES Liddington wished he hadn't said. The things he wished he hadn't done. All his life he'd been in the habit of replaying these, in all their terrible detail. He'd screw up his face in embarrassment and mutter, 'You fuckwit, Des.'

As he was doing now, at the wheel of the Saab. In full dress uniform, service ribbons and medals, the lot, driving home from Nuriootpa, where, at 8 p.m., he'd been awarded the National Police Service Medal. Shaken hands with the regional superintendent; posed for a photographer from the *Barossa Weekly*. The usual garbage. His selfless commitment to ethical and diligent service as a protector of the community. His tireless work on behalf of sporting clubs and welfare organisations. His many years of dedicated advocacy on behalf of his fellow police members…

Or, put another way: you've stuck it out for forty-two years, now piss off and put your feet up. Join the bowls club.

The thing was, why the fuck hadn't he simply said thank you and stepped away from the microphone? Instead, he'd rattled on for fifteen minutes, none of it funny or profound, most of it clichéd and self-serving. He sank further into the seat of his Saab, trying to disappear. 'It was a privilege to be part of the police family for so many years, sharing in all the victories as well as the grief and disappointments that are so often the lot of so many dedicated officers.' Why hadn't he stopped there? Why had he gone on to say, 'In pursuit of offenders I've bush-bashed, swum creeks and jumped fences. I've commandeered cars, I've commandeered a speedboat, I've even commandeered a quad bike and the back of a ute.' And the look on the super's face when he said, 'I don't know of any other job where I could've gone to work, jumped in a car with my mates, driven around looking for trouble, and been paid for it!'

And the way he'd droned on about all the roles he'd had over the years. How the different challenges had always kept him keenly honed. 'Keenly honed!' Jesus Christ.

He'd thanked his wife—'Who couldn't be here tonight'—his inspector, all of his colleagues and, of course, the superintendent.

Whose acknowledging smile was a kind of bleak twitch.

'You fuckwit, Des,' he moaned again, heading home across the moonlit hills, the road a pale ribbon unspooling beneath his probing headlights. The night was empty of life except for his car and an owl banking and diving. He supposed it was an owl. Funny how he'd lived in the country for years and knew so little about its creatures. What did he know in general, come to that? Who'd even want to give him a police medal?

Brake lights ahead, a car slowing for a turn-off. He overtook and continued into the night until he was alone again. Then, as he rolled down into a little hollow and up the other side, he sensed movement behind him, and checked the rear-view mirror. A bulky shadow dominated the mirror, too close, running without lights. Suddenly he was blinded: three spots on a roof bar lit up the Saab, burning his eyes.

He switched the mirror to night mode and then felt a sharp nudge, his head whiplashing: they'd shunted his rear quarter panel. He veered, fought to correct the slide, put his foot down and drew ahead. That lasted for about five seconds and he was hit again, and together they raced downhill towards an old Lutheran church that had been converted into a craft centre.

Another nudge, harder this time, the Saab twitching left, then right, as Liddington corrected, finding himself almost at right angles briefly, the car tipping, close to rolling. But he had speed on, and the gravel verge was loose, and now he was sliding, slaloming through a line of white parking posts, snapping the last one and spinning full circle until he was facing the way he'd come and his headlights were illuminating an old Jeep fitted with a nudge bar.

His motor had stalled. Hoping his dashcam was recording everything, he turned the ignition key. Nothing: he was still in drive. He shifted to park and tried again. The engine fired but now his door was being yanked open and a confusing mess of hands and arms swamped him. Two men, masked, yanking the keys out of the ignition, tossing them into the shadows, slicing him out of the seatbelt with a blade, dumping him in the dirt.

Now they booted him, and his first, stupid thought was what Josie would say about the state of his uniform. The dirt. The ripped sleeve. His bloodied knee and the greasy toecaps driving against his kidneys, his jaw and his balls.

He curled up, tucking his knees and chin into his chest and the pain kept coming, stabbing behind his eyes and flooding his groin. Now his feet burned: one of his attackers was smashing a metal bar against the thin soles of his best shoes. Now the ankles, his shins, and, unless he moved, the crown of his head. He rolled onto his back, stabbed by stones, then onto one side, the other, sometimes kicking out wildly.

The kicking stopped. A voice said, 'Someone's coming.'

Headlights swooped, then steadied, lighting up the men, who retreated a couple of steps. Liddington, on his back, heard the blast of a horn, a revving motor, a muttered, 'Jesus,' so he rolled onto his side and glimpsed a black, maybe blue, dual-cab ute—and it wasn't fucking around. Stationary one moment, charging the next, it smacked meatily into one of his attackers and flipped him into the air.

Stiffening his right arm, Liddington propped himself up and watched the dual-cab pull back and wait, the engine note screaming and dropping as if the driver itched to charge in again. Should he do something? Attempt an arrest? Thank the driver? His body a mass of slow, creaking pain, Liddington got to his bloodied hands and knees, his rocky feet. But he hurt too much, he was too old, too tired, too woozy, and could only sway there as the injured man was collected by his mate, taken to the Jeep and bundled into the passenger seat. No plates. He didn't recognise it. Didn't recognise the men, either: masked, bulked up by puffa jackets.

But no prizes for guessing.

Then they were gone and their dust billowed over him and he felt blindly for the ground again. Lowered himself to the welcoming dirt and flopped onto his back and presently soft hands tended to him and a soft voice murmured.

28

GRACE WAITED UNTIL she heard sirens and saw the unnerving pulse of red and blue lights coming in and out of view on the dark hills, then she gave the policeman's hand a final squeeze. She'd rolled him onto his side and checked that he was breathing freely. Anxious about concussion, she'd continued to talk to him, urging responses. Blotted the blood from his eyes. Squeezed his hand between her gloved hands. She supposed she was doing some good. He didn't pass out exactly, but nor did he seem to be conscious of her, outside this old church at a crossroads in the middle of nowhere. 'Forty-two years,' he murmured at one point. And: 'Pete fucking Patmore.'

And now, police and ambulance. Squeezing his hand, slipping his phone back into his pocket, she rushed to his car, leaned in, yanked the dashcam from his windscreen. Raced to the Triton, took a moment to check for damage—nothing: thank Christ for the bull bar—and sped away with a spurt of gravel as the lights and sirens grew more pronounced behind her.

How soon before the policeman recovered his wits? Was able to describe her? Galt's voice returned to Grace again: *Know when to walk away*. She didn't want to overreact, but nor did she want to be complacent. She'd attacked two men who were bashing a policeman. *They* might want to know who she was, even as the police surely would. Alerts would go out, roadblocks go up.

She began to map out her next few seconds, her next few hours and days. First, she reduced her speed from a panicky 130 km/h to a lawful 90 km/h. A few minutes later she reached the outskirts of Angaston and dropped to 60 km/h, then took the first empty side road and swapped the NSW plates for a Victorian set. Trundled through the town. Saw no action at her motel. Didn't pause.

She drove for an hour, keeping her speed below the official limit, and by 10.15 was standing at the check-in counter of a motel in Medindie, a stone's throw from the Adelaide CBD. She told the receptionist that her phone was playing up, or she'd have called ahead to reserve a room.

She said she'd have reached Adelaide from Melbourne a lot earlier in the day but had had to visit her grandmother in a nursing home. And wasn't that drive between Melbourne and Adelaide the most boring in the world?

The receptionist's eyes glazed over. She could barely summon the interest to say she didn't know; she'd never driven it.

At 10.45 Grace hid the Britton haul under the motel room's spare blankets and pillows, put on the overalls and bucket hat from her backpack and walked three kilometres to an alleyway behind a strip of shops on Main North Road. Destroying the policeman's dashcam, then discarding it with its SD card in one dumpster and her break-in clothing in another, she walked back onto Main North Road, where she tried a handful of convenience stores and service stations before finding a payphone. Called triple zero and reported the presence of child pornography in Jason Britton's house. Her face averted, her voice a low, rasping monotone, with long pauses between each word, she said no, she would not give her name.

Then pausing to stuff the overalls and hat in a charity bin, she set off back to the motel in her tights and hoodie. Her head was full as she walked. The hours until tomorrow morning. The yawning hours until tomorrow evening, when Erin would expect her home again.

Expect her to have attended the auction...

—

A night alone, somewhere unknown, is a long night. Headlights washed the curtains of the depressing motel room through the unrelenting hours and Grace tossed in the bed, challenged by voices that lobbed proposals, counterproposals, suggestions and accusations. Erin saying, *I believed in you*. Adam snarling, *Found you*. The bloodied policeman looking up at her and saying, *I know what you did*. Galt and his rules for thievery and escape. And she dreamed of running, but obstacles mired and tangled her feet. 'All I want is a normal life,' she said, but no one was listening.

She woke in the early hours of Sunday morning with that claim in her head, *a normal life*, and lay on her back watching the mottled creep of light across the ceiling, thinking of her life in the hills. She was an immigrant there, just as she'd been an immigrant everywhere else. No birthplace roots to give her a sense of identity—let alone bring her comfort. No maternity ward that she could name, no kindergarten, no primary school. No café where she'd first waitressed. No first driving lesson. She couldn't name parents, cousins, kindergarten friends or high-school sweethearts either—only Adam. Her old country had been a place of bleak foster homes and volatile affiliations with carers, foster siblings and policemen—not to mention crooks, all posturing like they were in an episode of *The Sopranos*. Nothing had been home-like in any of that. And—who was she kidding?—home also wasn't her life in the Adelaide Hills. She was rootless, disconnected.

Whenever she *did* connect it was fleeting, and entailed different deceptions for different situations.

I'm not whole, she thought, I'm split. Split between the present and the past; split between who she wanted to be and who she, inescapably, was.

Sunday, 7.30 a.m. Dressed now in the skirt and top, Grace restored the Triton's original plates and headed back to Gawler, driving with an unresolved notion of herself and not coming to her senses until after she'd dropped the keys in Off-Road Paradise's return box and discovered that the Angaston bus didn't run on Sundays. The kind of everyday hiccup endured by everyday people, she thought, logging into her fake Uber account. A bulky, cheerful man picked her up five minutes later, subjected her to a sustained explanation of the adjustments a person makes when he's retrenched at fifty, and dropped her off outside the Lutheran church in Murray Street. Settling her backpack of Jason Britton treasures on the footpath, he wished her a good day. Called her 'love'. She hoped he wouldn't notice how tense she was.

But Angaston that morning was merely content to sleep in, drive to church or walk the dog. The sun was mild. No one looked at her sideways. So she walked up the church steps, gave the Uber guy a vigorous wave goodbye, watched until he was out of sight, and cut around the side of the building. Then out across the yard at the rear and through side streets to the Vigneron Motel.

No one had been in her room. And no one cared as she returned the keys and checked out, having first rumpled the bedclothes and run the shower. She would find somewhere to lie low for a few days, then disappear. Or get as far away as possible. But her head was full of loose threads. Erin would soon contact the police. And the police, learning of a Barossa Valley connection, would make a further connection, to the Britton break-in. She'd be better off attending the auction.

She was halfway to Runacre Hall when her mobile rang. 'Only me. I'll…quick, I know the…about to start.'

'Sorry, you're cutting in and out again,' yelled Grace. 'I'll call you on my way home this afternoon, hopefully where the reception's better.'

A crackle. '…luck!…dinner?'

She parked behind the hall again and went in. No browsers today. A more hard-nosed crowd, experienced auction bidders, seated in ranks of chairs in the great hall, facing the auctioneer and the items he was spruiking. She settled in, took part in the bidding, and so the day passed. Outbid on the cedar chiffonier and other items Erin had wanted, she shifted tack and came away with a 1961 first edition Julia Child cookbook with an intact dust jacket for $1,850 and an unmarked 1962 Gibson Dove acoustic guitar—a mother-of-pearl dove inlaid in the pickguard—for $8,500.

She was paying with the Mandel's Collectibles credit card when Erin called. 'Can you hear me okay?'

'Loud and clear this time.'

'How did it go today?'

Grace told her.

'A guitar? Huh.'

'Don't worry, it's collectible.'

'Fair enough. You did well.'

'It all came to a bit more than ten thousand dollars, so let me pay the extra amount,' Grace said. It was what a normal person—in a normal relationship with a friend or a boss—would do.

'We can work that out. I tried to ask you before, if you get home in good time, would you like to pop in for dinner?'

Say yes. That's what a normal person would do. Return to your life in the hills. Grace plotted the drive. Road-blocks? But she had the perfect cover story, she'd spent both days buying stuff at Runacre Hall. 'Sounds lovely. I should be there by early evening,' she said, which was vague enough to account for anything that might fuck her up in the next little while.

29

EARLIER THAT SAME Sunday, Des Liddington told his inspector: 'They're letting me out after lunch.'

'Uh huh.'

The inspector, standing at the foot of the hospital bed, was not really listening to Des. Peter Renshaw was a man who listened to God. He was wearing a suit and tie, having popped in on his way to church.

But Liddington's wife, in the chair beside the bed, wasn't about to let Renshaw get away with it. 'He's lucky they didn't kill him!'

Renshaw blinked. Turned to her as laboriously as a ship at sea and said, 'Right.'

'Cuts, bruises, a cracked rib. He's lucky there's no internal bleeding!'

'Right.'

'Or concussion.'

'I understand.'

Josie gave a cross little sniff. Liddington squeezed her hand. And then Gabi Richter came bustling in with a grin and gift-shop flowers. Switched to flustered deference when she spotted Renshaw. Eyed her flowers desperately, as if wondering if they were appropriate.

Josie saved her. 'Let me find a vase for those.'

The relief was palpable. 'Thank you,' Gabi said. Then, breathlessly: 'Sorry to hear what happened, sir, Des...'

Meanwhile Renshaw looked on as if everyone was mad. He was a thin, dry, rustling man and, flicking his wristwatch into view, said, 'Time I was off. Get better soon, Des.'

'Sir.'

Now in the doorway, Renshaw said, 'Take tomorrow off. Take the week off, in fact. Friday's your last day anyway.'

'Sir,' Liddington said, having no intention of taking time off.

When Renshaw had gone, Des turned to Gabi and said, 'Thanks for coming.'

She winced. 'Actually...' She wouldn't look at him. Bit her bottom lip and eyed Josie plumping up the flowers, which were sorry-looking chrysanthemums threaded with baby's breath and eucalyptus leaves.

Suddenly he understood: 'The sergeant sent you.'

She rolled her shoulders, shot him a pained look. 'Sorry.'

'I gave a statement last night.'

'He wants to know if you've remembered anything more.'

'Fair enough, I'd do the same in his shoes, and, to answer your question, I don't really have anything to add. Have you checked my dashcam?'

'It's missing.'

Liddington had to think. 'The woman must have taken it.'

'Why?'

'Good question. Witnesses often don't stick around, but to take my dashcam?'

'We need her statement.'

'Plus I'd like to thank her,' Liddington said. He paused. 'You'd better have them print my car.'

'Okay.'

'What do you know about the triple-zero call?'

'She used your phone.'

Liddington was hurting all over. He shifted against the plumped-up pillows and smiled at Josie, who was back in her chair, squeezing his hand. Then he turned to Gabi again and said, 'Did anything else happen last night?'

'Like what?'

'I don't mean ordinary Saturday night pub brawls; I mean something more serious or out of the ordinary.'

Richter cocked her head. 'You think the woman…?'

Liddington shrugged. 'Maybe.'

'I'll check the logs.'

'She was driving a dual-cab ute, not sure what brand. Dark blue or black. Hard to tell.'

Richter checked her notes and nodded, confirming Liddington's earlier statement. 'Early model? Recent? Did you see the plates?'

'Not the latest model, but not too old. New South Wales plates.'

'Roof racks? Bull bar? Stuff like that?'

'Bull bar.'

'And she rammed one of the men?'

Liddington nodded and that hurt like buggery. 'She did, so if or when you find a vehicle, check for dents, a cracked headlight, the usual. Course, if she hit him with the bull bar, there might not be any damage.'

'How fast was she going?'

'Not fast, but she hit the guy hard enough to knock him off his feet.'

Gabi Richter said, as if it hurt to ask: 'And you think it was the Patmores?'

'I do.'

'They all said they didn't go out last night. Didn't know what we were talking about.'

'Naturally. But was one of them in pain, by any chance?

Limping? Bruised?'

'No.'

'Check them all. Second and third cousins. Drinking buddies.' He paused. 'Clinics, hospitals…'

'The boss said—'

'The boss said not to indulge my fantasies,' Liddington said. 'It's okay, Gabi, I know what I know.'

Richter shifted her shoulders uncomfortably. Looked at her notes. 'Can you remember anything else about the woman?'

'Like I said last night, slight build, maybe mid- to late twenties. Fair hair, what I could see of it under a cap. Wearing gloves, I just remembered, so forget prints.'

'Tatts? Piercings?'

'I was lucky to spot that much,' Liddington said.

Gabi Richter got to her feet. 'Get well soon, sir. I mean, Des.'

'Thanks, Gabi. You're doing a great job,' Liddington said, a corner of him thinking that his whole career had been like that. Saying well done to others.

30

THERE'D STILL BEEN no word from Melodie by the time Adam Garrett crawled into bed Saturday night, which probably accounted for another restless sleep, dreaming of lost keys, dead phones, cars with flat batteries, hands that slipped from his grasp.

And nothing when he checked his phone on Sunday morning. He called and texted her again. Waited. No reply.

He felt twitchy as he showered and shaved in the bathroom at the end of the corridor. It didn't ease as he dressed in his poky room and downed coffee and toast in the downstairs kitchen he shared with a bunch of students. She's pissed off with me, he thought. She's not stupid. She'll have twigged that I tipped off the police about the Calnan kid, and she's probably cooking up something special for me. Would she tell Ivan Varga? What would she tell him?

Garrett's jitters grew. There was only one thing to combat that: face it full on. Returning to his room, he put on a hi-vis jacket and bike helmet and slid one of his most useful props, a clipboard, into a pannier. Opened his door; checked both ways along the corridor. Sunday morning in a boarding house: the old place slumbered, the air suggestive of the lentil soups and curries of the Asian and Middle Eastern kids who lived in the other rooms. He wheeled his bike to the head of the stairs and carried it down, every step creaking beneath his weight. Past the kitchen and laundry, before pausing at the back door. The vast yard, still partly in shadow. The landlord's spotless Renault van marked *Saggio Smallgoods*, and the old coach house he lived in. Three small lemon trees; casuarinas; a crumpling incinerator; a tattered trampoline from when the Saggio kids were little. And the laneway gate, closed.

Garrett left the house and crossed the yard, badly spooked. Opened the gate, checked the lane, wheeled his bucking bike over the cobblestones to the end. Then around to Studland Street, where he paused again. He recognised almost all of the cars. And the remainder seemed innocuous, no heads showing, no exhaust smoke, no unmarked vans or brutal black Range Rovers.

—

Thirty minutes later he was in Tusmore, making a quick pass along Melodie's street before dismounting at the far end as if to adjust his chain. The area seemed peaceful, just another mix of home units, small tan-brick blocks of flats and older 1930s bungalows morosely shadowed by oleanders and stubby bullnose verandas. None of the cars spiked his interest and there were no pedestrians, so he got back on his bike and coasted down to number 16.

Clipboard in hand, he knocked on Melodie's door. Waited. Nothing altered. The air remained dappled and mild, no nearby curtains twitched, no one attended to the lawn sprinkler ticking in a garden across the street. Checking that he was unobserved, Garrett walked along the side wall of the house, peering into dark rooms, before pausing at the corner to survey the yard. No one waited or gardened there, no one was escaping over a fence, no one had bled out among the tomatoes.

He drew on thin latex gloves. The first thing he'd done when he'd come into Melodie's clutches was look for her spare key one day, when she was out on a case. Now, using the copy he'd made, he let himself into her house. Listened. Let his ears and nostrils test the atmosphere.

Her bed hadn't been slept in. The shower base was dry. The kettle was cold, the sink and benches wiped clean.

She had a home office. He went through her drawers and files, checking for anything that referred to him or the cases he'd worked for her. Everything he found related to her domestic life: home and car insurance papers; electricity invoices; a receipt for a new refrigerator; a birthday card from a niece in Sydney.

Then, in a bottom drawer, an A4 envelope marked 'Elite'. Inside it, a sheaf of business registration papers. The proprietor of Elite Investigations was one Adam Garrett of 44 Studland Street, North Adelaide, 5006.

Fucking old cow.

Fired up now, Garrett searched again, more closely this time. Nothing. He took the envelope to the kitchen sink, opened the back door and a window and made a little bonfire of the business papers. Ran the tap for several minutes. Flapped a bone-dry dishcloth to clear the smoke.

Ten minutes later he was chaining his bike to a rack outside a newsagency on Norwood Parade.

Melodie was on the floor behind her desk, the chair at a crazy angle three metres behind her, as though propelled there when she jack-knifed in death. The blood pooling beneath her torso was not large, it didn't glisten, it looked old and dry—but he itched to remove one of his gloves and touch it. He didn't want to touch her.

Otherwise, her office had been torn apart, a mess of upended drawers, jemmied-open cabinets and scattered files. Garrett stepped back to the hallway door and listened. The only other business on the first floor was an immigration agency. He'd never met, seen or heard the woman who ran it. The ground-floor businesses—a dental lab and a marine insurance broker—didn't operate on weekends.

No one to hear a shot. Or the damage as the place was roughly searched. Or to see strangers coming and going.

Closing the door again, he began his own search for records relating to his work for Elite Investigations. Melodie had always paid him in cash, either literally or by reducing his debt. But she'd surely need some records for the tax office—his travel expenses, for example. Insurance. And he'd submitted quite a few surveillance reports with his name on them. Not to mention glossy photographs with his prints on them. He'd worked for her since February. One job a month, on average, most of them genuine tailing assignments—husbands, wives, druggie kids.

These files were still intact, either on the floor or in the damaged filing cabinet. He crammed them into a bin bag that had lined the office wastepaper basket and left it by the door, then started the hunt for official paperwork related to his employee status. There was none. Either Melodie had never kept any or it had been nicked. Nothing related to his grey work, either: the 'retrieval' of Craig Tolhurst's son, for example; the Calnan surveillance. No surprise there.

Just then Garrett felt the tug of the CCTV camera Melodie had mounted at ceiling height in the far corner of the room. It wasn't top of the line—it recorded to a hard drive under her desk, not the cloud. He crouched to look. The drive had been removed.

Time to leave. He wiped everything he could remember ever touching, grabbed the bin bag and checked the corridor again. Quiet, empty. He headed downstairs, knowing how futile his actions had been. The police had other ways to identify him. A digital record connecting him to the business. Melodie's phone records. CCTV footage from other businesses along the block. But it could be days before her body was discovered. He'd be long gone by then. If he *was* cornered in the next thirty minutes, he could flash his one set of fake but solid ID and claim to be a client, looking for the mother who'd abandoned him.

Reaching the back door, he paused. Went back upstairs and pocketed Melodie's phone and purse. $260. Every little helped, and she had no further use for it. He tried to summon some regret or sadness. The truth was, she was an awful person who'd screwed him over on every job he did for her. The main thing was: he wouldn't have to pay the rest of the money he owed.

Feeling again that he was being watched, Garrett pedalled back across town to the boarding house. At the entrance to Studland Street, he dismounted as if to adjust the height of his saddle. Only one alteration in the meantime, a little rental Kia parked outside the psychotherapist's consulting room next door to the boarding house. Remounting, he spurted to the end of Studland, checking the Kia and the front yard of number 44, then headed around to the laneway, walking his bike over the cobbles. The back gate was open. Not unusual: it meant Mr Saggio had gone to the market.

But Adam Garrett paused a while, his bike propped against the sagging yard fence. A wisp of smoke from the incinerator. Again, not unusual. Mr Saggio was yet to embrace the concept of recycling, and his tenants knew not to hang their washing out on weekends.

The rear of the old house looked tranquil. Everyone still in bed. So Garrett wheeled his bike in through the gate and, with one eye on the back door, started feeding his surveillance files into the incinerator. Mr Saggio's smouldering egg and milk cartons loved it. They popped and snapped hungrily and the smoke surged up into Garrett's eyes so that he coughed and jerked his head away, and that was what saved his life.

31

CRAIG TOLHURST'S NEXT shot whanged off the chain ring as Garrett reached for his handlebars, and the third chipped the old wooden gate, so he dropped the bike and ran into the laneway. Scooted to the end, weaving, half-crouched, over the tricky cobblestones, as one last shot hummed past his ear and then he was flicking left, down a short side street.

I *knew* the guy looked pretty handy, he thought. Melodie should've listened to me.

As he ran, Garrett thought it through. Tolhurst had

found his address in Melodie's office, or she'd given it up before he shot her. And gaining access to the boarding house would have been easy—just knock on the front door with a convincing story. One of the other boarders—maybe even Mr Saggio—would have told him the room number, it was that kind of place. Or even said, 'His bike's not here but his car's still out the front. He'll probably be back soon, if you'd like to wait.'

And Tolhurst had waited—probably on the licheny old garden chair beside the hot water service. Perhaps by then he'd stopped caring about witnesses. He'd lost his son; been ripped off to the tune of a hundred grand. He'd simply get his revenge and accept the consequences.

But he'd found Melodie and he'd obtained a pistol—and someone happy to supply him with a pistol might be happy to help him in other ways, too. Keep watch, for example. Drive him away afterwards.

Minutes passed. No sirens. Maybe there wouldn't be: Tolhurst had shot at him with what looked like a little .22 target pistol; not very loud. And the people in the neighbourhood of the boarding house mostly liked to keep to themselves.

Garrett made a loop around the suburb, trotting for fifty paces, walking for fifty, careful not to attract attention by running flat out but covering ground quickly and conserving energy, his senses alert. Vehicles coming in from behind; the body language of pedestrians. Was anyone unduly interested in him? Walking as if concealing a weapon? Too nonchalant? Turning away too abruptly to sniff a rosebush?

But nothing happened. This was a suburb of grand old residences become specialists' rooms or fading behind thick hedges. Life along the broad streets was unhurried, the sun was lazy overhead, the air was still. A taxi searching for an address. A tradie's ute with Lady Gaga blaring. A woman in jodhpurs walking a dog. A young father saying, 'Come on, buddy,' to a toddler crouched to inspect an ant. An old man rugged up on a veranda.

Garrett approached his Mazda from the top end of Studland Street and realised that his sleeve felt wet, his upper arm hurt and his hand when he lifted it was dripping blood. He blinked; shook all of his adrenaline-blunted senses back into action. If he'd not recoiled from the smoke in Mr Saggio's incinerator, if he'd not jerked to his left, the bullet might have gone into his heart instead of his arm.

He felt dizzy. Sat abruptly on the kerb. But he couldn't stay there, dripping blood. Someone would notice. Say something like, 'You're bleeding,' or, half-jokingly, 'Who shot you?'

Garrett removed the hi-vis jacket and rolled the sleeve of his T-shirt up over his shoulder, craning to view the damage. He poked gingerly. A shallow groove, not a hole. Oozing blood, though.

Get in the car, he thought. Drive away—leave Adelaide and don't come back. He mentally scanned the belongings in his room: just clothes and toiletries, easily replaced. But he couldn't leave the laptop behind. If Melodie's murder or reports of shots fired brought the cops to Mr Saggio's house, they'd have a long, hard look at that.

Still no sirens. Garrett risked getting to his feet, swayed a little, and then, with his bloody hand in his pocket and his good hand across his chest to clasp and hide the bloodied sleeve, began to close in on the boarding house across the street.

He froze. Ducked behind a Golf belonging to one of the boarding-house kids: he'd almost stumbled into the man who wanted to kill him. Tolhurst was in the Kia rental car, just sitting there, slumped as if exhausted. A part of Garrett wanted to climb in with him and say...

Say what, though? Sorry? Sorry I ripped you off? Sorry your son died? Sorry I didn't go in there and save him?

A moment later, Tolhurst started the Kia and drove slowly down to O'Connell Street. Garrett, unwilling to trust that, stayed crouching for a few minutes. He was more conscious of the pain and bleeding now. Soon he'd attract attention—for crouching behind a car, if nothing else. He stood rockily. Trotted across the street and through the front gate.

He passed one of the Malaysian students on the creaking stairs, yawning her head off. He smiled and nodded, keeping his shoulder towards the wall, and asked, 'Did you hear that car backfiring?'

'Car?' she said dazedly.

'Bloody racket.' Garrett smiled more broadly. 'Woke me up.'

She'd already lost interest. But when he was on the top landing, she called up, 'You're bleeding.'

'Fell off my bike. All good.'

She grunted and disappeared from view. Garrett continued along the dim hallway to his room. Listened at the door. Unlocked it, then, his spine flat to the wall, swung it open. Darted a look, then entered swiftly, at a crouch. Nothing. He grabbed a change of clothes and, checking that the bathroom along the corridor was free, washed and bandaged the groove in his shoulder. The bandage was too small; a seam of blood began to show again. He'd need to call in at a chemist for a larger bandage and some antiseptic.

Finally, wincing as his shoulder rolled and flexed, he pulled on clean jeans and a T-shirt and returned to his room. Crammed his bloodied clothing into a rubbish bag, stepped into an oversized pair of overalls that he'd thought might come in handy one day, and packed his laptop and a selection of jeans, pants, shirts, underwear and toiletries into an overnight bag. Stood at the edge of his window, looking out at the front gate, the street, the roof of his car.

All clear. He left the house for the last time. His rent was up to date. Mr Saggio would soon find another boarder. And landlords dealt with abandoned belongings all the time.

—

Everything would be subterfuge now, even a visit to the chemist. To hide in a football crowd, you wear a scarf and strike up asinine conversations with like-minded strangers. You become what strangers expect you to be. And so, to explain the seep of blood on his upper sleeve, Garrett smeared oil from the Mazda's dipstick here and there on his overalls and became a mechanic who'd scraped his shoulder under a car. The chemist tut-tutted. Her assistant hurried off to find bandages and antiseptic. A woman waiting for a prescription said, 'My husband caught his sleeve in a cog once—nearly lost an arm.' Garrett was the centre of a little drama, but it was drama of the mundane kind, soon to be forgotten. He belonged, right then, and smiled. Rolled his eyes at his own bad luck, said thank you, enjoyed the attention.

Then he drove to a shopping centre where he used the parents' room to clean and dress his arm. Pulled on a fresh shirt and a hoodie from his bag and stowed the bloodied T-shirt and overalls under oily pizza boxes in an outside bin.

Back in his car, he tried to think his way through the next stages of his life. Tolhurst had found and lost him, but there was no reason to believe he'd abandon the hunt. If the guy had found a photo in Melodie's files, all he'd have to do was flash it around and say, 'I'm looking for my son. He's bipolar and suicidal and I'm worried about him,' and people would jump at the chance to help. The police would not be far behind: on his trail as soon as Melodie's body was found, doorknocking the streets around the boarding house and Melodie's office building. And now that she was dead, his main income stream no longer existed. He'd also lost Anita—Grace—who might or might not be still in the Adelaide Hills. No point looking for her, she could be anywhere. Anyway, the Hills were too close to the city. He needed to be hundreds of kilometres away.

His remaining set of ID was in the name of Louis Denton at an address in an outer suburb of Perth. He'd been nursing it for a long time, flying to Western Australia twice a year to shop with the credit card, borrow and return library books, take out RAC membership and use a carwash loyalty card.

Which made redundant everything currently in his wallet. He leaned onto one hip to fetch it from his pocket, wincing again as his shoulder flexed, and searched every compartment, knowing that even a scrunched-up receipt could sink him. Cards, licence, Melodie's business cards, a dentist's appointment card…

He waited until he was an hour north of Adelaide before scattering them to the wind. The hours passed and evening came, and he was alone in a black and eternal vastness. He stopped at a roadhouse for a steak sandwich and a Coke. Sitting where he could keep one eye on the door, the passing headlights and the occasional highway motorist stepping in from out of the dark night, he checked the news on his laptop. There was no mention of Melodie, or of a shooting in North Adelaide.

But Craig Tolhurst's name came up: arrangements had been made to fly his son's body back to Australia. He'd have been giving soundbites if he hadn't been taking pot shots at me, Garrett thought. He pictured Tolhurst's bearing in the driver's seat of the Kia, parked outside the boarding house. Maybe he'd just been informed. Something had gone out of him anyway.

His arm ached.

32

GRACE CALLED GAYNOR Bernard to arrange a delivery time for the watercolour then headed home, taking an indirect route in the lengthening shadows of late afternoon, turning at Murray Bridge and later, in Mount Barker, using a system of back roads through the little towns. Her instinct for self-preservation was more acute now, after the events of the weekend, and she replayed everything as she drove. Had she covered herself? Could anything be fixed at this late stage?

The break-in, first. She'd driven and returned,

undamaged, a rental vehicle sourced with fake ID from outside the Barossa. False plates—both sets now silting up in a roadside dam.

But what of that one major drawback, rescuing the policeman? She didn't know what he'd remember. She didn't know what his attackers would remember about her either. Or if they'd followed her.

Next, she tested her cover story. She'd had a legitimate reason for being in the Barossa Valley: to attend a clearing sale as a buyer for Mandel's Collectibles. She'd driven a vehicle belonging to the business. Her accommodation had been paid for by the business. And there was clear evidence that she'd been active on both days of the sale: witnesses, goods, receipts.

A solid series of dead ends? She wasn't reassured, and pulled into a layby near Lobethal to check the news feed on her phone again. The policeman was okay: his name was Desmond Liddington and he'd been released from hospital after being monitored for concussion. Witnesses to his assault were being urged to come forward, particularly anyone with dashcam footage. And police would like to talk to a young woman motorist who might have witnessed the incident.

Grace looked away from her phone, staring at the darkening hillsides. She saw Liddington in her mind's eye. He's at home with his wife and kids making a fuss of him, but that won't last, he'll soon go back to work, keen to track down his attackers and the woman who saved him.

Where does he start? With the fact that his rescuer didn't stick around. He'll wonder why. Then he'll move on to the fact that she was driving a dual-cab ute fitted with a bull bar and New South Wales plates. And if he recalls the plate number, or even part of it, he'll contact the DMV in Sydney and learn that it belongs to a black 1998 Commodore registered in Hay. His curiosity grows. He speculates: either the woman was an everyday grifter dodging fees, fines and tolls, or she was engaged in something more serious.

And so, he checks the overnight logs—and finds the Britton break-in. Listens to the triple-zero recording.

Jesus, she was getting soft. Why hadn't she waited before tipping off the police? Too fired up by Britton's kiddie porn. Wanted the cops to find it before it was destroyed.

She returned her attention to her phone. Scrolled further down the news feed, finding no mention of the Britton break-in. Maybe the police hadn't attended yet. Maybe they'd thought she was a crank. Maybe they were keeping it quiet until Britton returned from overseas.

She envisaged the policeman again. Saw him speculating that it was more likely a sophisticated burglar would do their research and find a specific target than drive around the back roads of the Barossa hoping to stumble across a house worth breaking into.

Spend a night or two in the area, in other words. Maybe in a motel.

Grace pulled back out onto the road, full of shadowy foreboding.

—

At 6.14 she drew up at the kerb fifty metres past Erin's shop and settled in for a few minutes to watch it in the rear-view mirror. Checking out observation posts: cars and nearby buildings. Movements in the darkness. Pedestrians who didn't belong.

But she was too jittery. She restarted the Subaru and drove home to Landau Street. Idled outside number 22 for a few beats, tamping down her nerves enough to carry out another scan. The night here was not fraught in any obvious way, but she didn't know if she'd even spot anything, the way she was feeling. She sighed, drove in, parked, unlocked her flat and stood for a while in the hallway, testing the atmosphere. Then a wash of light spilled into the yard behind her and the dark spell was broken.

'Oh you're home,' Erin called. 'Can I interest you in some pumpkin soup?'

Ten minutes later, with the soup—at this stage still a chunky blob of orange ice—thawing in a saucepan, Grace was distributing her Runacre Hall purchases across Erin's kitchen table. Erin touched them one by one, a little gleam of anticipation in her eyes. 'You did well. I'm really pleased.' She lifted the Blamire Young watercolour and tilted it to catch the ceiling light. 'I see what you mean, it needs a clean. And a better frame.'

'I'm taking it to the restorer before work tomorrow. She's expecting me.'

Erin looked apologetic. 'A busy day. You still okay to take the car in for its service?'

The plan was, drop the car off after work, collect it sometime on Tuesday. 'Sure.'

Erin set down the painting and glanced at the other items. 'I still can't believe you got us a guitar.'

There was that word again: *us*. 'I'm confident it'll sell,' Grace said. 'But I'm sorry I had no luck with the furniture. Bidding was pretty brisk. Not really any bargains.'

Conscious that she was close to babbling, and knowing that lies need only skirt the truth a little to be accepted, Grace took up her wine glass and sipped from it, watching her boss and landlady over the rim. Erin looked shy and awkward. She doesn't have friends, she doesn't have visitors, Grace thought.

A hiss from the stove. Erin, flustered—worse than me, mused Grace—rushed to check. Poked at the soup-berg with a wooden spoon. Said, 'We're halfway there. I should have taken it out sooner.'

Grace could smell the soup now. 'No hurry. I'm looking forward to eating something not cooked by me. I'm hopeless in the kitchen.'

'I used to be hopeless,' Erin said, her face shutting down as she returned to the table.

'You had lessons?'

'I had a husband.' The tone was flat and bleak, and that was enough.

Grace visualised the husband—demanding,

controlling—and she visualised Erin escaping, starting anew. Her guardedness and agoraphobia: it was on the tip of Grace's tongue to ask about it. She wanted to reach out her hand and squeeze Erin's forearm. Instead, she gestured at her Runacre Hall purchases. 'Let me take all this back to my place, then I'll set the table.'

Relieved, Erin said, 'Sure,' and, when Grace returned, they sat half-companionably until the soup was hot. They ate it with wine and hunks of bread, and made small talk that skirted all that was hidden in their lives. Then Grace got up to go, pleading tiredness, and on Erin's back step received a brief, incisive goodnight hug. It was a welcome alteration to the warp and weft of her life.

33

MONDAY, AND GRACE awoke to gentle rain. Her little house was a cave whenever the sky closed in and the trees huddled and dripped. She opened her bedroom curtains, checked the yard, padded through to the kitchen.

Later, propped up in bed against cushions and her pillow, she logged on to the Mandel's Collectibles website and listed for sale everything she'd obtained from the Runacre Hall weekend. She left the guitar and the Blamire Young watercolour unpriced, tagging them *Expressions of interest invited* and *Available soon*.

She was showered and dressed by 8.30, which gave her time to deliver the watercolour to the conservator before opening the shop at 10. She peered out at the yard again: the rain had stopped but her veranda was dripping, so she folded the watercolour in bubble wrap and grabbed the umbrella from the chipped vase beside her front door. She locked up, splashed across the yard to the Forester, stowed the painting and the umbrella, checked that her haul from Schiller Lane was still securely in the lockbox, then ran back for her bike. She'd wheeled it to the car and was lifting the hatch when Erin appeared, wearing a dressing gown and rubber boots, shoulders hunched under a huge tartan golfing umbrella. Her face was deathly pale and her eyes unreadable, but possibly panicked.

'You gave me a fright!' Grace said. 'Is everything all right?'

Erin worked at clearing her expression. 'What if it's raining when you drop the car off?' She looked pointedly at the bike. 'You'll get all wet.' Looked at Grace again and said, 'I won't be able to come and collect you.'

This is significant, Grace thought. Erin prepared to leave the house; prepared to leave the house for me. 'I'll see how I go. If it *is* raining at the end of the day, I'll get an Uber.'

Erin tried to hide her relief. 'If you're sure? I'll pay for it.'

'I'm sure,' Grace said. 'And I'll start looking at used cars this week.'

'Ask the garage, they might have something.'

'They might,' agreed Grace, thinking that she should wait a bit before spending any of Jason Britton's cash.

A few minutes later she was winding the Forester through the leafy towns. Reaching the parking bay at the base of Gaynor Bernard's steep driveway, she locked the car and laboured uphill with the Blamire Young watercolour tucked under her arm.

A dripping old world, she thought, knocking on Bernard's front door and turning to gaze awhile at the trees and shrubs as she waited. An unpainted concrete garden gnome sat darkened by the rain. A wheelbarrow had gathered rainwater overnight and a lone tea towel sagged on a clothesline. But bellbirds beeped and, on the other side of the misty valley, sunshine struggled through a hole in the low, fat clouds. Whether that meant good or bad luck, she didn't know.

Grace knocked again. No answer, so she crossed the yard to the studio and this time her knock was answered. 'Oh. Hello.'

Gaynor Bernard wore stained overalls, spotted Crocs, a hairnet and smeared glasses. Her hands were flecked with old paint, and again her eyes blinked with vague irresolution, as if Grace hadn't been expected.

Grace glanced past her at a small painting on the workbench. Two images, the head and shoulders of a man wearing a shirt and neckerchief, and, seeping into one side of his head, a team of straining draughthorses pulling a wagon. Bernard was removing the top layer, Grace realised.

'Self-portrait, 1889,' the conservator said, noticing the direction of Grace's gaze, 'and it's the better picture, so why he painted over it, I don't know. Perhaps he thought there was room in the nineties for one more bit of arcadian crap.'

Grace shifted her attention. The conservator was twinkling at her. She'd used the mild expletive almost daringly.

Grace grinned in return. 'Oh, I don't know, you can never have too many horse-drawn wagons,' she said, unwrapping the Blamire Young and handing it to Bernard, who barely glanced at it.

'Would you like a coffee?'

'That's kind of you but I need to get going. As I explained on the phone, if you could—'

'Oh, just a quick one. If you're going to be bringing me such interesting challenges'—Bernard gave the Blamire Young a little shake—'we should break the ice.'

Grace tensed. The strain didn't ease, even as she gave a tight smile, said, 'Just a quick one,' and sat through a polite, low-key grilling. Where do you live? Where did you grow up? Do you know so-and-so? Grace fielded the questions deftly but almost trotted back down the hill afterwards, half-expecting hands to clutch her shoulder and spin her around. She sped away with a little spurt of the tyres on the sodden road.

When she reached Battendorf, Grace stowed Britton's cash, Chagall painting and iPhone collection in her safe-deposit box before crossing the street to open the shop. The day passed and her heart beat heavily. Long, quiet hours: perhaps people feared more rain. The shop bell rang only once, for a tourist from Dresden, who looked at but didn't buy a set of Meissen Blue Onion porcelain knife rests.

Seeking a distraction, Grace dusted and tidied, pondering Gaynor Bernard's behaviour. Lonely? Not in the way Erin was lonely. Curious—a nosy, intrusive kind of curiosity.

I'm not that fascinating, she thought, moving on to remove the antique knitting-basket display from the shop window. She replaced it with colonial-era chisels, hammers, pliers, wood planes and handsaws arranged on, and in, a few side-on wooden crates, and at 5 p.m. checked the emails. Two people had put in offers for the Gibson guitar: $8,750 and $8,500. Grace googled their names. One taught at the Conservatory of Music, the other was lead guitarist for a country-rock band called Whole Spectrum. She didn't know who'd be more deserving. Let Erin decide. Or wait for further offers to come in.

At 5.05 she locked the front and rear doors and walked out to Erin's car. The sky was clear again, and everything looked cleansed by the rain—the air, the streets, even the light.

By 5.10 she was unloading her bike and handing the Subaru's ignition key to Mark Dinakis, Battendorf Motors' proprietor and head mechanic. About fifty, dark and burly, with bushy eyebrows, he said, 'Regular service, got it.'

'Call me tomorrow when it's ready?'

He nodded. 'Should be done by late morning, early afternoon.'

Grace smiled, strapped on her helmet and pedalled away, taking the short cuts through to Landau Street.

34

BRODIE HENDREN HAD taken the 9.10 a.m. Virgin to Adelaide and wasn't impressed with the city. Rain. Plus it seemed to move at glacial speed for such a small place. What would Seb Verco say? Patience. It took nearly forever to collect his luggage and do the paperwork for the black Hertz Mustang he'd reserved in the name of Michael S. Davies. The real Davies had bought an SS badge from Hendren a few weeks earlier—unwittingly revealing practically everything but his shoe size—and, just for the fun of it, Davies paid for insurance on the Mustang, too.

First step, Apex Mail on Enfield Road. Difficult to find a park, and, owing to the overnight rain, Hendren ended up having to splash through two hundred metres of puddles before he could shove open Apex's front door, a big man with important business. Offered his Davies ID again and walked out with a padded envelope containing the barrel for his Glock.

Next stop, AAA Commercial Services on Dequetteville Terrace, where he claimed an envelope containing the slide and recoil spring. Finally, Box Office on Magill Road. Where, according to a kid who had so much metal in his mouth he was practically incomprehensible, the parcel for Michael S. Davies had not yet arrived.

'What do you mean, it's still in transit? I tracked it here on the app. It says awaiting collection.'

The kid swivelled his computer monitor towards Hendren. 'See? In transit. Be here tomorrow.'

A pistol without its clip and bullets wasn't much good. 'Jesus fucking Christ,' Hendren said, banging out again: a big man thwarted.

Fury, frustration and dumb people—they'd made him hungry. Subway was the closest you'd get to anything healthy in this backwater so he ordered a chicken teriyaki wrap and a Coke Zero in a branch down the street from Box Office.

The place was quiet for a fast-food joint. Too early for worker drones on their lunch breaks, so he was able to sit in a corner where he could watch the room, the staff and the front door while he worked his phone.

First, Serial Treasures. Someone was offering $250 for the Ivan Milat crayon drawing; Hendren accepted. Next, Third Realm. The helmet remained unsold, probably because so many of them were floating around the various marketplaces, but some hero was offering to swap Heinrich Himmler's glasses for the edelweiss patch. Fuck off. Plus, he'd be a millionaire if he had a dollar for every pair of Himmler's glasses listed on auction sites.

Finally, the socials. He was curious to see how Seb Verco was dealing with all the shit being heaped on his head.

Jesus: the poor guy had been given the flick by Twitter. Hendren checked Instagram. At least he was still active there—hitting back, in fact. 'Can't they see I was playing a comedic role?' And: 'These keyboard warriors who say I hate women conveniently ignore the fact I have gone on record saying my mother is my hero. I give to charities supporting women and I teach people of all genders and races to respect one another.' And: 'I was proving the falsity of all the negative narratives about me, showing the world tolerance and encouraging respectful discourse. My platform is a beacon of light and tolerance, and, somehow, I'm the villain?'

So fucked up. A man couldn't be a man anymore.

Hendren pushed the wrap aside, only half-consumed, banged out to the Mustang and used the navigation app to take him up into the Adelaide Hills. At a fair speed, too. There were probably cameras the whole way, but that would be Michael S. Davies' problem.

One of five TradeWorks hardware stores in the Adelaide Hills. That's all he'd been able to get from his google trawl through news stories of the Alisha Kennedy abduction and murder. He reckoned Oakbank and Battendorf were the most likely, but he couldn't rule out Lobethal, Echunga or Stirling. He could always call at each one—flash Karen's photo and a fake cop ID, but what if a store clerk saw through it, or he struck someone who knew Karen? Anyway, it was a long shot—the CCTV footage would probably have been deleted after all this time.

Hendren had a theory that your behaviour was determined by where you lived. You weren't likely to buy serial-killer memorabilia if you lived in Vaucluse or Toorak, for example. If you were a junkie burglar, you burgled your mum, the house next door, or your housemate's room. And if you were a housepainter, always on the go, you stocked up at your nearest hardware store.

The business address of Balhannah Brushstrokes proved to be a garage at the rear of a weatherboard house in a street behind the primary school. You'd think a painter would be houseproud, but the timbers were flaking and patched with filler, and the flimsy front door was sun-faded and clawed to shreds at the bottom—a big motherfucker of a dog, Hendren thought, glancing around uneasily.

But he knocked. A dog started to go wild on the other side of it; a woman screeched. The dog shut up but Hendren could hear it in there, straining to rip his throat out.

'Who is it?'

Hendren leaned his mouth close to the door. 'I was hoping to speak to someone about painting my house.'

'He's not here.'

'When will he be back?'

'How would I know? End of the day, probably.'

Business must be good if you can afford to be rude to a potential client. 'Is he on a job nearby? Maybe I could drop in.'

'The empty shop next to the baker's,' the woman said, her voice, and scrabbling claws, fading as she withdrew.

Useless bitch. Which baker? Which empty shop? Which town? Hendren drove to the main street and, talk about luck, there was a bakery with an empty shop next to it. He entered, finding an apprentice on his hands and knees, painting a skirting board with the tip of his tongue curled into the corner of his pimply upper lip for concentration.

'Boss around?'

The kid didn't dare stop. The brush moved one centimetre as he said, strain in his voice: 'We ran out.'

Hendren tried another tack. 'Maybe I can catch him. Where does he buy his paint?'

The kid knew the answer to this one. 'TradeWorks.'

Balhannah was halfway between two TradeWorks

outlets, and not close to either one. Hendren said, 'The one in Oakbank?'

The kid seemed to think this was a dumb question. 'Battendorf.'

'Battendorf. And that's the one he usually goes to?' Hendren asked, thinking the boss man might have shopped at one of the other branches the day Alisha Kennedy was murdered, simply because he had a job nearby.

Now the apprentice seemed to struggle. First, here was this random interrupting, asking questions. Second, it hadn't occurred to him to think about the boss in this way, a man who might prefer one hardware shop over another.

'S'pose,' he said.

It would have to do. 'I'll see if I can catch him there,' Hendren said.

'Sure.'

Hendren left. That kid'll forget I was even here, he thought.

He drove to the TradeWorks in Battendorf. It was near another large structure, a self-storage yard, in the far corner of an industrial estate at the edge of the town. Parking opposite an Officeworks and a JB HiFi, he crossed a broad carpark and went in. Stood for a while, irresolute. What was he even doing there? It wasn't as if the painter—if he was here right now—or a staff member would remember a customer from almost two years ago. This was a waste of time. He needed to deal with Karen quickly, then scarper, leaving behind nothing that would tie him to her or the town. Hide her body, race back to Melbourne and fudge an alibi for when the police finally started tracking down ex-husbands and boyfriends. It was too great a risk to show her photo around. It would get him remembered.

Hendren returned to the car and made his way to the town's main street. Parked behind the supermarket and nursed a green tea in a café along from the Commonwealth Bank. Did Karen live locally? Evidently she had a lawn that needed mowing, and you wouldn't drive hundreds of kilometres to buy a mower, you'd go to your nearest hardware. She might live some distance away, of course—maybe she'd passed the Battendorf TradeWorks on her way home from work or seeing a friend or whatever.

But what work, what friend? She'd always seemed a city type to Hendren. On the other hand, she was in hiding. As for making friends, how would she go about that? Join a club? What were her interests, come to that? For the past two and a half years, Karen had simply been an all-purpose bitch living rent-free in his head. Now he tried to conjure up the woman he'd once loved enough to marry.

Okay, she had a thing for vegetarian food. She had a thing for bags, too: not enough bags in her life, always on the hunt for something perfect to hold her phone, water bottle, purse and general crap. And she liked Subarus: her father, the old cunt, had told her you can't go wrong with a Subaru.

Work...back then she had some kind of backroom job

for an auction house. Research? Valuations? Something like that. They'd met at a deceased estate auction. He'd seen her name tag, realised she worked for the firm running the auction, and asked if she could tell him more about one of the listings, an antique Colt revolver purported to have belonged to Ben Hall, the bushranger. She'd leaned in to answer, so that their heads almost touched, and, her voice low and her breath soft against his ear, had told him that her boss was a shithead, the pistol couldn't possibly have belonged to Ben Hall. 'No provenance,' she murmured, 'and the date's wrong, you'd be throwing away good money.'

Her face, her voice, her body—instant fireworks.

More than likely she'd have looked for work in the area of art and antiques since she fucked him over. Hendren drained his tea, paid and walked out into dampish, dappled spring sunlight.

Christ—looked like half the main street of Battendorf was dedicated to selling old junk. An antiquarian bookseller. Two antique furniture barns. A bric-a-brac joint. A place selling vintage clothes and toys, another a mix of collectible antiques and knick-knacks.

He began his hunt, confident that Karen wouldn't recognise him until it was too late—if she was here, in one of these shops. He'd lost a lot of weight in the past two years. Flab gone, abs and pecs ripped. He'd ditched the jeans and T-shirt look for linen pants, jacket and collared shirt; heavy-framed non-prescription glasses. Cut off the ponytail.

He checked out the shopfronts. Three of the places didn't open on Mondays. As for the other three, one was a rumpled old bookseller who said she'd never employed an assistant. Nor had the rakish, snobbish twenty-somethings who sold vintage clothing and toys. Easy enough to find that out—all you had to do was gaze around looking impressed, and remark on what a big staff they must need to run a place like this.

That left Mandel's Collectibles. Karen's surname was Michael, so that was close. It would be easier for a Karen Michael to morph into a Karen, or maybe a Helen, Mandel than call herself Rosemary Hickinbotham.

He strode in busily, cast a cheery smile and a 'Beautiful day!' at the woman—not Karen—who was flipping through the pages of a catalogue behind the counter, and immediately wheeled around to peer in at the vintage Stanley block plane on display in the window.

Behind him, her voice: 'We're having a special on old tools this month.'

He turned with his ready smile. 'So I see. The Stanley plane: it doesn't come with the original box, by any chance?'

'Sorry, no.'

'How did you come by it, may I ask? Clearing sale? Trade-in? I might be able to track down the original owner.'

Slight, trim, the woman could have been Karen's younger sister. 'I don't know, sorry. I'd have to ask the boss.'

'Ah,' Hendren said, crossing the shop floor and leaning on the counter. Glancing hopefully past her at the door leading to the back rooms, he asked, 'Is he—or she—in today, by any chance?'

The woman shook her head. 'If you like, I'll ask her after work and give you a call?'

Ask *her*. Hendren felt the first tingle.

He made a show of checking his watch—a man with a busy schedule—then, to ensure that she forgot him, he said, 'Nah, that's okay. The wife would kill me if I came home with another bit of old crap, her words.'

It worked. The woman smiled politely and returned to her catalogue as he left the shop. Then, in case she was watching him through the window, he strolled across the street and along it to the next intersection, just an everyday guy going about his business. Simple psychology.

He used the first side street to begin a broad loop around the town centre, ending with a pass along the laneway behind Mandel's Collectibles. A small museum, an RSL hall, a couple of dumpbins and a handful of cars and back doors.

Among the cars, a white Forester. He eyed it quickly as he walked past. In the rear compartment, a bicycle on top of a shallow lockbox. South Australian plates, not surprising, but...yep, a dent in the tailgate. He'd caused it himself—and a Sunshine Coast antiques fair sticker in the back window.

He hurried back to the Mustang in the supermarket carpark and drove it back to the alleyway. Reversed into the narrow strip of parking outside the RSL hall, beautifully obscured by a big old Falcon station wagon. Even so, as he discovered when he climbed into the rear of the Mustang, he still had a clear view, through the side windows of both cars, down to the Subaru. If challenged, he'd simply say he'd dropped his credit card between the driver's seat and the centre console. But the minutes passed and he saw no one.

Until, at 5.12 p.m., the Mandel's Collectibles woman appeared. She locked the back door of the shop and headed, key in hand, towards the Subaru. Lights flashed. She climbed behind the wheel.

Hendren watched from the back seat of his Mustang, his head barely showing, as the Subaru reversed, then swung away from him and down the alleyway. When it reached the intersection, he squeezed through the gap between the seats, got behind the wheel and started the engine. Nosed out carefully. The Subaru was waiting at the give-way sign. Then it turned right, and Hendren sped after it, pausing at the end to nose out until he spotted the Subaru again, a couple of hundred metres down the road. He waited for half a minute, then followed, and shortly after that, near the edge of the town, saw brake lights flare. The Subaru was turning. He cruised on by, eyes apparently intent on the road ahead.

The woman had pulled into a place with a sun-faded sign saying Battendorf Motors. Two petrol bowsers at the front, a big, open service bay with a car on a hoist, a rack of tyres, a trailer for hire. And the woman, talking to a man in overalls wiping his hands on a rag.

Hendren drove a hundred metres down the road to a garden centre. He'd always been baffled by places like garden centres, but this one was busy, cars coming and going, and no one paid him any attention as he tucked the Mustang behind a line of small trees in black tubs.

He settled in to wait for the Subaru to emerge again. After he'd been there for five solid minutes he remembered the bicycle. The car's in for repairs. She's riding home. Fuck, fuck, fuck.

He spurted back onto the road. Cruised the garage again. The big roller door was coming down, closing for the day, but not before he glimpsed the Subaru being driven into the service bay. He shot to the next corner and braked, looking both ways and up towards the shops. No sign of the woman. She had a head start and could have gone anywhere. Shit, shit, shit.

Okay. There was always tomorrow. He didn't have the rest of the gun yet anyway. Google Maps took him across to the M1, out of the hills and down onto Greenhill Road, where he pulled over, checked his Airbnb app and found a place five minutes away. Settling in half an hour later, he checked the mail-drop tracking app: the Glock's clip was awaiting collection. Well, he'd believe it when he saw it. In the morning.

Then evening drew in and Brodie Hendren didn't know what to do with himself. Unfamiliar city. There'd been a chocolate on his pillow but the TV didn't even have

Netflix. Strange priorities. He flicked through free to air and found a David Attenborough. Big creatures devouring small ones, and he tried to find something positive in that. Maybe pass the observation on to Seb Verco. Anyway, feeling vaguely better, he logged on to see if Brie Haven was having a sesh with her vibrator.

35

AS DES LIDDINGTON said to his wife when he drove off to the police station that Monday morning, it was a bit anticlimactic, having had your retirement function, to go back to work for another week.

Strictly desk duties, however, especially given that he'd had the crap beaten out of him, but Liddington also understood that no one quite knew what to do with him. They certainly didn't want him wading into any further paperwork-generating strife. Didn't want him underfoot, either. And they'd said their official goodbyes.

So he was stuck in a little back room with a desk, a computer, a landline phone and masses of unimportant files to collate, sort, reject, copy and turn into paper gliders. Some of his colleagues stopped by to check on his bruises and a bored kid from CID asked, with frank disbelief, why he thought the Patmore clan was behind the assault on him, but mostly he was left to his own devices.

Which suited Liddington just fine. Anyone passing along the corridor or hanging on to the doorframe to say hello would see good old cheesy-grin Des, a harmless old bloke, slightly overweight, just days away from watching *Footy Classified* in his carpet slippers. But Liddington was wide awake under that veneer. He was hunting the woman who'd saved his life.

He wanted to thank her, naturally. He also wanted a witness statement. He wanted his dashcam back. He wanted her dashcam footage, if available. And if she'd committed, or gone on to commit, a serious crime that evening, he wanted to know about that, too. The last arrest of his career?

According to the weekend's overnight logs, the house of a home-loan guy named Jason Britton had been broken into on Saturday evening. Two factors made that case interesting: the burglary, on a little-used back road near Rowland Flat, might have gone undiscovered for days if not for an anonymous call to police; and the caller had advised that there was child pornography on the premises. Attending police had confirmed the break-in and the porn.

Furthermore, the caller had been a woman, as had an earlier triple-zero caller that evening, on *his* phone, requesting ambulance and police to save his sorry arse.

He worked the landline then, wheedling, cajoling, calling in favours and playing on the fact that this was his last week on the job. Eventually he got hold of both audio files.

The same woman had made both calls. He'd have staked his life on it. She sounded young, and indistinct, as if muffling her voice with a handkerchief. She spoke economically and precisely—if jerkily. No over-explaining, no er-ums. He thought there was a hint of cold disgust in the call about the kiddie porn. He'd like to find her ahead of the federal police. Sooner or later, he knew, they'd move on from thinking only about Jason Britton to also thinking about her.

Liddington laced his hands behind his head and stared at a stain in a ceiling tile. The woman who'd saved him might simply have been a passer-by who didn't stick around because she was running from a husband or boyfriend, or on her way to a rendezvous with a secret lover, or shy, or drunk, or high. He made a note to have the lab run a diagnostic test to see if the voice prints matched. But if it *was* the same woman on both calls...was she the burglar? The burglar's getaway driver? Girlfriend?

Too many variables. A more solid lead was the ute. Work out what make it was, trace its movements on CCTV, find the owner and hence the driver. And so Liddington entered 'dual-cab ute' into Google Images and came up with a range of examples. He switched between them, ignoring older models, occasionally closing his eyes to conjure up the night of his attack—the lights, voices and blurred outlines—then peering at the images again. If his life depended upon it, he'd claim that his saviour had been at the wheel of a dark-coloured Mitsubishi Triton fitted with a bull bar.

Maybe an Isuzu. But stick with the Triton for now.

How to find it? Liddington knew he might be way off base, but it would save him a lot of time if he assumed that the break-in and his rescue were linked. The same woman. The same vehicle. The same manner of reporting.

According to Gabi Richter, the Britton break-in didn't have the hallmarks of a smash-and-grab by druggies or opportunists. The thief, or thieves, had probably jammed the electronics before breaking in, and had left behind easily transportable items of some value: an Italian leather coat, a set of golf clubs, expensive wines and spirits.

Liddington googled Britton, and found a *Home Beautiful* article. He scrolled through, examining text and photographs, noting that the guy owned silverware, a small Chagall oil painting and a collection of never-opened first- and second-generation iPhones.

Ten minutes later he was sputtering across the Barossa in his tired and dented old Saab, passing through Rowland Flat and then, halfway to Lyndoch, turning off onto back roads that led to the Britton house on Schiller Lane. He drove past slowly, noting the presence of police vehicles, and came to an open gateway a hundred metres beyond an old shed in the adjoining paddock. He pulled over, parked and got out to look. He could see tyre impressions in the roadside dirt, the grass between the gateposts, and back along the fence, towards the shed. Someone had driven in and out again, he thought, noting the each-way flattening of the grass.

Rather than compromise any of these traces, he walked along the road and climbed through the fence at the rear of the shed. Grass grew hard up against the rear and side walls; no one had walked here. He edged along the wall closest to Britton's house and peered around the corner, half expecting—or hoping—to see a vehicle that didn't belong. Just an old shed, with an open side facing away from the road, and empty but for a few fuel drums and a grain auger.

But a dirt floor. Soft dirt holding clear tyre tracks.

Liddington returned to his car, swung around and turned in at Britton's driveway. Four police vehicles including two marked *Crime Scene*. They were parked haphazardly in the driveway and on the lawn, and one had knocked over a garden tap. A crime-scene officer in overalls and overshoes emerged from the house with a laptop in an evidence bag as Liddington got out of his car.

He didn't know her. 'Is Evie around by any chance?'

She didn't pause as she passed him. 'Evie who?'

There were several crime-scene experts in the Valley, but Evie Bonnard was the one Liddington knew best. She was a wine buff, and she'd never treated him like a dickhead. Smiling pleasantly, he walked up the veranda steps and into the house. Gave his details to the uniformed constable on the door—didn't know him either—and followed the busy sounds.

Doors and drawers banging; voices calling. Liddington made his way along a short hallway that led to an open-plan living area, and found strangers searching cupboards, fanning the pages of books and magazines, upending drawers and removing the backs of photo frames. He took out his phone, called up the *Home Beautiful* article again, just as Evie Bonnard emerged from a side room and said, 'Des?'

'Evie.'

'I thought you'd retired?'

Her tone wasn't accusing, exactly, but she was looking at him sharply, as if he represented some fresh hell. Mostly her working face was mild and vague, as if pleasant music played in her head, taking her far from the miseries she combed through every day. Right now she was scowling.

Because he shouldn't be here? 'Friday's my last day,' Liddington said. He paused. 'Is everything okay?'

'You tell me.'

The scowl deepened. She glanced covertly over her shoulder at two men—detectives, Liddington thought, although he didn't know them. Dressed in suits, they stood hip to hip, huddled over an iPad.

Returning her attention to Liddington, she gave a little jerk of the head and said, 'It seems that we have two crimes and therefore two crime-scene teams, ours and federal. Guess who muscled in on the other?'

'Because of the porn?'

Evie lowered her voice and leaned in, her hairnet brushing Liddington's cheek. 'Apparently our householder was already on their radar.'

'Does he know he's been burgled?'

'No. He's on holiday in Thailand, due home later in the week. There's a tight lid on everything so he doesn't get spooked.'

And because he's part of a paedophile ring, thought Liddington. 'At least they're letting you work the burglary angle.'

'For now. My fear is they'll take over everything and put the burglary on the back burner.'

Liddington showed her his phone. 'I found this. It might help you work out what was taken. I'll send you the link.'

Evie gave him a steady look. 'Thank you, I appreciate it, but may I ask why you're interested?'

'A long shot,' admitted Liddington, 'but I think the woman who saved me the other night is your burglar.'

'You think.'

'Like I said, a long shot.'

Evie stared up at his face, her gaze tracing his forehead,

eyes, cheeks. 'Nice technicolour bruising going on there.'

'You should see the rest of me.'

She shuddered. 'No thanks.'

'I don't blame you. But getting back to the woman, I'm pretty sure she was driving a Triton dual-cab, and I found a fresh set of tyre tracks in the dirt floor of the old shed on the other side of that side fence.'

He gestured. Evie frowned, grabbed his sleeve and led him to a corner of the room. The action alerted the detectives, who looked up briefly, before returning to the screen of their iPad.

'Des, I know you want to find this woman, but I can't have you wandering into my crime scene on the off-chance you find something that relates to her. Yes, I'll check the tyre marks, but I'll have to pass it on to these guys'—she gestured—'and then it will be out of my hands, and yours.' She paused. 'And it's not as if you were attacked *here*.'

'No, you're right. But it happened not all that far from here. I was on my way home from my retirement do, in fact.'

'Coincidence. She could have been anybody.'

'Look, if you could do two things for me'—he saw the irritation in her face—'related to your investigation. Not favours, as such.'

'Like what?'

'A voice-print comparison of two triple-zero calls—one reporting the burglary, and the other the attack on me—and check if the tyre treads could possibly have been made by a Mitsubishi Triton dual-cab.'

'Or any other dual-cab. Des, you're a victim, you can't investigate your own attack.'

At least she hadn't said no. 'I understand. It's just that they've got me filing witness statements for the rest of the week and it's driving me bonkers.'

'If I find anything, I'm not necessarily telling you, Des.'

'Understood.'

Liddington returned to his cramped room in the police station and, after sorting a few witness statements to keep his sergeant happy, began hunting down CCTV footage that might show a dark-coloured dual-cab fitted with a bull bar. Knowing that it would take hours, days, he started with public and private cameras near Rowland Flat and the church crossroads first. Then he worked his way out, eventually taking in the main towns of the Valley, including Angaston, Tanunda, Nuriootpa and Lyndoch. Service stations, supermarkets, major intersections and public buildings were the best sources. By late Wednesday morning he'd located a black Triton parked near a cage of barbecue gas cylinders on the side wall of a twenty-four-hour service station in Angaston. He gave thanks to the gods. It might not be *his* Triton, but it was a start.

Wishing he could enlist the help of a forensic video technician, Liddington sipped his stomach-souring tearoom coffees, gave his harmless old-fart smiles to the occasional colleague passing his door, and watched the

Triton ute on fast-forward until early afternoon. According to the time stamp, it had first appeared in the early evening of last Friday. Despite the poor video quality, he could see a yellow New South Wales numberplate as it entered the forecourt and wound its way around to the parking bay at the side of the building. The driver alighted. Slight; youthful. Probably female.

The ute sat there all Friday night and most of Saturday. Then the same figure got behind the wheel soon after 8 p.m. Saturday evening, drove away and did not return. He kept watching. The Triton did not return on Sunday, Monday or Tuesday.

By coordinating with CCTV from an intersection on the outskirts of Angaston, he was able to obtain a clear image of the plate number. According to the NSW Department of Motor Vehicles, it belonged to a black 1998 Commodore that had been written off in 2017.

At 2 p.m. he stopped for a late lunch, eating in at a deli a block from the police station. The shop's wall-mounted TV was showing breaking news: Jason Britton had been arrested by Border Force detectives when he touched down at Sydney airport on his way home from Thailand.

The next bit of good news came mid-afternoon, when Gabi Richter arrived in his poky office, flushed, eyes burning. 'Guess what?'

'You got them.'

'You're no fun,' she said, giving him a half-humorous, half-disappointed scowl. 'Drew Patmore's second cousin took himself to Tanunda hospital with a cracked kneecap. The doctor wasn't happy with his story and informed us. As soon as we show up in his room, he spills his guts. Wants us to protect him from Drew and Pete.'

'Who was the other one?'

'Nathan, another vague cousin.'

'Keeping it in the family,' Liddington said.

'Yep. Anyway, they torched the Jeep, we found it over near Tanunda. No forensic joy there, and testing your car and your clothes will take a while, but we do have a confession.'

'Thanks, Gabi, that's great news.'

When she was gone, Liddington returned to his CCTV viewing, this time trying to trace the movements of the driver, not the car. She seemed to walk west after parking the Triton on Friday evening, but had approached it from the south-east on Saturday night. Suggestive behaviour. Cautious. Both stretches of that main road west and east, and the north–south cross streets, were poorly covered by cameras, as Liddington discovered when he took a scout around in his Saab. For all he knew, the mystery driver might have parked a second car nearby and stayed Friday night elsewhere in the Valley—or even in Adelaide. Or she'd walked all the way across town to some motel out on the road to Nuriootpa. Or, like any normal person, she'd saved herself the bother and stayed in the Vigneron Motel, five minutes' walk from her vehicle.

—

Liddington spent most of Thursday viewing the Vigneron's CCTV and running checks on the guests. Grey nomads, travelling sales reps, a couple of German tourists and four women and two men who worked in antiques and were in Angaston for the Runacre Hall clearing sale. No one had a criminal record. All were driving legitimately registered vehicles. But three of the women resembled the driver of the dual-cab in size and shape: a tourist from Hamburg, a cosmetics rep and a buyer for Mandel's Collectibles in the Adelaide Hills. The tourist had since flown to Cairns with her boyfriend, the rep was still visiting pharmacies in the region, and the antiques buyer had checked out on Sunday morning.

He called the German woman's mobile number. She and her boyfriend had dined at a winery restaurant on Saturday evening. Liddington made a call: the restaurant confirmed they were still in the restaurant an hour after he'd been carted off to hospital. Likewise, the cosmetics rep, who'd dined with a local pharmacist and his family.

That left Grace Latimore, the antiques buyer. She was driving a white Forester registered to her boss. According to the motel's CCTV coverage, she'd parked the Forester outside her motel room on Friday afternoon, driven out on Saturday morning, back again that afternoon, and out again Sunday morning, when she'd handed in her room key.

Unfortunately, her room was at the far end of a wing, farthest from the camera and obscured by shrubbery, a veranda trellis and the vehicles parked outside the intervening rooms. Liddington peered at the vague shape that was all he could see of her room. She certainly came and went from her room, but not in the lead-up to the Schiller Lane burglary, or after the time he was attacked.

On Friday he obtained limited CCTV coverage of the Runacre Hall carpark, and saw Grace Latimore come and go on both days of the sale. She'd parked the Forester and entered the hall each morning, and when she left between four-thirty and five each afternoon, had been loaded with items she'd bought and won at auction. She was legitimate. And yet…He felt a tingle as he watched her.

If she had been the burglar, and his saviour, what would she have done immediately afterwards? Unlikely that she'd want to stick around the Barossa in a recognisable vehicle, or park it back at the service station and walk down the road to her motel. Attending the Sunday auction had taken nerve, but it had been a necessary part of her cover story. On Saturday night she'd have wanted to clear out of the Barossa and find somewhere to stash the dual-cab ute.

In the dwindling hours of his last day as a policeman, Desmond Liddington searched wider afield and found the Triton on the Northern Expressway at 9.47 p.m. Saturday. Fitted with Victorian plates this time, and possibly headed for the city. He was calling car-hire places and motels when five o'clock rolled around and he was dragged out for a desultory round of farewell drinks.

Beer. He hated beer.

36

TUESDAY DAWNED FREE of rain clouds. Grace cycled into Battendorf from Landau Street, locked her bike to a pole outside the shop and crossed over to the café to sip a soy latte at her regular table in the back corner. As always, the woman who served her indicated one of the better tables, and, as always, Grace declined.

'I'm fine here, thanks.'

Her table gave her a view of the whole place, including the front door and part of the main window adjacent to it, and an escape door was at her shoulder, leading to a short corridor, a backyard, an alleyway leading to a network of side streets. Familiar locals—no strangers at this hour—came and went. The Mount Barker bus. Kevin in his hi-vis jacket, picking up gutter and footpath rubbish with his grabber tool. A kid late for school, a power walker checking her Fitbit: the usual sights and signs. But Grace couldn't shake the jitters.

Finishing her coffee, she crossed the street to the shop, dumped her bag on the counter, touched her treasures in the cabinet drawer for reassurance and opened for business. A slow morning: a bid of $8,850 for the Gibson guitar, an email thanking her for the Vassilieff tip, and a mini-bus load of CWA women touring the Hills antique centres. They spent five minutes buying nothing and when they left the silver Art Deco dragonfly hair comb left too, stashed in someone's handbag or pocket.

Otherwise, Grace dusted, tidied, answered correspondence and checked the news feed on her phone. Nothing about the policeman, but the Jason Britton arrest had generated a long article on sex tourism in the *Guardian*. She tightened her fists, muttered, 'Yes.' Wished she could share it.

Battendorf Motors called at 12.45. The Forester was ready for pick-up.

'I'll come now,' she said.

Placing a *Back Soon* note in the window, Grace locked the shop and cycled to the garage, where she spotted Erin's car in a parking bay at the edge of the forecourt. She dismounted, wheeled her bike across, propped it on its stand and settled her helmet on the saddle. She was shaking out her hair when the jitters returned—a more tangible sense this time that something was wrong. A quality of stillness and expectation in the atmosphere. And the junior mechanics, one under an old Holden, fitting a new exhaust, the other on a truck tyre, eating a sandwich in the sun, seemed overly focused on her.

Grace checked herself uneasily. Inoffensive jeans and T-shirt. No embarrassing stains. She pulled her bag out of the pannier, hooking it over her neck, and crossed her arms over her chest as she walked into the office.

Mark Dinakis looked up. He had the invoice resting on top of the counter and spun it around to face her as she crossed the room. 'Have a read through, see what you think.'

Her name was there, Grace Latimore, the Landau Street address, the amount due, and a short account of the work undertaken. 'Looks good,' she said, absently taking the Mandel's Collectibles credit card from her bag. She paused, looking up from the page. 'Change the sparkplugs next service?'

Dinakis nodded. 'They're fine for another six months,' he said, his tone faintly stressed. She looked at him. He looked at her. And then she was alerted to his right hand: tense, the fingers like a claw around a small, black rectangular device. 'I also found this.'

37

GRACE'S MIND RACED. Playing for time, she put on a little frown.

'What is it?'

'A tracking device.'

'*Tracking* device?'

Dinakis nodded. 'It's not the first time I've found one, but this one's slightly more sophisticated. It was plugged into the OBD.'

'I don't know what that is.'

'It's a port under the dash, near the steering column.

It's where we plug in a diagnostics gizmo when we service or repair a car.'

'Perhaps it was fitted when the car was made,' Grace said, still playing dumb—but thinking: it was Adam or the police in the Barossa. Or just about anyone from her past.

'Absolutely not,' Dinakis said. He grew uncomfortable, as if regretting what he was about to say. 'I have to ask, is there a controlling boyfriend in the picture? Husband, partner? Someone keeping tabs on you for whatever reason?'

'No,' Grace said, thinking: I have to get out of here.

'It's just that I had a young woman in that situation late last year and we contacted the police. They did the right thing by her.'

Grace smacked her forehead with the heel of her palm. 'I know what it is! It's not my car, it's a work car—Mandel's Collectibles, up on the main street?'

Dinakis nodded that he knew it.

'We're always out and about, deliveries, auctions, clearing sales, sometimes for days at a time, with valuable things in the back. Erin—Ms Mandel—must've had the tracker installed to keep tabs on the car.'

Dinakis seemed doubtful. 'Okay.'

'Would you be able to put it back, please?'

'Sure.' He paused. 'I can show you if you like.'

She paid the bill, followed him out to the car and watched him open the driver's door and reach under the dash. 'It goes up in here, see?'

'Okay.'

Then he was uncoiling and she was stepping back to let him out.

'Good to go.'

'Thank you.'

Aware of the other mechanics' continued attention—either Dinakis had told them about the tracker, or one of them had brought it to his attention—Grace stowed the bike in the rear of the Subaru. She drove out onto the road sedately, her mind still racing, and headed back up to the roundabout as if returning to the main street. When she was confident that she couldn't be seen she turned right, not left, and followed the intersecting road down towards the little park adjacent to the town's leisure centre.

Parking beneath a massive gum tree next to the skateboard ramps, she got out and stood back from the car, contemplating it gloomily, first speculating that Erin had, in fact, fitted a tracker and not told her—but that only seemed feasible if Erin didn't trust her, in which case Erin wouldn't have let her drive off on buying trips with a credit card and cash. Or someone was tracking Erin? Doubtful. Erin barely ever drove the car. Adam, the cops, or someone else from her past.

Other questions arose now. When and where had the bug been installed? She recalled the sudden onset of signal interference when she was in the Barossa Valley a few days ago: Erin's calls dropping out; scratchy sounds on the line. The car was bugged recently, she thought. Here in town?

At home? That first night at the motel in Angaston?

Then she recalled the day she'd delivered the Whiteley to be cleaned. It hadn't bothered her at the time—she wasn't used to the car—but she hadn't heard the snap of the door locks when she pressed the key fob's lock and unlock buttons. She'd never met Gaynor Bernard; it couldn't have anything to do with her…Had she been followed?

Dinakis had found only one bug. But if there's one, there could be another, Grace thought, glancing about uneasily. The sky seemed far away, remote from her. No skateboarders until school got out. The air was mild and magpies warbled and nest-builders were busy as she went over the Forester.

Under the bonnet, every corner of the boot, inside the wheel arches. The chassis. In the glovebox and under the seats. She found nothing. She brushed herself down and began to weigh her options.

The car, first. She could simply drive off in it. Chuck the tracker into the Onkaparinga River and just go. Whoever was monitoring her movements wouldn't necessarily be alarmed: the Subaru was always being used for shop business. And right now, lunchtime, they wouldn't necessarily be alarmed that she'd driven it to the little park beside the leisure centre.

She felt foggy in the head, as if she'd used up all of her smarts in the Barossa Valley. But she did know she should go: run and not look back. It was entirely possible that two surveillance teams were on her, one keeping tabs at Mandel's

Collectibles, the other at Landau Street. She couldn't return to either place. Goodbye granny flat, goodbye job, goodbye both sets of treasures and her safe-deposit stash.

Goodbye Erin.

She unplugged the tracker from the OBD port, turned off her phone, removed the sim card and headed back to the main road, then through to the highway that would take her down into the city. Dump the car at the airport; rent or buy another, or take a train or a bus to Western Australia or the Northern Territory.

Five minutes later, approaching the M1, she cursed her brain again. She had no money with her. She had the business credit card, but, if the Battendorf Motors mechanic happened to follow up with Erin, there would soon be a stop on the card and an alert issued for the Subaru. Meanwhile, whoever was monitoring the tracking device would have thrown themselves into action when the signal vanished. For all she knew, someone was on her tail right now. She braked suddenly, shot to the kerb without indicating, and checked her mirrors. An angry toot as the car immediately behind her swerved to pass, the driver waving his fist, but the subsequent cars sailed on by.

She was a mess; she couldn't think straight.

Keep the Subaru, but fit it with new plates? But she'd jettisoned her remaining two sets.

I'm stuffed, she thought.

Then she found herself thinking about her haul from Jason Britton's house. There was no reason why anyone would be watching the bank. A quick in and out. And so she turned around and headed back to Battendorf and the park beside the leisure centre. Reinstalling the tracking device, she dug out the change of clothes she kept permanently in the Subaru's lockbox—loose cream pants and a pale blue shirt—and entered the leisure centre's women's changeroom, in a corridor next to a yoga class. Working quickly, before she could be seen, she redressed, trashed the clothes she'd removed, then washed her hands and flicked her hair into shape.

Before returning to the car, she stood inside the centre's main door for a while. Nothing out there that bothered her. Getting behind the wheel finally, she drove up to the main part of town and into the laneway behind the shop. Cruised along it from one end to the other: no strangers or strange cars. She went around and came in again, parked in her regular spot and unloaded the bike, then pedalled across to the carpark behind the main-street shops. Here she locked the bike to a pole, stuck her helmet on the saddle and, shouldering one of the panniers, crossed to the side street that would take her up to the town's main drag. Still she could not shake off the sensation of being observed.

At the corner, she darted a look along the main street, taking in the bank, Erin's shop, the other shops. She waited a moment, risked another look—at cars and pedestrians this time. A couple of figures in the distance, walking away from her. Parked cars, all apparently empty. She left the security of the side wall and headed along the footpath to the bank, feeling exposed.

Up the steps, through the heavy wood and brass main doors, and into a dimly lit tiled foyer decorated with an old vase—bought from Erin's shop—for umbrellas, and a second set of glass doors leading into the main section of the bank. Grace had her shoulder to one of the doors and was part-way through when she spotted Erin in there, arms braced on the counter, a couple of small weekender bags at her feet, speaking urgently to a teller.

Standing next to her was a uniformed policeman. Grace stiffened, began to back out again. And bumped into the mechanic, Mark Dinakis. He was with a woman wearing plain clothes and the flat, unimpressed look of the law.

38

FEELING HER THROAT close, Grace gave a faintly puzzled frown as she glanced from one to the other. Had they witnessed the way she'd faltered just then?

Play the innocent, she told herself. 'Mr Dinakis. Is there something about the car…? The payment? I used a work card…'

Dinakis shook his head; he was embarrassed, hating to inconvenience her. 'Ms Latimore, this is Detective Sergeant Swanwick. She—'

Swanwick stepped forward, her hand out. She seemed

to alter shape, her thin, scowling, raw-boned face now folding into a smile. 'Alanna. We were worried about you.'

Play it dumb, Grace thought, shaking the outstretched hand, which felt cool, hinting at strength. 'About me?'

The detective took a step back, still smiling; smoothing her creased grey linen shirt and dark trousers as if the movement of her hands would guide what she said next. 'The tracking device found by Mr Dinakis,' she began.

Dinakis cut in: 'Grace, we looked everywhere for you.'

Grace's mind raced. He hadn't been satisfied with her explanation about the bug. He'd called the cops. And the cops would have checked with Erin. But was she in trouble? She couldn't tell yet. 'Such a beautiful day,' she said, 'I decided to have lunch in the park.'

'And then came here to the bank?' Swanwick said.

The detective was pleasant, all smiles; mostly an act, Grace thought. 'I'm off on a buying trip soon. Patchwork quilts. They're popular. The woman who makes them likes cash.' She paused. Added, for deflection: 'I'm sure she declares it to the tax man.'

'I'm not the tax police,' Swanwick said, staring at the pannier on Grace's shoulder. 'So you came here to the bank, and then what? Changed your mind about going in?'

Grace half turned to the glass doors and gestured towards Erin, who was still talking to the teller. 'I saw Erin and assumed *she* was getting the cash out. No sense doubling up.'

A weak story, so she fixed Swanwick, then Dinakis,

with a harder look: a reasonable woman being quizzed about something yet to be clarified. 'Not sure what that's got to do with you being worried about me?'

'Not here, not now,' Swanwick muttered, staring past Grace's shoulder. Erin had come pushing through the swinging glass doors, tailed by the uniformed officer.

'Grace! You're okay! Thank God,' Erin said.

Grace turned to her. 'What's going on?'

'I needed some running-away money.'

'For what?'

'I wanted to warn you, but I was scared my phone was bugged,' Erin said. She proffered one of the bags. 'Here: I packed a few things for you.'

Grace threw up her hands. 'Nothing's making any sense.'

'Please, everybody, not here, not now,' Swanwick said. 'Wait till we're in the car, all right?' She nodded to the uniform, who stepped away to speak into his radio. They all waited, looking at their shoes, and when the uniform said, 'It just pulled up,' Swanwick said, 'There's a white Hyundai SUV parked right outside the bank. Ms Mandel, Ms Latimer, into the back seat—quickly, please. Mr Dinakis, thank you for everything, we'll be in touch.'

The mechanic smiled, nodded, gave her an ironical little salute. 'My pleasure.'

The uniformed policeman left first, glanced both ways along the street, and, a moment later, Grace found herself following Erin down the stone steps to the footpath, with

Swanwick hard on their heels. All she wanted to do was run—a quick dart left or right. She'd mapped out all of the town's side streets, hedges and backyard sheds when she first started living here, and she could hide close by until they finally assumed she was long gone. But then what?

'In you get,' Swanwick said, opening the kerbside rear door of the SUV. The engine was idling. Another uniform was at the wheel, watching the road and his mirrors.

Erin slipped in first, sliding across until she was behind the driver, before smiling tensely at Grace. 'Really sorry about all this.'

Be patient, Grace told herself. She settled in behind Swanwick, who'd taken the passenger seat and was murmuring to the driver. Grace saw him nod, check the mirrors again and pull away from the kerb. His gaze was restless: road, side roads, cars, mirrors.

Swanwick was no less focused. Leaning into the gap between the seats, face half-turned to Grace, she lifted her voice above the road-surface and engine noises. 'This is the situation. Someone bugged Ms Mandel's car.'

'I know, Mr Dinakis showed me,' Grace said. She touched Erin's wrist. 'Sorry, I assumed you'd had it fitted—a work thing.'

Erin began to speak, but Swanwick got in first. 'In fact, Mr Dinakis found two devices.'

No wonder he reported it. 'God, really?'

'So, Grace, before we get to where we're going, I need you to check your pockets, your phone, your shoes, your bag...You're looking for anything that doesn't belong. Don't worry about the things Ms Mandel put together for you—they've already been checked.'

'God, really?' said Grace again, patting her pockets, her jeans, taking off her runners. 'My phone's okay,' she added, not wanting Swanwick to look at it. 'It never leaves my side.'

Swanwick grunted. 'You'd be surprised how small some tracking devices are. I helped a woman and her three kids last month who were bugged a dozen ways they weren't even aware of: an app on her phone, an Apple AirTag inside a teddy bear, and bugs in the lining of a parka, the handle of the baby's stroller...'

'I'm good,' Grace said eventually.

But she could sense an edgy vibration in Erin. She turned to her and asked, 'Is someone after you?'

'My ex,' Erin said tremulously. 'His name's Brodie—Brodie Hendren, and he—'

Swanwick interrupted again. 'Before we go down that path...Ms Latimer, you've been the main driver of Ms Mandel's car recently, is that correct?'

'Yes.'

'Can you think of anyone who would want to know your movements?'

Grace paused as if to search through her past. 'No, no one.'

'Has anyone shown any interest in you lately? Showing up in various places unexpectedly, for example? A customer, boyfriend, ex-partner, neighbour...?'

'Nothing like that.'

Erin leaned into the gap between the front seats. 'Sergeant—Alanna—it's me, *I'm* the one. My ex.'

'Yes, probably,' Swanwick said, 'but I need to be sure.'

'It's the kind of thing he'd do,' Erin said. 'He's a tech nerd. Anything IT. And it would be just like him to fit *two* trackers, in case one didn't work or fell off or something.'

'Yes, well, that's what alerted Mr Dinakis,' Swanwick said. 'He's serviced plenty of fleet vehicles fitted with professional-grade tracking devices. He's never found a vehicle fitted with two devices. Either both were fitted at the same time, or the second was fitted by someone who didn't know about the first.'

And it was just like Adam to have fitted two devices, thought Grace, mentally dismissing Erin's assertions. She glanced restlessly through the windows, left, right, and ahead, aware that they were about to leave Battendorf by way of one of the narrow, winding roads heading north and slightly east, towards Lobethal and Gumeracha. The trees on either side reached branches across the road, so that they were speeding down a shadowy tunnel banded by greenish light. She turned to Erin. 'Your ex is certainly determined,' she said, keeping up her innocent and confused act, hoping it was convincing everyone.

Before Erin could respond, Swanwick broke in with another of her back-tracking questions, proving to Grace that she needed to stay on her toes. 'By the way, where is Ms Mandel's car now?'

Thank Christ I didn't leave it at the leisure centre, Grace thought.

'Where I usually park it, behind the shop.'

Still watching the road ahead, Swanwick seemed to think about that. 'We may need to take it to the police garage.'

'Okay.'

The car rolled on smoothly and Grace, settling into her seat, turned to Erin again and said, 'Sorry about your husband, I had no idea.'

'I should have told you about him, but after two years of nothing happening, I started to think I was safe, so there was no point telling anyone. I was beginning to relax, in fact.' She shuddered. 'Just as well the car needed a service, or I could be dead now.'

'He's violent?'

'Yes.'

'But the fact that he *hasn't* done anything yet could mean he's only just fitted the bugs,' Grace said.

'Yeah, maybe.'

'Anyway, a good thing Mr Dinakis told the police.'

Swanwick had been listening. 'In fact, he told his wife first, and she told me.'

'Why…?'

'Mrs Dinakis runs a refuge,' Swanwick said. 'We often coordinate: we send family violence victims to her, and she alerts us to potential or ongoing situations.'

It was Grace's turn to lean into the gap between the

seats. 'Is that where we're going? The refuge?'

Swanwick nodded. 'They have a room free, which is not often the case. And given Mr Hendren's propensity for violence—confirmed by Queensland Police—I didn't want to take any chances.'

'Just until he's arrested,' Erin said. She patted her bag. 'And I took some money out for us.'

Grace settled back in her seat. 'Thanks for thinking of me—but I'm not in danger.'

'You could be,' Swanwick said. 'The fact that you live and work with—Hang on, I need to read this.' She turned her attention to her phone.

They travelled on, wrapped in a green world broken up here and there by open stretches where the trees had been felled for crops and fallow ground. And then Swanwick was passing her phone to Erin through the gap in the seats. 'I've been waiting for this—it's a still from CCTV footage, dated yesterday. The camera outside your shop.'

Erin took the phone, bent her head to the screen, enlarged the image. Hunching now, tight as a spring, stress in her voice as she said, 'He's lost weight…but yep, that's him.'

'Show it to Ms Latimer.'

The phone felt warm and sleek in Grace's hand. The CCTV camera, slightly angled along the footpath, had picked up the guy who'd checked out the antique tool display. His flash young-real-estate-agent look—pointy shoes, tight-fitting pants and jacket over a grey V-necked

T-shirt. His scalp, raw and pale over the ears, topped by a patch of sculpted oily hair.

'He came into the shop yesterday,' she said, some of her tension draining away. She'd thought she was the prey. The irony: she'd been in hiding with a woman in hiding.

Swanwick fired questions at her. 'What did he want? Did he say anything, want to know where Ms Mandel was, anything like that?'

'No. He was interested in our window display, some old hand tools, and asked about one of the planes, wondering if we had the box it came in. I said Erin might know more—sorry, Erin.'

'No problem.'

Swanwick stuck her face between the seats again. 'Grace, you didn't tell him where Erin lives? Anything at all?'

'No, course not.'

A grunt and Swanwick faced the unfolding road again, saying, 'It's possible he knows that, anyway. We'll sweep everything in case he broke in and planted more bugs.'

Grace's tension returned. Would a bug-sweeping device pick up either or both of her stashes? 'Good to know.'

Everyone moved quickly this morning, she thought. Maybe Erin's car had been the first to be serviced. Then Dinakis told his wife, who told Swanwick—who probably went straight to Erin.

Before or after running a background check on me?

She found her knee jiggling up and down. Feeling

more confined by the second, she said, 'How will you catch him? By watching the house and the shop?'

Swanwick turned to peer in at her. Screwed an expression of apology onto her face and said, 'In an ideal world, yes, but…resources. I'll ask the local station to send a car past now and then, but mostly we'll be trying to find out where Mr Hendren's holed up. Erin, do you happen to know where he lives now? According to Queensland police, he's no longer in Brisbane.'

'Sorry, no.'

Swanwick turned away. 'We'll check local hotels, motels and Airbnbs.'

They rode in silence. It worked on Erin, so that she touched Grace on the wrist and said, 'Really sorry about all this. Everything happened so quickly this morning. And I didn't know if it was safe to call and warn you.'

Grace smiled. 'That's all right,' she said, glancing at the world outside their windows. They'd reached Gumeracha and she tried to memorise their route as the driver turned off the main road and into a network of small residential streets, sometimes doubling back. Finally he entered a street of older houses and slowed to 20 km/h. Drove to the end, turned around and made another sweep. She spotted a two-storey weatherboard with barred windows, a reinforced front door and security cameras at each end of the veranda. A Honda people mover had been parked nose out in the driveway as if for a quick escape.

She said, 'Were we followed?'

No one answered her, and, as the driver continued to the end of the street, she tried to anticipate the next few hours in the refuge. The front and rear doors would be kept locked, no one getting in unless they were known to Mrs Dinakis and her helpers—but surely the residents could let themselves out if they wanted? Or if the building was on fire? Plenty of scrutiny, however: cameras, people on duty. She'd have to slip out of a window and shimmy down a tree. Except that the windows, top and bottom, were fitted with bars. Barred to keep men out, barred to keep me in, she thought, as the SUV pulled into the kerb and Swanwick made a muttered phone call.

39

THEN SWANWICK WAS ushering them along the garden path to the veranda steps. Grace took note of the keypad at the front door, the CCTV cameras and the tamper-proof lights under the veranda roof. She tensed as the door opened.

The woman who stood there darted her gaze from Swanwick to Erin, Grace and the SUV idling in the street. 'Tracey Dinakis,' she said, beginning to shake hands before the sergeant could make introductions, and soon after that Swanwick and her driver were gone.

'Let's get you inside.'

Grace had time to notice a push-button alarm halfway down the hallway before she and Erin were ushered through the first door on the right. Marked *Tracey Dinakis Director*, it led to a cluttered room: shelved books, framed prints and certificates, filing cabinets, chairs, a desk with a computer, another push-button alarm on the wall near the desk, and a sheer curtain to conceal the interior from curious pedestrians.

'Have a seat.'

Dinakis's voice, a low, uninflected growl, belied her smile. In her jeans, T-shirt and sockless black sandshoes she seemed to Grace brusque and competent. A woman who knew about violent men, and the kind who might track their partners to a refuge.

When they were settled opposite her on old wooden chairs, Dinakis said, 'As you can no doubt tell, this is more of a halfway house than a fully outfitted refuge. Short-term crisis accommodation, and very communal.' She paused. 'I know your situation. Mark called me, and I called Sergeant Swanwick. Alanna's good, she doesn't muck around waiting for situations to get worse, so here we are.'

'Thanks for taking us in,' Erin said.

Dinakis nodded. 'I'll see if I can rustle up a couple of personal duress alarms later, but right now I want to assure you we've got the exterior and interior pretty well covered with cameras, lights and alarms, and there's always someone on duty, twenty-four seven.' She paused. 'Me, tonight. Poor Mark, doesn't see me for days sometimes.'

Grace thought she should say something. 'So glad he found those trackers on Erin's car.'

'Happens more often than you think,' Dinakis said.

She was eyeing Grace. She doesn't know how I fit in, Grace thought. Or maybe she sees something I can't hide. My old paranoia.

'Right.' Dinakis seemed to shrug away whatever it was. 'First, I need to know if either of you informed anyone—however tangentially—that you were coming here?'

They shook their heads.

'Good. Now, as I said, our accommodation is short-term, two weeks at the most. Demand is high. And I can't give you separate rooms. Which raises the question: can you go somewhere safe when you leave here? A friend, a relative?'

They looked at each other; looked at her and shook their heads.

'Okay. We can deal with that later. If you like, we'll draw up care plans: counselling, legal aid, outreach services. Right now I'll show you how everything works, introduce you to some of the others—if they're in the common areas—and show you to your room.'

'Thank you,' Erin said.

Dinakis's phone pinged. She snatched it from her desk, read the screen and said, 'Back in a jiffy.'

She left the room, leaving the door half ajar behind her, and Grace followed and interpreted the sounds. Murmurs—Dinakis and another woman—then footsteps receding along the corridor and up the stairs.

Dinakis returned, saying, 'Sorry, that was our doctor. She carries out forensic examinations on behalf of the police and the courts. One of our women…' she added, with a gesture of her hand.

They understood. Erin said, 'Good to know. It was a doctor in Brisbane who helped me get away, actually. It was all arranged. My ex thought I was going in for a pap smear—things like that made him queasy, so he didn't come with me—and the doctor took me through to a lawyer and a family violence advocate who set up a safety plan for me.'

Dinakis nodded. 'I wish it were that easy for all our clients.'

Grace saw Erin go tense. Did she feel dismissed?

'That was the second time I left. The first time I had no one.'

Tracey Dinakis gave Erin a look, infinitely sad, came around from behind her desk and embraced her briskly by the shoulders. 'Let's make sure he never finds you again. Come on, I'll show you where everything is.'

They filed into the corridor. The ground floor of the creaky old house consisted of three bedrooms, a sitting room, a kitchen and a laundry. A young woman and a listless child were watching afternoon cartoons in the sitting room, and two women in their forties were measuring out milk, flour and butter in the kitchen. They smiled at Dinakis; narrowed their eyes at Grace and Erin.

Then through to the laundry, just inside the only door leading to the backyard. Grace formed a quick impression of tree canopies, vegetable patches, a sandpit and a swing set before Dinakis said, 'I see that neither of you brought much luggage. We'll get you some more clothes tomorrow, but you can feel free to use the washing machine whenever you like, there's a clothesline out there,' she added, gesturing.

'Thanks,' Grace said.

Dinakis paused. 'But maybe try to avoid doing any washing mid- to late evening? It's just that one of our residents likes to do her washing then. She's here with four kids and she's very shy and a bit…a bit OCD.'

She fixed them with a hard look then, as if to say everyone in the house had had a shit time, and been affected in different ways.

Grace nodded.

Their bedroom was upstairs at the rear of the house. 'Have to warn you, the door's very noisy,' Dinakis said.

A deafening screech, in fact: the first thing Grace would attend to. A large room, with a double bed and two singles, a flimsy plywood wardrobe, two chests of drawers, an armchair, a small TV on top of a three-drawer dresser. A desk and a kitchen chair in one corner, a frieze of nursery-rhyme characters around the walls. A mobile turned lazily above the single beds and paperbacks and picture books stood upright or at a lean on a shelf above the main bed.

Grace crossed to the barred window. It looked out over the backyard, but was no use to her: the bars, the narrow gaps between them and the tamper-proof screws fixing them to the wooden frame. Behind her Erin said, 'Thank you. Plenty of room.'

'Pretty basic, I know,' Dinakis said, 'but you're safe here.'

Grace rejoined them as Dinakis added, 'Shared bathroom down the hall, sorry. Needless to say, please don't hog the shower or the loo.'

'We won't. Thank you for everything,' Erin said, and she glanced keenly at Grace then, as if to nudge her.

She's wresting back some control, Grace thought. Dutifully turning to Tracey Dinakis, she said, 'Yes, thank you, everything's great and it's good of you to take us in.'

Dinakis waved that off. 'I'll let you get settled. 'I'll be in the office if you need me for anything.'

Grace watched her leave, closing the noisy door behind her, shutting off the sounds of voices and the TV downstairs, then turned to Erin, who was rattling the wardrobe's flimsy wire coathangers and saying, 'Half each?'

'Sure.'

'Not that we've got much. Hope you're okay with what I grabbed from your place.'

'Fine,' Grace said.

Not as if I'll take any of it with me, she thought.

40

BRODIE HENDREN'S TUESDAY started badly. Somehow, Airbnb beds—unlike hotel beds—reminded him of all the people who'd been there before him, sleeping or doing whatever the hell they did. And he woke up feeling out of sorts. With any luck he'd be confronting Karen later, but even so he felt somehow…

He couldn't quite name it. It seemed to be a jumble of discontent, sullenness—which he hated in himself—and dissatisfaction. Back when he was a kid, a teacher had written 'Brodie possesses a disorderly mind' in his report card. Yeah, well, fuck you—he'd come a long way since then. You didn't achieve that if your mind was disorderly.

Even so, as he lay in a bed used by strangers, staring up at the dawn light smearing the ceiling, he had a shot at ordering the things he was feeling. First, he hadn't been sticking to his diet. He needed to buy some probiotics to offset the fast-food toxins compromising his gut health. Offset the breakfast crap he'd bought at the convenience store down the street last night because he didn't know where the fuck else to go: a yogurt stuffed with sugar, a floury apple and rice crackers too close to the use-by date. He nearly picked up an energy drink, too, but the energy came from sugar and caffeine, and fuck that for a joke. Should've packed a couple of litres of Hendro's Headers.

What else? The Glock pistol was still minus its clip which, the way his luck was running, wouldn't be waiting for him at the mail centre on Magill Road.

He stuck a couple of pillows behind his back and opened his laptop...and a shameful memory came flooding in. He winced, groaned, shut the lid. He shouldn't have jerked off last night, watching Brie Haven. He'd been weak. All she'd done was walk around in a dressing gown, tidying up before bed, but he'd pumped himself desperately in anticipation. He should be above that kind of thing. It defiled him, defiled his body and his core character.

What would Seb Verco do? Hendren took a deep breath to build character strength and, without a second thought, opened his laptop again and deleted the bitch's video link.

He could get it back up again if he needed to. But he wouldn't need to. He'd moved past that.

Okay. Feeling more in control, he checked his listings—sluggish—then checked in on Seb to cheer himself up.

Fucking hell, now the poor bastard was being ganged up on by some #MeToo slags. Forced to attend Los Angeles police headquarters to face rape and inappropriate touching charges—photographed on the steps with his lawyer.

Looking pretty good, actually—fit and healthy—he summed the whole matter up in a nutshell: 'I'm rich and successful, so is it any wonder unscrupulous people want a piece of me? People who know me know that I like and respect women.'

Brodie Hendren shut down his laptop and stepped into the shower, wondering if maybe the reason he'd woken up feeling so shithouse was because his body had absorbed Seb's bad luck through the airwaves overnight.

With a renewed appreciation for his body and its sensitive antennae, he lathered up vigorously, treacherous cock included, an act of excoriation to rid himself of toxins, negative thoughts and all the shit that women heap on you. Their arrogance and entitlement. The way they never take responsibility for their own poor choices. The way they program themselves to be victims. And how they block and ignore you. It was as if you could hardly afford to look at a woman these days without being accused of rape.

He thought of Karen telling the cops he was responsible

for her bruises when she was exactly the kind of bitch who'd hurt herself to get a man into trouble. He told the cops that, but they took her side anyway. Woke cunts.

He was well into it by now, almost chanting as he soaped himself…

Then the water went cold. No pressure, either—just when he needed it most, just when he needed to feel the full, lashing force of hot water sluicing all the poisons down the drain. Shivering under a weak dribble, he was forced to splash impotently at the lather with his hands.

Stepping out, reaching for a towel, he caught a glimpse of his body in the misted mirror. Looking good. The looks-maxxing regime was paying off: exercise, diet, a bit of Botox and filler, a bit of cheek and jaw sculpting with a little hammer.

But Jesus, was that a hint of belly? After just a day or two of crap food?

Feeling utterly pissed off, he headed out in the Mustang. He was halfway to Box Office on Magill Road, window down, waiting to turn left at a traffic light, when a toned woman on a bicycle came alongside, propped one foot on the ground and took a swig of water from the bottle mounted to her frame. He turned his head to check her out, and quickly away again. He was having a shit day, and really didn't want to see contempt on a woman's face just then.

She said, 'Cool car.'

He chanced a quick look. She actually looked like she meant it. 'Thanks.'

'See ya!' she said, streaking ahead when the light changed.

That was a mood-lifter. It must have sharpened his cognitive abilities, too, because he thought: Who else has looked at this car and noticed it? Anyone in the Adelaide Hills, for example?

He headed for a side street and googled motorbike rentals.

The nearest place—called, in some kind of anti-marketing flex, Mid-Life Crisis—was in the next suburb. Renting a Kawasaki took a while, and when he reached the parcel joint, he was ready to thump someone. But his envelope was ready and he rode to a quiet park to open it. There was no sign that it had been opened or tampered with. He took out the ammunition clip. It slid into the butt of the Glock with a click that spoke of expensive, finely calibrated engineering and death.

He checked his watch: 1.30 already. Time to get in a few practice shots.

Google Maps took him to the Scott Creek conservation park, not all that far from where he needed to go in the Adelaide Hills. There were no parked vehicles when he arrived, and no rangers around when he set out to walk the Almanda Mine Loop. He passed the Engine House and an old stone chimney, but instead of turning left at Bagot's Shaft he turned right, climbing into an isolated clearing surrounded by gum trees, dense shrubbery and a low, rocky cliff face. Useful sound absorption. With last night's orange juice bottle propped on a mossy log as a target, he fired ten shots—three hits and seven near-misses. That would do: he was familiar enough with the weight and balance of the pistol now, and he'd be shooting point-blank anyway.

He walked back to the Kawasaki, alert for random day-trippers and rangers. With any luck the shots would be put down to feral animal control. According to the website, the Wildlife Service carried out these purges once or twice a year.

He checked his shoes. Damn, dust on the toecaps. Grass seeds in his socks. He took a few minutes to sort himself out.

It was almost 4 p.m. by the time he arrived in Battendorf. He cruised the motor repair joint first. No white Forester, which he'd pretty much expected, so he headed up to the main street and made a slow pass of Mandel's Collectibles. There was a *Back Soon* note on the door. He rode to the end of the block and turned left, then paused at the entrance to the one-way alley behind Karen's shop and spotted the Subaru.

So: they were around somewhere. He wheeled the bike into a narrow gap between dumpbins and walked through to the main street. He was hungry. He needed sugar and carbs. No: he *didn't* need sugar and carbs, he needed protein. He needed to feel good inside and out. He needed something to cure his unease, his disquiet. Fruit. A mixed salad. A Hendro's Header.

But fucked if he could find a decent place on that miserable excuse for a main street. He stood indecisively at the window of a coffee shop. Buns, scrolls, Danishes. Would it kill him? He could easily make up for it. Do a few weights.

Be strong, he told himself. If in doubt, channel Seb Verco.

Five o'clock. Five-thirty, six, six-thirty. He walked from one end of the street to the other, then made a broad circuit, taking in various side streets, and, as evening darkness folded around the town, it occurred to him that he might be pulling an all-nighter.

Hungry again, he checked that Karen's Subaru was still parked behind the shop, then walked to the nearest pub. It was buzzing mildly. No one seemed interested in him, so he ate a parma in the dining room, and, holding a regretful hand over his poor stomach, returned to the alley. The place spooked him: dark clouds scudding across a rising moon, and a chill in the air. But the Subaru was still there.

Then: headlights. Tyres rumbling along the cobbles. He hurdled over the museum's scrappy hedge, crouched and peeked: a cop car.

41

IN AN UNCONSCIOUS synchronisation of their movements that afternoon, Grace and Erin finished unpacking almost simultaneously and found themselves facing each other on the single beds.

'Right,' Erin said, staring down at the stretch of worn carpet and gently thumping her thin upper thighs with her bony fists: steeling herself.

Grace smiled and nodded. 'Right.'

Erin looked up. 'My real name's Karen Michael.'

From Karen Michael to Erin Mandel: not far enough,

thought Grace. Her old name, Anita, had been suffused with fear and baseness and shame, and she'd had to grow into a name quite unlike it. A braver, better name.

'Okay.'

'I'm from Brisbane. I did fine arts at uni and got a job with a company that specialises in buying and selling art and antiques. I did research for them. Provenance checks. Catalogue entries. That kind of thing.'

'Okay,' said Grace again.

She was listening to Erin, but also to the creaky old house. The voices of six other women and their children; footsteps on the protesting stairs; the squeaking of other door hinges. She was mapping everything: the rooms and corridors, the residents, not knowing what might help or hinder her later. Could she escape via the backyard? When were the children allowed to play there, and how closely were they watched? Could she simply say, at some quiet point in the remains of the day, that she was going out for a stroll around the garden? To do a spot of helpful weeding?

'I met Brodie when he came to examine an old revolver we were auctioning. We got talking and one thing led to another and we ended up getting married.'

He's interested in handguns, noted Grace. She gave Erin another encouraging nod. 'Okay.'

'He was no pin-up, but then again, nor am I.'

Grace looked at Erin as if for the first time, and decided: a woman who is not plain but thinks of herself as plain.

Meanwhile Erin had switched from bothering her

knees to pinching at the seams of her jeans. Then, catching Grace's scrutiny, she stilled her hands. 'That video clip of him outside the shop: he looks different now—kind of better toned and more dress-conscious—but it's definitely him.'

'What did he used to look like?'

'A bit fat, a bit sloppy, always in old jeans and T-shirts and cheap runners. Long hair that he didn't wash often enough. Didn't shave every day.'

Grace didn't know where this was going. 'Do you think he's trying to win you back with his new look?'

Erin shook her head violently. 'God, I hope not. Actually, he started working on his image towards the end of our time together. He joined the gym, changed his diet, that kind of thing. But until then he was just a bit of a slob and always a bit flat and demoralised; needing reassurance. He seemed to think there was no point making an effort because women didn't find him attractive. When *I* hooked up with him, it was like there must be something wrong with me. Crazy.'

'Sounds insecure,' Grace said.

She cocked her head: voices in the backyard. The shrill delight of small children and the low patience of a woman. She longed to know what they were doing, but remained seated, fixed on Erin.

'He *was* insecure,' Erin said. 'Especially about women. He'd say they didn't find him attractive because he'd lost out in the genetic lottery stakes—I mean, hello, I married him, didn't I?—then turn around and say they were all shallow, manipulative bitches. Or slags. We'd be in the car and he'd see a woman and her kids on the footpath and go, "Welfare slut." Or he'd see a teenager and say, "I'd do her." Or an older woman and it'd be, "Not her, she's probably had too much dick." As if I wasn't right there in the car with him.'

Here Erin paused. The silence was awkward, as if she thought she'd said too much.

Grace cleared her throat. 'You said earlier he's a tech nerd…'

Erin seized the conversational lifeline. 'Anything involving computers and IT. Probably a bit of hacking now and then, and he was always buying and selling stuff. He'd be on his computers—he had more than one—day and night. It brought in a bit of money.' She rolled her shoulders, embarrassed. 'But mostly he used my money.'

'I had that happen to me,' Grace said, thinking of Galt.

'Anyway, I had some shares my dad bought me when I first left home. Some little corner of me somehow knew not to tell Brodie about them, and they brought in just enough to get me started here. When I left for the last time, I also cleared out one of the accounts—not that there was much in it.'

Grace had done that, too. 'Did he usually work from home?'

'He had three or four proper jobs early on, but he

always quit—probably before he was sacked. Never his fault, of course—always some dickhead boss.'

'The things he bought and sold…Just old guns?'

Erin shook her head. 'Swords, bayonets, uniforms—military memorabilia in general. That was one thing we connected on, after he'd had his fingers burnt with a couple of fakes. Brodie getting his fingers burnt, not a good scene. I showed him how to spot fakes and do valuations and provenance research.' She paused. 'One time he exchanged some rare Japanese memorabilia, belonged to a general or an admiral, someone high up, for a few netsukes. They're worth a lot of money.'

Grace went still: she knew about netsukes. 'I'm guessing you didn't benefit.'

'Kmart, Target and lukewarm tea,' agreed Erin. 'He let me have an allowance, but it was never enough.'

Grace thought of Galt again, as Erin went on: 'He'd check the shopping when I got home. Why didn't I buy home-brand cheese, kind of thing; why buy normal toilet paper instead of the double-length ones. Wore me out. I was actually in a shop once, buying a bra, and he must have been monitoring the credit card at that very moment, because he called and abused me for not going to Kmart.'

'Was there anyone you could talk to?'

Erin shook her head and blinked at Grace, her tears an almost metallic gleam. 'We were both kind of cut off from our families. At the start, that was another thing we shared.' She shrugged. 'My dad's in Mount Isa, he's a Subaru dealer, and my stepmother doesn't want me around—not that I could tell either of them what was happening, anyway. And Brodie—classic abandonment issues. His mother left when he was six and his father just got depressed. He was barely there for him.'

Grace knew the control game plan: Brodie Hendren shutting Erin off from friends and family, dictating who she could spend time with, demanding to know where she was. 'I suppose you couldn't see a shrink; he'd have known.'

'He knew everything,' Erin said. She gazed calmly at Grace and said, 'I've never told anyone any of this before, not really. There was never anyone I could trust, let alone try to contact.'

Grace flinched. Erin, you can't trust me, either, she thought. Not long term. Right now, yes. I'll listen. A shoulder to cry on. But later tonight, I'm running.

'I'm so sorry,' she said.

Erin shrugged. 'What can you do? Things got gradually worse, and then one day the police came around and charged him with selling stolen goods.'

'What happened?'

'Charges dropped,' Erin said, in disgust. 'Worse luck for me. He got more paranoid after that, calling and texting a hundred times a day. Where was I? What was I doing there? Who was I with? Who was I fucking?'

Bafflement replaced the searing emotion. 'One day this parcel came for him. It was an infidelity test kit. He started testing my underwear for semen.'

'God,' Grace said, thinking of Galt. He hadn't trusted either, but he'd used his fists to get at the truth.

'It was all tied up with what I could or couldn't wear,' continued Erin. 'My T-shirts were too tight, my bathers too small, my blouse too sheer. As though I was constantly trying to make myself attractive to other men, when that was the *last* thing on my mind. I didn't want *anyone* to look at or touch me. And he wanted sex all the time. He got so angry if I wasn't enthusiastic enough.' It was all pouring out of her now. 'If I stacked the dishwasher the wrong way, or let the peas touch the gravy, there was hell to pay. He woke me once to say I was sleeping too loudly. Another time, when I was asleep—probably being too loud—he used my finger to unlock my phone so he could see who I was texting or calling.' Erin gave Grace another of her direct looks. 'The constant belittling. It turned me so full of self-doubt about everything—how I looked, my cooking, even just relating to people—that I got sacked for taking too many sick days.' She gestured at her torso. 'Look at me, still skin and bones.'

There was a scream from the backyard. Both women crossed to the window and watched a young woman wearing shorts and a hoodie bending to lift a small boy who'd fallen. Another child looked on, fear and guilt on her face. Grace took note of the yard's layout and dimensions. No street access. No back gate in the high enclosing wall.

They returned to their seats on the edges of the beds,

Erin smoothing the doona unconsciously before settling. 'Thank God I never had children, eh?'

But the tone was wistful.

She went on: 'An old story—I'm such a cliché. He apologised, blah, blah, blah, I gave it another go, got another job, but it soon started up again.'

A knock on the door. Erin tilted her face. 'Come in!'

Tracey Dinakis poked her head in, wincing at the squeak of hinges. 'Sorry to interrupt. Would you like tea and muffins downstairs?'

'That would be lovely,' Erin said, looking relieved.

And Grace was relieved. Holding back a little, and waiting until the others were near the bottom of the stairs, she said, 'Start without me, I need a tissue,' and hurried back to the bedroom. Found a deodorant in Erin's kit and crossed to the door, listening. When she heard the others reach the bottom she sprayed the deodorant on the hinges of the door, then swung it experimentally to and fro.

Hardly any squeaking.

She clattered down the stairs and into the sitting room, where everyone was gathered around the coffee table. She sat, making barely a ripple in the room, thinking of the ripples she'd make later, when they discovered that she must have slipped away in the dark hours of the night. Thinking of the ripples if Hendren was soon arrested and she was still here: she'd have to give further statements to police, maybe even appear as a prosecution witness—exposure she really did not need.

42

HENDREN WAS PRETTY sure the cop car wasn't there for him. Maybe there'd been a spate of break-ins. He watched it spotlight everything as it passed down the alley. The effect was hallucinatory, a cone of misshapen brightness swooping, never settling, casting unnatural shadows, and so he kept low instinctively, even after the car reached the give-way sign at the end and disappeared.

He gave it a couple of minutes before he stepped out of his hiding place and crossed to the back door of Karen's shop. He was hoping for a quick in and out, maybe get lucky and find her home address on a scrap of paper, but the lock was serious-looking, and he didn't want to be exposed if the cop car came back. He had no choice but to wait for someone to return to the shop or the Subaru.

He walked back to the museum, this time checking its doors and windows. Spotting no alarms or security—probably the place was full of old teapots and sepia photographs—he forced the back door. A narrow hallway, with a bathroom on the right and an office on the left, led to a large display room. Sure enough, old crap in dusty display cabinets.

He returned to the tiny hallway office. Rummaged in the drawers and found a roll of red insulating tape. Excellent. Things were going his way.

Five minutes later, having placed a strip of tape over the Subaru's left rear brake light, he was back in the museum, seated in darkness at the front window, which gave him a clear view down to the Subaru. Appropriately, his chair was the kind you see in old photographs, the head of the household seated, the little woman behind him, her hand on his shoulder.

Except that he was alone, the time was dragging and he was uncomfortable in his own thoughts. Usually, his devices were there to comfort him. Checking his listings, posting a new item for sale. Watching Brie Haven. Creating a fake medical report, setting up a new crowdfunding scam. He needed to stay alert, he needed to watch the street, but he itched to swipe at his phone.

He hummed, his torso rocked, one foot tapped the floor: *If I'm not tough on myself, no one else will be. I don't invite or accept losers in my life. A loserish mentality makes for a loser. Grow as a man and be tough.*

'To be competitive,' Seb Verco had once said, 'live with your competitive equals.' Brodie Hendren stopped tapping his foot. He lived alone. He didn't know who his equals were. Seb Verco lived in a big house with guys who looked equally gym-fit and stacked, half-naked chicks lounging around the place; couple of Lamborghinis parked out the front.

Yeah, how likely was that? It hadn't been easy after Karen—the Tinder years. Women went for winners like Seb Verco. One chick—no model herself, actually; verging on chubby—thought she was being super tactful, the way she'd turned down a second date. Telling him all he had to do was be nice, be himself, and he'd find someone one day. She thought she had *standards*? Looking the way she did? He hadn't met her *standards*? Jesus.

And the whole thing with Brie Haven last May. He'd been working out regularly, feeling nicely toned, and one night as they were fucking he stopped and said, 'Who do you belong to?'

She'd just laughed and told him to get off her—like nothing meant anything. Like *he* didn't mean anything. He swiped her spare key as he left; returned the next day and bugged her flat when she was at work. But how was that a win if she didn't even know about the cameras in the first place? He yawned, stretched his shoulders—and froze. Dropped into a panicky squat beneath the windowsill.

Karen's shop assistant was out there.

He risked another look—and jerked back: she was now *inside the yard*. He waited, but curiosity got the better of him and he popped his head up again. The cop car was coming through, flashing its spot around, and she was using the hedge as cover, just as he'd done earlier. As soon as it was gone, she slipped back into the alley and raced down to the shop and in through the back door.

Yeah, that didn't look suspicious.

43

HOURS HAD PASSED BEFORE Grace was able to slip away from the refuge. Dinner, evening TV, lights out, teeth and bed—Grace in a single closest to the wall, Erin in the double on the other side of the room. In the semi-darkness—the backyard security lights through the curtains and a strip of corridor light beneath the door—she'd struggled to stay awake. Tiredness, a comfortable bed and the soft murmur of Erin's voice, still going.

'You must be bored, hearing all this.'

'Of course not.'

Not bored: tired. Although Erin did tend to go back over the same ground.

'It helps to talk about it. I feel looser somehow.'

'I'm glad.'

Grace shifted under the covers, everything freshly laundered, gently perfumed...Then, realising that her eyes were drooping, attention wandering, she propped herself on one elbow and gazed across at the window for a while. At one point, the backyard lights seemed to get brighter: the laundry woman, she thought, setting off a motion-detector light as she pegged out her washing.

Sometimes Erin did seem to drift closer to sleep. Longer pauses, drowsier voice. But then she'd rally, her tone often edged in dread as she relived her life with a violent, inept man.

'The first time I left, he found where I was living pretty quickly. I came home from work one day and there was a note at the bottom of my shopping list: "Take it up the arse, bitch." Another time he left his Brisbane Lions scarf on the table. The police couldn't work out how he'd found me, but it turned out he'd sent me a message I thought was from the tax office, and when I clicked the link it installed spyware on my phone. I got a new one after that.'

'Was he charged?'

'Restraining order. He wasn't allowed within a hundred metres, so he'd park a hundred and five metres away. He was basically living in his car, I think. But he could still get at me. He started transferring, like, a dollar into my bank account just so he could abuse me in that box where you can leave a message.'

Grace cast her mind back and realised that she'd rarely seen Erin use her mobile phone. And she'd seen her flinch when it pinged for a text from a parcel company.

Now Erin said, 'I suppose you want to know why I went back to him?'

'Erin, no one's blaming you.'

But the explanations were compulsive. 'He turned up one day and I could see he'd been trying, he'd lost weight and was dressing better, but he was in a state. Kept apologising, saying he hadn't been his real self because he was on painkillers after falling off his motorbike and blah blah, so *again* I gave him another chance. The things you tell yourself. At the bottom of it, I kind of thought, at least I'll know where I stand…'

Her voice faded, as though she had come to the end of a chapter. Grace heard footsteps on the stairs, a door open and close. A TV blared briefly, then was silenced. In the backyard, the sensor lights flared again.

Erin's voice came back, almost too low to pick individual words. 'It lasted about three months, then one day I caught him tapping his face with a little hammer. I wasn't meant to see that, and he hated it. He started rocking, which was one of the warning signs, and I tried to get out but…well. I wasn't quick enough.'

Until now, Erin's story hadn't surprised Grace. 'A *hammer*?'

'It's a thing: change how you look. Anyway, more to the point, you should've seen *my* face. I went to the police and the man behind the counter said, "Oh, this isn't your usual look?" I know that sounds terrible but he was actually quite kind and I think he was a bit shocked.'

Well, if that's how she wanted to read it…

But Grace knew there *were* cops who were capable of kindness. The night she was arrested, seventeen years old, the custody sergeant had waited for Galt to swagger off to the station tearoom before murmuring, 'Be careful there.' Concern in his eyes.

It didn't help, of course.

A sigh, a rustling of bedclothes as Erin turned over. A further ebb to her voice: 'Now you know why I'm a recluse…Jesus, how did he find me? Even if they get him, I bet he just gets a rap over the knuckles and I'll have to start all over again and…'

Grace waited for another thirty minutes, allowing time for Erin's breathing to stretch and slow and deepen. It was an unsettling half hour. She felt fearful and infected with Erin's ex festering away in her mind. Not to mention her own ex. She wanted to regain her old, sharp-edged self—and movement could help achieve that. But not until the time was right. Patience now. Stealth and luck in the dead of night.

At 11 p.m. she slipped out of the bed and into jeans, a T-shirt, a dark hoodie and trainers. Her keys. Her wallet.

Her phone. The pannier from her bike. All she owned in the world at that moment.

The door retained its blessed oily silence as she left the room and made for the top of the stairs. Keeping to the wall edge of each step, to reduce creaking, she came to a turning that gave her a view of the ground-floor hallway. It was empty. She completed her descent. Light showed under only one room down there, the office at the end.

She turned right, passing the darkened kitchen, and took several steps into the laundry. A washing machine on the spin cycle, a hamper of dirty clothes, another of damp clothes ready for the line, and a sheet trailing from the metal sink to the floor, one corner resting in pinkish water. Droplets everywhere, and a scent in the air that Grace associated with the bedclothes she'd just been wrapped in.

No sign of the nervy laundry woman. She peered through the window. Out there, queerly lit by a spill of security lights, was a clothesline, a heaped laundry basket, and the arched spine of a woman reaching up a sock in one hand, a peg in the other.

Grace welcomed those lights. They'd set up shapes and shadows that tricked the eye. Leaving the laundry, she crept to the back door and let herself out, down a set of steps to the lawn. Edging along the back wall, she soon became a tricky shadow herself, among the trees and a wheelbarrow and a neglected yellow bucket. She crouched for a while in the shelter of the side fence, watching the woman peg socks, knickers, a child's singlet. One last T-shirt and then she was lifting the empty basket and heading back indoors.

Grace ran to the wheelbarrow and bumped it along the ground to the darkest corner. Upended it. Stood on it and made a couple of failed leaps before managing to hook her fingers over the top of the fence. It was treated pine, and her knees and shoe caps boomed against it as she began her scramble up and over, into the lane behind the house.

She ran, dragging her shadow with her, wrapped in the scents of a dark night: soil, cooling air and springtime flowers in the neighbouring gardens. She ran for five minutes and then was on the forecourt of a Mobil station, tapping the Uber app on her phone. Of course, the police would track that part of her escape easily enough, but not until long after she was gone.

She was dropped off at the pub, which still showed lights; the rest of Battendorf had pretty much shut down until morning. Even so, Grace's sense of being observed was powerful as she crept down the alleyway behind Erin's shop. She checked over her shoulder, chanced a quick glance up and down the street, but saw nothing.

And then lights turning in. She darted into the front yard of the museum and crouched behind the hedge, her heart hammering as a police car prowled by. Parting foliage, she watched the car loop a spotlight at every back door and window, probing every shadow. Then it stopped, brake lights flaring, and an officer got out, removing her cap for a good scalp scratch as she crossed the road, flashed her torch into the Subaru, rattled Erin's back door.

From the local station, Grace thought. Briefed by Sergeant Swanwick to make regular passes throughout the night.

When the car rolled on again and turned left onto the main road, Grace slipped across to the shop. Using the glow of her phone's home screen—the torch was too bright—she let herself in and found her way through to the main room. Here there was sufficient ambient light for her to edge around the furniture to the old cabinet in the corner. She knelt, removed the bottom drawer, emptied it, prised up the false base.

Empty.

44

GRACE WASN'T EASILY thrown. She adapted swiftly to threatening situations and altered circumstances. But she was thrown now. She rocked back on her heels and stared into the empty gap. Stuck her hand in and brushed it around pointlessly. Adam? She looked back over her shoulder: if Adam had found her, he wouldn't simply pinch her stuff and disappear.

Erin's husband. Grace looked over her shoulder again, then climbed to her feet. She reached for a cricket bat (said to have been used by Bradman) and moved from shadow to shadow in the main room; in and out of the back rooms.

She was alone. Returning to the cabinet, she replaced the drawer, brushed off her knees and checked the till. The morning's seed money—$300—was still there. She folded the notes into her back pocket. Then she ran her gaze over everything on the floor and in the display cabinets: all of Erin's trash, all of her treasures, dimly lit by the streetlights outside the main window. She could hardly lug a dressing table around with her, even if it was worth five grand. The Meissen vase would get broken. The $3,500 Atkins Brothers sterling silver teapot would bulk up the pannier too much. In the end, Grace pocketed a matching pair of George V preserve spoons, $2,500.

But the cash, the spoons, didn't make up for what she'd lost. She couldn't hang around waiting for the bank to open: she'd simply have to wave goodbye to her Barossa haul. That left the stuff in the granny flat.

Unless Erin's ex had found that, too.

She didn't like this. She felt exposed, ready to run as she slipped through to the back and opened the door a crack. The air was mild and still; oddly, unpleasantly scented: no springtime perfume, just old-food smells from the noodle shop four doors down. The town was asleep.

She crossed to the Subaru and circled it once, flashing her phone torch into the footwells, front and rear, and the cargo compartment.

Someone had stuck insulating tape over the rear passenger-side brake light.

Her mind raced. If Erin's ex-husband had been monitoring both tracking devices, he'd know they'd been compromised. Now he was relying on a visual tag?

She crouched and ripped off the tape. Flicked it from her fingers and hurried around to the driver's door—and a man was streaking at her from out of the shadows.

He rammed a pistol into her belly before she could save herself. 'Where's Karen? Where is she, bitch?'

His breath was rancid, gusting in her face. Something he'd eaten was rotting inside him. 'What?'

Another foetid wave, a snarl: '*Where's Karen*?'

'Who, what? Don't know what you mean.'

Another jab with the pistol, doubling her over. 'Your muff-diving buddy. Where is she?'

Grace gasped in pain. 'You've got the wrong person.'

He seemed to give himself a shake, as if he couldn't believe where this confrontation was heading. In the darkness, in the alleyway's soup of sweet and foetid odours, he screamed, 'I have not got the wrong person. You work here, and I want to know where your boss is.'

'My boss?'

This time he took her right hand and pressed the tip of the pistol barrel against the pouchy flesh between the base of her thumb and forefinger. 'Where is she?'

'She's away. Buying trip.'

He pulled the trigger, and she said: '*Oh*.'

They both stared down at the bloody mess, before she thought to snatch her hand away.

And she was half deaf; it was a shock how loud a pistol could be. She was muddled suddenly: the new life she'd almost been living seemed like a far-fetched story. She was someone who stole and ran, stole and ran, that's all. It was miserably all for nothing, and now she was going to die.

She stood there numbly, and then the pain kicked in, and Erin's ex-husband was grinding the end of the barrel against the bone between her eyes, so that she could smell the gun smoke. The acrid stink woke her up.

Hunching away from him, playing a bewildered victim, she gasped, 'Why did you do that?'

'To remind you what I'm capable of.'

A part of her thinking, *You rehearsed that*, she smacked the barrel away with her good hand and punched him in the throat with the other.

Agony pulsed through her from hand to brain, a jolt of electricity punching her into full alertness. He reeled back, clutching at his throat but swinging the pistol towards her again, and she came at him, knees, feet, forearms and fists. Slammed her forehead into his nose and then, as he toppled, she found herself entangled with him, following him to the ground, and the pistol was trapped between them when it fired again.

Grace was dazed. And curious—strange how much quieter that next shot had been, muffled by their bodies. She wondered when the new pain would start to burn? Then she snapped out of it as Brodie Hendren jackknifed against her. He arched, headbutting her unwittingly, his terrible sculpted hair scraping against her nose and she pushed him away, and God that hurt. Down onto her knees as if in prayer. Her good hand probing frantically at her sodden stomach…

No. His blood, not hers.

There would be people and lights soon. She had to play it through. She couldn't just take his pistol and run: she was too sore, too tired, too focused on the future about to be snatched from her.

As Erin's ex flexed and groaned and his breath gusted, Grace searched his pockets. Took his keys and wallet.

But what if she was searched? Here in the alleyway or at the hospital? She was back inside the shop and out again before the first police car arrived. Whoever had found her hollow drawer was unlikely to search it again.

45

A BLUR. PARAMEDICS cleaned and sterilised her hand at the scene, a doctor stitched up the entry and exit points in the emergency department of Stirling hospital, and a nurse offered a sedative. Still dazed, Grace swallowed it. The next thing she knew, it was Wednesday morning.

The on-duty doctor came and went, and soon after that, Sergeant Swanwick and another detective were seated beside her bed, watching a nurse apply a new dressing, layers of gauze and flesh-coloured tape that made her thumb stick out.

'Useful for hitchhiking,' she quipped.

Humour, because she didn't know if she was about to be arrested. Swanwick responded with a wintry smile. 'Bone damage?'

Grace scanned the narrow, curtained space surreptitiously. Where were her clothes? 'No.'

'Nerve damage?'

'Some,' admitted Grace, thinking that a bung hand was going to be a problem if she was going back to her old profession, which had depended on some degree of sensitivity. She might have to go straight—and, in her nervous state, almost offered Swanwick this wisecrack, too. It's the painkillers, she thought. Said out loud: 'The doctor said it could take a while for the nerves to repair.'

Swanwick ran a scowl over Grace's face and arms, the bruises there. 'Well, it could have been a lot worse. They're letting you out this morning?'

Grace nodded. 'That's what the doctor said earlier.' She shifted; her butt was sore from rolling around on the cobblestones in the alley. 'Is Erin okay?'

'She's fine. At home, waiting for the hospital to call. She'll come in and collect you.'

Grace had a dim memory of Erin last night—how had she got to the alley?—holding her good hand in the police car that had taken her to hospital. Not an ambulance: only one was available, and it had taken Hendren down to the city. She also had a dim memory of a constable sitting in a chair outside the ward all night. Whether or not he was still there, she didn't know: Swanwick had drawn the curtain around the bed.

She glanced at the other detective, a kid in an ill-fitting suit. He was on the other side of the bed, a notebook in his lap. She glanced at Swanwick again. Waited. Then asked what someone in her position was bound to ask: 'I didn't get a good look. Was it Erin's ex who shot me?'

'Yes.'

Grace asked another innocent question, even though she knew the answer. 'Is he going to come after me again?'

A complicated look from Swanwick. 'No.' She sighed and added, 'The bullet went through his stomach and nicked his spine. He might not walk again. And he's facing a number of serious charges: assault, stalking, reckless injury, discharging a firearm…'

Grace leaned back on heaped pillows. 'Sooner him than me.'

'Yes. Look, I need a statement,' Swanwick said, with a glance at her colleague. He placed a digital recorder on the bed beside Grace's hip, then blushed and moved it to the bedside cabinet. 'We'll get it typed up and, when you're feeling better, you can come in and sign it. If you start to feel tired, we can finish it another time.'

'Sure,' Grace said, steeling herself.

'First of all, why did you leave the refuge? You must have known what might happen.'

Grace glanced at the curtain; she felt imprisoned. The sounds of the hospital were constant: voices, a crackling

PA call, the squeak of rubber soles. The smell: disinfectant, laundered bedding, pharmaceuticals. Even a faint whiff of Sergeant Swanwick's shampoo and the junior detective's aftershave.

She was relieved to hear a voice outside the curtain: 'Breakfast dishes?'

But Swanwick, tilting her chin up, directed her voice over the curtain rail: 'Come back in half an hour, please.'

'Right you are,' and squeaky footsteps, a wobbly wheel, as Grace told herself: Half an hour of questions? Better keep the answers brief.

She answered Swanwick. 'I was scared.'

'Of Ms Mandel's husband?'

'Not specifically him,' Grace said. She summoned memories and images of Galt and found herself no longer acting but sinking into the bed as if to hide. 'I've had DV troubles of my own. It all got to me.'

'What kind of DV troubles? Are you in danger?'

Grace tweaked the backstory she'd given Erin. 'I grew up in New Zealand. My parents were in the antiques business. I got married too young. Usual story, he turned out to have a temper, and when my parents died, he sort of ran their business into the ground and blamed everything on me. I just walked out one day.'

'Is he looking for you?'

'I don't think so. For him it would be too much effort. But Erin told me everything her ex did to her last night, and…I don't know, I thought if I could just drive somewhere far away…'

'In Ms Mandel's car?'

Grace shifted in embarrassment. 'Yes.'

'What happened?'

Grace shrugged. 'I was attacked before I could even unlock it.' She cocked her head a little. 'I guess he was watching?'

She could see that Swanwick knew what she was doing: angling for information. Swanwick's smile was still thin but less wintry as she said, 'I'd asked for a regular patrol. When they spotted a motorbike that hadn't been there earlier, they called it in. I checked, and it had been rented with stolen ID.'

She stopped as if she'd said too much.

Grace filled the silence. 'That explains why everyone got there so quickly.'

A level gaze from Swanwick. Grace could barely read it.

Time passed before the sergeant said, 'Indeed. Now, tell me about the attack.'

Grace told her. When she finished, Swanwick said, 'You got tangled up together and you both fell to the ground and the gun just went off.'

'Yes.'

'You weren't holding it?'

'No.'

'It wasn't your gun?'

Grace shuddered. 'I don't know anything about guns.'

Swanwick nodded slowly, her gaze flat.

Grace said, 'I should've stayed with Erin, I'm really sorry. I've caused a real mess,' she added, waving her bulky hand around as if it symbolised all that had happened.

'Yes, well, it is what it is,' Swanwick said curtly, sounding unsatisfied. Whether that was to do with her, or life in general, Grace couldn't say.

A nurse opened the curtain after Swanwick and her detective left the ward, and Grace felt lain bare to the world. The staff, the other patients, fixed on her with a hard curiosity. Was it true that she'd been shot? Was it true that she was a person of interest in something?

A waiting game, until Erin arrived at 9 a.m. bringing a change of clothes and an orderly with a wheelchair. Out to the Subaru, parked in the turning circle near the main entry, where Grace tilted her face to the sun. 'Good to be alive,' she said, and felt it powerfully, as if for the first time.

Erin laughed. 'Sure is.'

She seemed vibrant, her eyes bright and her thin frame almost enlarged by life and its possibilities. 'Buckle up, let's get you home.'

Home, thought Grace as her boss and landlady flicked the wheel and zipped through the carpark. Thoughts of home took Grace to the stash behind her bathtub surround. 'Have the police finished searching for bugs?'

Erin slowed for the exit; her eyes raked the main road

in both directions as if to scorch it. 'All good. Nothing found.'

In which case, would they have bothered to dust for prints? If they did run her prints, they'd know who she was. Anita—all grown up after her juvenile arrest in Sydney. Was Swanwick playing a waiting game?

They rode in silence through the hills, Erin still seeming to vibrate at the wheel. Eventually she said, 'Sorry about your hand.'

'Could've been worse.'

'Grace, it wasn't smart, what you did.'

A reversal in our roles, Grace thought. She usually looks to *me* for the smart thing to do. 'I know. I'm really sorry.'

'I told you how foul he could be.'

'Yes.'

Erin seemed to need more, so Grace added: 'I should've listened.'

'Yes.'

More silent riding, the morning sun slanting in against Grace's window, so that all she wanted to do was sleep.

'Have a nap if you like.'

It unnerved Grace that Erin should be watching her. She checked: Erin's eyes were still on the road. Some sixth sense? Maybe she glanced at me and I missed it…fuck, I'm losing my touch, she thought. My defences are down. She placed her head against the glass and sleep was upon her.

—

Then she was being steered through her front door and down the little hallway to her bedroom. She tried to look for any sign that the police had dusted for prints, and badly wanted to check behind her bathtub panel, but Erin, no-nonsense, propelled her into bed.

She slept through lunch and woke feeling groggy at 3.30. Erin was there, reading, in a kitchen chair that she'd dragged into the bedroom.

'You must've really needed that sleep.'

'Feel like I was hit by a bus,' Grace said.

All she wanted was to be alone, but Erin said, 'Tea? Coffee?'

'Tea,' Grace said.

She waited until she heard the tap in the kitchen before swinging her legs onto the floor. The world tilted; she waited for it to settle. Plodded to her bathroom, perched on the loo, finished that and grabbed the nailfile from the medicine cabinet. Then, crouching beside the bathtub, all of her limbs protesting, she undid the screws fumblingly with her left hand.

Nothing. The gold bar, cash, ID and Klee oil painting were gone.

Wondering if the world had shifted in the past twenty-four hours, she returned to her bedroom and was slipping under the covers when Erin returned with a mug of tea in each hand.

'Here you go.'

‘Thanks,’ Grace said, sounding hollow, even to her own ears.

Erin, settling onto the chair beside the bed again, kicked off her shoes and slurped at her tea. ‘It’s all safe,’ she said.

‘Sorry?’

‘All your stuff, both stashes. It’s all safe.’

46

GRACE SWUNG OUT of bed again, her mind racing.

'Relax,' Erin said. 'No one knows.'

Grace eased onto the edge of her bed, bare feet on the room's threadbare carpet. She wriggled her toes in agitation: she couldn't run far without shoes. And one ankle was swollen and bruised. Funny she hadn't noticed that until now. Maybe Hendren had stamped on it.

'When…?'

'I've known since soon after you came to live here,' Erin said. Her gaze was as flat and searching as Sergeant

Swanwick's—or any cop Grace had ever encountered. A newer, more self-reliant Erin, expecting the truth.

'That was ages ago.'

'Well, look at it from my point of view. You suddenly turn up at the shop, asking for a job. You didn't offer any references—I didn't ask, of course, I liked you straight away and you were quite knowledgeable. But I didn't know who you were or if you could be trusted.'

Grace nodded.

Erin leaned back in the chair, extended her legs and folded one pale foot over the other. Small, slender feet full of bones close to the surface. Grace concentrated on them, feeling a kind of feverish intensity as she waited for the story to finish.

'For all I knew, Brodie could've sent you. That's how I used to think—if anything out of the ordinary happened, it wasn't to be trusted.'

'I get that,' Grace said, pulling her gaze away, trying to look into Erin's mind this time.

'That first time I left him? Brodie bugged my new place. Cameras, microphones. So when you were settled, I did a search. The flat when you were at work, and the shop the day you went to Woodside Auctions.'

'Okay.'

Erin cocked her head. 'Interesting escape packages—if that's what they are.'

Grace said nothing.

Erin shrugged. 'When I finally left Brodie, I just

grabbed my phone and wallet and a couple of changes of clothes, and ran. If I'd been better prepared, like you must've been, I might have spent time putting aside more cash and other things worth money. I owned a nice Thea Proctor, for example. But clearly *you* knew what you were doing. I mean, how did you get those sets of ID?'

Lying was habitual for Grace. Practicable and easy. She would lie now—or offer a half-truth to facilitate this conversation, assuage Erin's doubts and save herself. And maybe even secure a future here. 'I used to know people who could supply those kinds of things. A long time ago.'

Erin nodded. 'Some dodgy characters in our field.'

'Yes.'

'Wish I'd known how to do that—then maybe Brodie wouldn't have found me.'

A lot I could teach you about that, Grace thought.

Erin sipped her tea. 'Are you cold? Let's sit in the sun.'

The sunlounges again, their mugs of tea on the slatted table between them.

'This might go better with gin and tonic,' Grace said.

Erin toasted her and took a swig of tea. 'No alcohol for you, young lady. You're an invalid.'

'Yeah, yeah.'

This was strange; Grace wished she didn't have to lie to Erin and felt a kind of breathlessness, waiting for a judgment to fall on her head. She drained her tea and closed her eyes under the sun, feeling suffused by light and heat.

The elderly man next door started mowing. Just a whirr, an electric mower, but she opened her eyes and glanced towards the back fence.

Erin had also responded to the sound. Eyeing the lawn, then the unwieldy TradeWorks mower in her lean-to shed, she sighed, 'It's time we mowed.'

There it was again: we.

'Yes,' Grace said.

Erin settled back in her sunlounge, turning her head to Grace. 'Has your ex ever come close to finding you?'

Grace shook her head. This was a part of the lying she wished she could avoid. On the other hand, there *had* been a cruel ex. Galt would abuse and belittle her then crawl for forgiveness, in a confusing dance that kept her defenceless and insecure. 'No. I think he's dead now.'

Something in her eyes made Erin turn away, nodding slowly, tilting her face back to the sun. 'I grabbed your stuff as soon as the police told me about the tracking device yesterday morning. I took an Uber and put everything in a locker at that self-storage place near TradeWorks.'

'Thank you.'

'I thought if Brodie didn't find them, the police might. I'll give you the key later. You might as well use it, I paid for six months in advance.'

Grace had mixed feelings about self-storage yards. They were secure, and accessible at any time, but rarely within reach if you had to run. Banks were generally easier to get to, but only during business hours. Both, it seemed, were more secure than a bathtub or an old cabinet. Come the morning, she'd amalgamate everything and stow it all at the storage yard while she worked out what to do next—worked out how to liquidate it, worked out what to do with her life now, in fact.

She said, hesitantly, 'With your ex incapacitated, you won't have to leave here after all.'

Erin toasted that. 'Fingers crossed. Of course, he might miraculously walk again, or arrange for killers to come after me while he's in jail—but I think I'm safe.'

How do I broach it? thought Grace: *What about me?*

As if to underscore the unvoiced question, Erin said, 'I look forward to growing the business. Getting out and about more—clearing sales, auctions…'

Grace shifted uncomfortably, a sack of bruised and battered bones, the chair's plastic webbing moist and sticky under her. She didn't know how to respond. 'I think I'm due one of the pills they gave me. Every four hours, and I missed at midday.'

Erin checked her watch. 'I can get it.'

'I also need the loo,' Grace said, and something in her tone must have registered, for Erin subsided again.

Tipping the dregs of her tea onto the grass, Grace crossed to the veranda steps and into the flat. Clunked her mug down on the kitchen bench, ran the tap, distractions as she stalked from room to room, thinking. She didn't want to take a pill and muddle her head. She didn't want to leave Battendorf. She didn't know what to do, but it occurred to her that she was in no fit state to make decisions.

She returned to the yard and eased herself painfully onto the sunlounge again. 'Erin—'

'You will stay on, I hope.'

The knot loosened in Grace. 'You mean, the flat and the job?'

'You're good at what you do. You'd be a great help, and we can maybe think about a more permanent arrangement.'

She didn't say 'partner,' but that's what she seemed to mean. 'Thank you.'

'Good.'

'There's a lot you can teach me,' Grace said, warming to the idea. A straight life and security.

'I think,' Erin said, 'it's a case of teaching each other.'

Grace looked down at her bandaged paw, resting in her lap, and lifted it briefly. 'I might not be able to polish any of your sideboards for a while. I probably shouldn't drive, either.'

'Not to worry.' Erin gave her an unfettered smile and cast her arms wide in the sunshine. 'I can do anything now.'

She's putting on a brave front, thought Grace. But it's going to take a while before she feels really safe.

The days passed and Erin changed Grace's dressing every morning and the doctor expressed satisfaction at the end of the week. The women drove to the shop together, worked together, returned to Landau Street together, and Grace's edginess flattened without disappearing. Ready to spike if she came under threat.

As when Sergeant Swanwick called at the shop. 'Just to catch up,' she said. 'Go over a few things.'

She didn't, though. She chatted, bought a beer stein for her husband and seemed unconcerned about Grace and all that had happened. So that Grace was ready when the sergeant switched gears. 'How's the hand?' she asked, her tone almost accusatory.

Grace said pleasantly, 'Not bad. Unless I knock it.'

Swanwick snorted and glanced around at the bulky furniture. 'Life's offered you plenty of things to knock against lately.'

Grace returned the laugh, thinking: Not knocking against a woman like you is all I want from life.

A week and a half later, Grace received a text: the Blamire Young watercolour was ready for collection.

'I'll go,' Erin said. 'Nothing to stop me now.'

Grace felt unsure. She'd been reserved—almost secretive—in her dealings with Gaynor Bernard. What would the conservator think if a different woman turned up to collect the watercolour? Probably nothing: after a few words from Erin, she'd soon understand the relationship. But it might be useful to let Bernard see them together.

'Why don't we both go?'

47

IT WAS TWO weeks into Des Liddington's retirement, and over breakfast one morning, his wife said, 'I have to admit, I'd been dreading it, having you under my feet all day, but you're hardly ever here.'

They were in the sunroom, a screened-off section of their back porch, overlooking roses, a lawn, a clothesline and staked tomatoes. Liddington, his bruises fading, sipped his morning coffee. Tore out a bite of jam toast, chewed and said, 'All in good time. Slippers, a recliner in front of the TV.' He patted his belly. 'A slab of beer, a bowl of peanuts.'

'Yes, well,' Josie said, gesturing at the exercise bike in the far corner.

Lingering over the paper, toast and coffee, the ABC murmuring from the transistor—they were comfortable with each other. Liddington treasured this, after years of early-morning call-outs. He finished the *Advertiser*'s sports section, made a stab at the sudoku and said, 'Gabi called. Forensics told her the tyre tracks at Britton's house could've come from a Triton.'

Josie was reading the letters to the editor. 'Someone in Rostrevor says her rent went up forty per cent in two years. What about DNA?'

Theirs was a free-form conversational dance worked up from a lifetime together—at the table, in bed, in the car. Hints, abbreviations, ellipses, shorthand outlines and imaginative leaps. Josie Liddington knew that her husband would be interested in the rental crisis because their poor son had just moved out into a place of his own. And Des had always told her everything about his police work—hopes, fears, mistakes, little victories, speculations and suspicions. Right now, she knew that he was trying to track down the woman who'd saved his life. In about an hour's time he'd be off in the car again, knocking on doors.

'Nothing,' he said, switching to the cryptic crossword.

A little while later, Josie said, 'What about a bus?'

Liddington went still in his chair, the biro in his hand poised over 4 across as he made Josie's leap. 'Good point.' Had the woman rented the Triton somewhere *outside* the

Barossa? Taken the bus there, taken the bus back again?

'CCTV,' Josie said, turning the page. 'He says his brain fog's got worse.' Their son.

Liddington shrugged sadly. 'It'll take time, I guess.' He bent over the paper again, absently reaching for his toast—but he'd eaten it. 'Bail denied, by the way.'

'Good. Insurance scam?'

'Insurance scam. I mean, Patmore and his boys were pricks to begin with, but the pandemic made it worse. They just got deeper into debt.'

Time passed, then Josie grabbed their cups and plates and said, 'Good luck today.'

Luck, meaning finding the woman. Getting a statement from her. Getting her to stand up in court and describe what she'd seen, who she'd seen, what she'd done. Liddington nodded. 'Gawler could be a good start.'

'There's a bus from Angaston,' Josie said.

'What are you doing later?'

'I can't today,' Josie said. 'Book group tonight and I haven't even started reading it. Tomorrow?'

Liddington looked out at his yard, its neatness and order. Beyond his fence line it was all untidiness and *dis*order. Potholed asphalt and dusty roads sharply winding. A mess of trees and untamed grass. Clouds of all kinds—sometimes all kinds in the sky at once—and buildings all higgledy-piggledy. The disorder that might worsen in his son as he tried it alone in the world. The elusive Triton driver, who was a good person but maybe also not a good person.

Goodness was his wife in the patched-up Saab beside him tomorrow, tapping address details into an app to show him the way.

And so, on a Tuesday in late October, Desmond Liddington—wearing his old uniform but not feeling too much like he was pulling a swiftie—found himself watching CCTV footage in a Gawler car-rental place called Off-Road Paradise while Josie poked around in a nearby dress shop.

'Pause it?' he said.

The clerk complied. Liddington peered at the screen. The woman who'd registered at the Vigneron Motel as Grace Latimer, of Mandel's Collectibles in the Adelaide Hills, had just been handed paperwork and an ignition key.

Des said his thanks and returned to the Saab. Josie was already there.

'Success?'

Des turned the key. 'Success.'

'Dangerous,' Josie said. She was stating the possibility; she'd been stating it for as long as she'd been married to him.

48

ADAM GARRETT HAD reinvented himself once before: he could do it again. Where this time? Victoria? He had good Western Australian ID in his wallet and the chamois pouch strapped to his waist—birth certificate, driver's licence and even a marriage certificate—but did he want to drive all the way to Perth? What he could do was find a place to live in Melbourne, maybe Geelong, and start using the WA documents to build a legitimate Victorian ID. Get a job, pay rent, then, over several months, establish local connections—drinking buddies; movies with a casual girlfriend;

weekend hikes with a bushwalking club—and, bit by bit, apply for a licence, a library card, a replacement Medicare card. *Become* a new person, not just fake it.

But he spent most of the first week laying false trails for the police to follow. Using Melodie's Visa, he bought petrol in Port Augusta, Whyalla, Ceduna and finally Tarcoola—clearly this fugitive was crossing the Nullarbor Plain to Western Australia. At Tarcoola he turned around and came back, this time using cash to keep his car fuelled up. At Broken Hill he swapped his eyesore green Mazda 2 and $875 cash for a Holden ute and headed deep into New South Wales, topping up the fuel whenever he could, dining in the kinds of roadside eateries that had a back-door exit, staying in the kinds of bush motels that didn't ask questions. And always, wherever he stayed, he kept a change of clothes in the ute and the ignition key nearby—under a garden-border stone, a beer crate—in case he was forced to dive out of a window in his jocks.

In Dubbo he bought a new phone and in Bathurst paid a photographer for a range of portraits and full-body shots. 'Kind of a joke,' he said, 'to hang up at my wedding reception.'

Garrett with and without glasses. With and without gel-spiked hair. In shorts, a T-shirt and thongs, in jeans and a hoodie, in a suit and tie. 'So she knows what she's getting,' he joked.

The photographer smiled without interest. 'You don't need wedding photos, by any chance?'

Garrett was regretful. 'Sorry. Wedding's in Perth. My future father-in-law has all that arranged.'

'Too bad. Hope it goes well.'

It was all part of creating a life, and as he drove further east and south, it occurred to him that Anita was probably good at that kind of thing. Slipping in and out of different guises. Creating different stories.

He listened to the news on those long stretches between towns, and if there was wi-fi he checked his phone before he slept at night. Craig Tolhurst featured now and then. The latest story had him standing on the tarmac at Sydney airport, welcoming the return of his son's body.

Bet that cost a bundle, Garrett thought, peering at his phone. He saw Tolhurst shrug off reporters. The guy didn't look like a gunslinger now, just a tired old parent.

He tossed the phone aside, flopped back on his pillow. He felt shitty, frankly. Guilt, pity and a profound hope that Tolhurst would forget him.

Then, shortly after that, Melodie was in the news.

The story broke in stages, over several days. First, a private investigator had been found murdered in her office in the Adelaide suburb of Norwood. Then: she'd been discovered following reports of a suspicious smell in the building. And: the private investigator found murdered in her office had been identified as Melodie Pithouse, 54, originally of Sydney. And: Pithouse had not been licensed to operate in South Australia. Finally: police wished to speak to an associate of Ms Pithouse, Adam Garrett, 29, last seen driving a 2015 lime-green Mazda 2.

Spooked, Garrett pulled over and checked his wallet and document pouch again. He was Louis Denton now. There was nothing to tie him to Adam Garrett.

Still continuing south and east, he stopped for a day in Bega, where he swapped his numberplates for a set bearing a similar combination of letters and numbers. The Victorian border was not so far away, yet he felt a curious hesitation about making the crossing. It seemed to propose permanency of some kind. He might stay there forever. Never see Anita again. Was that what he wanted?

He got back on the road and was 150 kilometres from the border when Gaynor Bernard messaged him on Telegram: *Is it true what the police are saying about you?*

Garrett pulled over again. *I did a bit of surveillance work for her, that's all. She hung out with some very dodgy people.*

No reply. He set out again and crossed the border and the hours passed and night drew in. At 9 p.m., deeply fatigued, he found a room above the bar of a pub that smelt of beer, old nicotine and misery. A warm night, summer would soon be opening, offering hope, but Garrett was simply assailed by loneliness and indecision.

Then, at close to midnight: *This Grace person: are you going to hurt her?*

Adam Garrett thought long and hard. *No. She made a dent in my heart.* He didn't know if he was lying or not.

Time went by, silence from Gaynor. And after a while, he realised that he half-believed what he'd written. He felt the sting of regret for the lost years. Neet—she'd been a victim too.

He didn't know what he wanted to do—about Neet, to Neet, for Neet. He was tired of running, his nerves were shot. She'd been his only true friend; she was his only chance in life. But at the same time, he'd like to hear her acknowledge that she'd hurt him; say she was sorry about it. At the very least, he really wanted the watch back. If she still had it.

He continued to wait for Gaynor's reply. Maybe she was up there in the hills laughing at his dented-heart bullshit.

When he woke in the morning, there it was. *She came here with her boss. Mandel's Collectibles in Battendorf.*

49

GRACE FOUND HERSELF playing a nervy waiting game. She believed everyone had a story, and hers was always having to move on—when what she really wanted was to settle in one place and make a life there. As things stood, it was stupid to think that Battendorf—her job, her flat, Erin—offered that. For a start, she'd have to give evidence against Brodie Hendren eventually, and what if his lawyers decided to investigate her background before the trial?

She'd found no evidence of fingerprint powder in the granny flat or the shop, but that didn't mean that the police weren't also looking into her background. They seemed to be viewing Hendren's attack on her as incidental to the main story—Hendren and Erin—but someone, somewhere, might decide they wanted to tie up loose ends.

If she ran, though, she'd be more than a loose end. The police would be certain to dig deeply, and the pursuit of her, across country, would be intense. Even if she gave an 'innocent' explanation before she left—that she wanted to look for new job opportunities, or that being shot had traumatised her—it was likely that Swanwick would insist on keeping tabs.

And so she tensed up when Swanwick walked into the shop on a blustery day in early November.

The sergeant's eyes were streaming as she held a tissue to her nose. 'Happens to me every spring,' Swanwick said.

'Me, too,' Erin said.

'What about you?' Swanwick demanded, turning to Grace.

Grace stopped what she was doing, which was tightening and loosening her grip on a soft rubber ball. She did it habitually: watching TV; being driven to work by Erin; serving customers if Erin was out on an errand. Sensations had returned—patchily—but her hand felt most comfortable in its cupped shape. Stretching her fingers was agonising. She'd be able to drive again soon, her fingers curled around the Subaru's steering wheel, but placing her palm flat? Forget it.

'Allergic to work,' she said breezily, glancing through

the window for back-up officers or a paddy wagon out there in the street.

'Just thought you'd both like to know, Mr Hendren has decided to plead guilty.'

Grace, expressionless, decided to wait. She saw that Erin didn't trust the news either.

Swanwick, switching her attention from one to the other, said, 'Not quite the overabundance of joy I was expecting.'

Erin said, 'Brodie's always got an angle.'

Swanwick cocked her head. 'Meaning?'

'Why'd he plead guilty?'

'According to his lawyer, he'll be in a wheelchair for the rest of his life,' Swanwick said. 'He didn't want to go through a trial on top of all that.' She paused: 'Plus he gets a discount on his sentence.'

Erin snorted. '*That's* the Brodie I knew and loved.'

Swanwick looked on amusedly. 'We still don't know where he's been living, and he won't say. Didn't have keys or a wallet on him. Insists he's between addresses.'

Erin shrugged. 'Can't help you, sorry.'

'Not to worry,' Swanwick said. 'And that's me for now. Back to the grindstone.'

Grace heard the disclaimer, *for now*. Then tensed as Swanwick about-faced at the door and came back. 'Forgot to ask, how's the hand going?'

Grace resumed squeezing her rubber ball: tighten, one two three; release, one two three. 'Slowly.'

Swanwick nodded. 'Good to know,' she said, and, with a gesture of finality—a smart little slap of both hands against the countertop—turned to go.

At lunchtime Erin said, 'I've been thinking.'

She said it often these days: plans for the shop, the business. A bigger vehicle, like a Mercedes van. A more professional online presence. Perhaps specialise in just two or three areas. There was more colour in her cheeks, too, and earlier in the week she'd said, 'I've put on a kilo!'

Grace, expecting more of the same now, said, 'Okay…?'

'A massive sale,' Erin said, gesturing at the miscellany that surrounded them. 'Everything that's been here longer than a year. Everything that's pretty but cheap. Everything that's ugly but expensive. The incomplete dinner sets. The chipped vase, even if it is a Meissen.'

She turned to the Blamire Young watercolour, which she'd hung behind the cash register and didn't intend to sell. 'Fine art, quality furniture and good silver, that's who we'll be.'

'Sounds good,' Grace said.

Erin stalked through her shop and rapped her knuckles against the corner cabinet, where Grace had stowed her treasures. 'This ugly thing can go to the tip for a start.'

Grace went red with embarrassment. Erin, twinkling as she came back through the jumble in her new, confident way, said, 'Memories, eh?'

Grace coloured some more. 'Something like that.'

—

As the days passed, Grace dared to hope more confidently, and her mind rarely strayed beyond her flat, the shop and helping Erin price their sale items.

But one morning, as they emerged from the driveway on their way to work, she heard Erin say, 'I've been thinking. It would be best if you found your own place to live.'

Grace felt her heart thump. Her breathing grew irregular. Not knowing what to say, she made her own automatic check of Landau Street: passing cars, parked cars. Nothing had altered overnight, but *this* alteration, being asked to leave, swamped everything.

'Are you…' she managed to say.

Erin shot her a look. Registered the dismay, jammed on the brakes and grabbed Grace's wrist. 'Oh my god, sorry, nothing like that. It's to mark the shift. I'm not getting rid of you.'

'Okay, that's a relief…'

'We work well together, we've become friends, I'd like to formalise a *partnership*—if that's okay with you. I've been thinking about it a lot. We're two independent women. You can't keep living in a poky granny flat at the back of someone's house, you need a place you can call your own. And I no longer need the security of having someone living in that flat.'

Grace began to fit her mind around the changes. 'Yes, makes sense,' she said.

Her independence. A friendly professional distance.

—

But a week later, when she could drive again and was coasting down the main street after delivering an ugly hallstand at fifty per cent off to a faux Cape Cod house near Woodside, she saw a police car pull away from the kerb in front of the shop. They've come for me, she thought. A summons; request to come in for further questioning. Feeling undecided, she continued around to the alley, parked behind the shop and sat there for several minutes.

Erin emerged from the back door, looking stricken. Grace got out, locked the Subaru, crossed hesitantly. 'Everything okay?'

'I heard you pull up. Why didn't you come in?'

She's really upset, Grace thought. 'Waiting for a song to finish.'

'I just had a couple of policemen here.'

'Oh?'

'It's Brodie. He's accusing me of stealing from him. The car'—she nodded at the Subaru—'and money from his accounts.'

'Can he do that?'

'Just when I thought it was all over,' Erin said, weeping now, her new-found assurance vanished. 'The gift that keeps on giving, right?'

'Let's get you inside,' Grace said.

Into the familiar clutter, the afternoon light through the street window, the furniture polish. 'Has he got a case?'

Erin seemed to fold in on herself. 'Kind of,' she said, collapsing into the chair behind the cash register. 'I emptied a small account when I left. And though I paid for the car, it was in his name.' She blushed. 'When I got it registered here, I told motor vehicles that I was Brodie.'

One of those unisex names, Grace thought. 'So what did the police want?'

'A follow-up for the police in Brisbane. They asked me to come in and give a statement.'

Agitation ripped through Grace. 'Your ex is fucking with you, Erin.'

'I know.'

Grace rattled off suggestions: 'Get Sergeant Swanwick onside, get a lawyer, and make sure everyone knows what he did to you.'

But Erin seemed stunned, far away, lost among memories. 'You're probably right,' she said tiredly, as if she'd reached a terminus.

'I *am* right.'

Erin got to her feet. 'I need to go home for a while.'

'I'll take you.'

'No, stay here. Get an Uber home and I'll pay for it.'

As soon as Erin was gone, Grace began researching lawyers. Head down, deeply absorbed, she ignored the customer who entered the shop a few minutes later. Didn't even look up when he said, 'Hello, Neet.'

Grace pirouetted, streaked towards the corridor and slammed the connecting door in his face. A few winged steps to the alleyway door, her weak right hand turning the knob, shoving hard. It moved an inch and sent a jolt through her arm, as if she'd punched a boulder. The shock of it bounced her back. Adam had rolled a dumpbin up against the door.

And he was in the corridor with her now, filling the little space. She whirled around, charged, shrieking and flailing. He hadn't expected that. Retreated a step, his hands up. 'Neet...'

She tried to knee him, striking his thigh. Whacked him left and right and her fingernails clawed. His expression altered: no longer shocked or stunned, he began to punch her steadily: her jaw, her shoulders and breastbone, and a deep, midriff drive that would have doubled her over if she hadn't turned aside at the last moment.

But he'd connected with her hipbone, spinning her around, and their struggle spilled back into the main part of the shop. Grace, straining past an island of back-to-back hallstands to reach the front door, felt his hands snatch at her arms, the neck of her T-shirt. Then his arms were around her waist and she smacked face-down onto the floor. She kicked away, half-crawling now, and he had her by the left foot, wrenching her sandal off. She tottered upright, slammed into a small desk—and there went the handpainted Art Deco vase, French, 1904, with a tiny chip in the handle, $795 marked down to $400, and she saw, too late, that he'd turned the door sign to *Closed* and knew that he'd have locked it, too.

She stumbled to the floor again, got to her knees, and he kicked her, tipping her onto her side. Immediately rolling onto her back, she windmilled her legs at him. His face was so altered: big, red, and his spit was flying as he knocked her legs aside, stood a moment straddling her, then thumped onto her stomach. She flailed at him as he began to smack her face steadily, left and right, bitter curses with each blow.

Her dud hand connected with the side of his head and she cried out, an awful wail, as the pain flared not just in the webbing of her thumb and fingers but also behind the left eye; she didn't know why that would be so.

He froze, as if her cry had shocked him, then grabbed her forearms and pressed them to the floor. Leaned in and said, 'Neet, don't,' his voice urgent.

That sobered her. She stared up at him as he stared down, each gauging what the other would do, until she heaved at him slightly with her hips. He rolled off and scooted away. Sat with his back against a sideboard and watched her.

Exhausted, Grace managed to slump against a club chair: brown leather, ex-Adelaide Club, marked down to $375 according to the sticker she'd slapped on one of the arms that morning. 'You bugged the car.'

'Yes.'

'What do you want Adam? Revenge? Have a laugh about old times?'

'Neet, don't.'

They stared at each other. She said, 'My name is Grace now.'

'I know.'

'How do you know? How did you find me?'

'Doesn't matter.'

It was an awful truth that too much time had passed for her to feel anything. Finding the energy to climb to her feet, she said, 'I'm sorry, for what it's worth.'

A twist to his mouth; a singsong voice: 'Of course you are. It was a different time back then, things change, we're different people now. I quite understand.'

She shook her head at him with dislike. And when he put out his hand for a boost up from the floor, she ignored it. He rolled onto his side and bounced upright neatly and brushed his hands. 'Now what?'

'You tell me. You came looking for me, not the other way round.'

Tiredness rolled through him again. He collapsed onto the club chair. 'What happened to your hand?'

'Hurt it.'

'I saw you that time, the stamp expo in Brisbane.'

'I know.'

'What were you doing there?'

'What do you think I was doing there?' Grace said. She paused. 'I didn't know you'd be there, if that's what you mean.'

He shrugged as if he didn't care. 'My life's gone to shit.'

She didn't tell him about her life.

He said, 'I hated you for years.'

She said nothing. Felt something, though. That she'd loved him. Imperfectly, and a long time ago.

'But then I heard you had a hard time with that cop. Galt. Did you shoot him?'

She didn't reply but remained silent and watchful, her slight body poised in case he turned on her again. She wanted him gone. She didn't know if he would go.

Then he was looking at her with a light in his eyes, not quite rueful, not quite respectful. 'You took the watch that time, right? The Jaeger?'

'Do you want it back?'

That was the simplest thing she'd ever said to him, and he replied simply.

'Yep. It's mine.'

She pulled on a denim jacket and they walked half a block down the street to his car, an old Holden ute. Grace approved: it was invisible. Waiting on the footpath as he walked around to unlock his door, she glanced both ways along the street automatically, thinking that she'd also give him some cash—perhaps quite a bit of cash. It would help to send him away. It would announce a permanent goodbye.

The street was as unremarkable as ever: a bus pulled away, a security van idled outside the bank, a woman pulled a shopping cart, a man pushed twins in a stroller.

And an old red Saab came trundling along the street, the driver peering left and right.

50

GRACE DUCKED BEFORE the Barossa cop could spot her, crouching hard against the flank of the ute.

She heard Adam's bewildered voice: 'Neet?'

'Get in,' she hissed. 'Unlock my door.'

The old Holden rocked on its springs as he settled behind the steering wheel. As soon as her door was open, she piled in, first removing a daypack from the footwell and tucking herself under the dashboard. 'Go!'

Adam turned the ignition key. 'Like to tell me what's going on?'

She looked up at him, wondering what story to give. The sun, still high, angled across the windscreen and lit up his face and torso. He looked skittish, intense, his gaze switching from her to his windows and mirrors as he pulled away from the kerb. 'You saw someone?'

'Just go,' she said. 'Turn right at the roundabout.'

When they were off the main street, she climbed into the passenger seat and strapped herself in. It's over, she thought. She'd been daring to hope...Never dare to hope. She checked her side mirror, then turned her head to peer through the back window. A silver SUV followed by a tradie's van, but no red Saab. Had the cop spotted her? Was he putting the word out? Was he following them, in fact, at a distance? He'd tracked her down as she'd feared he would. He'd approach Erin, advise the local police. After that, her prints would be lifted and checked for sure.

Adam said with a tense laugh, 'Should we be worried?'

There's no 'we' about it, Grace thought. She was just tired of him now. He'd come here looking for justice, and she *was* atoning, but she resented it. All she wanted to do was pay him off, watch him drive away, then—old story—pack up her gear and run. She felt bleak. The lonely months and years ahead.

'Neet? I said—'

'Nothing you need to worry about.'

'Someone's after you?'

Grace checked again: no red Saab. The silver SUV was still there, but the tradie's van was turning off and she saw a black Range Rover and a yellow Beetle loom up in its place.

'Grace?'

'Later,' she muttered, directing him downhill to the leisure centre, then around the little stretch of parkland and into the industrial estate. She pointed. 'Keep going to the end, then turn left at JB HiFi and park outside Officeworks.'

'You're the boss,' he said.

She didn't want to be the boss. She didn't want any kind of relationship with him. Little waves of feelings lapped at her insides: the comfort of her life here; the security of solitude and the open road. She tensed as Adam made the turn, passing a Spotlight and Vacuum City on the left, an Aldi and a Colonial Furniture Barn on the right. Plenty of cars, plenty of tired people shopping at this time of the day, early afternoon. Now they were approaching the Officeworks. Beyond it, behind a high cyclone fence, SecureCo Storage.

'Park here.' She pointed to an empty space between a dusty white van and a small dead tree inside a concrete border, one of many scattered around the centre's carparks. More people entering and leaving the nearby businesses.

She checked the windows and mirrors again—no red Saab—then upended the contents of Adam's daypack into the footwell.

'Jesus, Neet!'

'Wait here.' She reached for her door handle.

He grabbed her arm. She looked into his face, her door

half-open. Saw, eventually, pain and acceptance. 'This is it now,' she said gently. 'We're done.'

He let her go. 'Yes.'

'Okay then.'

With a strap of the daypack on one shoulder, she walked the hundred metres to the storage yard, which sat at the end of a broad, mostly empty parking area. She keyed in a code at the gate. It swung open and she walked through; heard it click shut behind her. The larger storage units—some containing vintage cars or enough furniture to fill a house—were at the front and down the sides. The smaller units—Grace's was the size of a bar fridge—were at the rear. She knelt, unlocked it, and saw that she'd never fit it all into the daypack. Choose, she told herself. Cash, the gold bar, Adam's beautiful watch, the icon, the Klee painting and two sets of ID. Leaving Jason Britton's iPhones, Chagall and lesser coins and stamps, she locked up again and returned to the front gate.

Come back for the rest a few months from now, she told herself, and was halfway across the paved area, her gaze flickering from Adam's old ute to the many nearby vehicles and bag-carrying pedestrians, when she saw a tall man with a hooked face step out of a black Range Rover. He advanced on Adam's side window, a pistol held down against his thigh. She changed direction slightly, cut away from Officeworks and across to Vacuum City. She was thinking, irrelevantly, that the shop's Miele needed a new brush head, when she heard a shot. She froze, ducked, scuttled away. *Was she going to be next?*

Then everything erupted. Shouts, more shots—a short, sharp fusillade—and a swarm of tactical response police. Where had they come from? Confused, badly rattled, Grace huddled behind the rear tyre of the nearest car. Or should she put the engine block between her and the shooting?

A policeman yanked her to her feet. He was padded, masked, helmeted, bristling with belts, pouches and metal. 'I need you to come with me,' he said, his voice harsh with anonymous authority.

51

IT WAS A MOMENT before she realised he wasn't arresting her. The carpark seethed with movement, people ducking and scuttling and some, like Grace, stumbling as they were shepherded across the asphalt by armed policemen.

Her cop was combative, urgent, impatient with her. '*Come on!*' Into the shelter of a service lane that ran behind Vacuum City and other small retailers. '*Move*,' her cop said, practically shoving her towards a huddle of men, women, toddlers and babies in prams beside a delivery bay halfway down. Some were whimpering. All stood close to the wall.

Another shove. Grace whirled around on him. 'What's going on?'

But he was looking away from her, tense with fear or eager for combat, she couldn't tell. Then he snarled, 'Stay put,' without glancing at her and lumbered back the way they'd come. She saw him slow when he reached the corner. Flatten his back against the wall; dart a look at whatever might have been unfolding near Adam's ute.

Grace kept watching. More shots, then the black Range Rover streaked past at the end, heading for the exit, so close to the cop that he jerked back. Both side windows had been shot out, holes peppered the rear, and it rocked and tilted as the passenger-side front tyre smacked over a concrete parking divider. A figure appeared ahead of it, darting out to fling a tyre-shredder across the exit lane. The Range Rover jerked too sharply to the right and collided with a truck that had been barred from entering. Police swarmed, pulled two men out flat onto their faces and cuffed them.

Grace began to retreat further, edging around the people still crouched behind the delivery bay. They didn't notice her, probably didn't care, everything was too volatile. But order would be restored eventually, the whole place shut down. No one in or out until everyone had been questioned. *Why are you here today? How did you get here? Did you come alone?* And if they'd checked the CCTV footage, the questioning would be much sharper. *What did you do at the storage yard? Why didn't you park closer to it?*

What is your relationship to the driver? Do you know the man who shot him?

For Grace was certain that Adam had been shot.

Reaching a delivery bay marked Bubs Warehouse at the far end of the service lane, she took stock. A broad strip of lawn set with small flowering gums separated her from the main road and the parkland and leisure centre beyond. Two hundred metres to her right was an intersecting road and a set of traffic lights. To her left, another entrance to the industrial estate. A police car, its roof bars flashing red and blue, straddled the entry and exit lanes. Armed police stood nearby, some stopping vehicles from entering or exiting, some standing around, alert.

She turned for another scan of the area near the traffic lights on the main road—and a woman was there. Young, scared, her uniform cap slightly tilted by the mass of hair piled beneath it. With her nose piercing and a tattooed bird's wing peeking from beneath her collar, she was a cross between a frightened young police probationer and a street-wise kid. She held up one hand.

'Sorry, madam, it's not safe, you need to move away from here.'

'What's going on?'

'Perhaps head up there?' the young cop said, pointing, her gaze skittering from Grace to the people behind Grace, then to the roadblock, where an ambulance had pulled up, its siren an unearthly dying cry, and back to Grace. 'Madam?'

Grace gazed around wildly, a distressed and bewildered woman who'd just popped in for a bit of shopping. Flinging an arm up at the Bubs Warehouse sign, she said, 'I was in there, looking at prams.' Rubbing her belly, she added, 'I didn't see anything and I don't even know what's happening.'

Now she gestured towards the leisure centre on the other side of the main road. 'Look, my daughter's over there doing kinder gym, she's only four.' She checked the time on her phone. 'If I'm not there when it finishes, she'll start to panic.'

The young constable chewed her bottom lip. Police work had suddenly become very real. She was attending at a major incident, and she'd been asked to make an on-the-spot judgment call.

'Okay, but be careful and don't get in anyone's car. If you get turned back by my colleagues, too bad—there's nothing I can do about it.'

'Thank you, thank you, thank you,' babbled Grace. Turning to go, she added: 'You be careful too.'

Taking advantage of the police car reversing to let the ambulance in, Grace slipped across the road, through a tiny copse of black wattles, and—just in case the young cop was watching—into the leisure centre. Staff members and women in leggings were standing at a window.

'What's going on over there?'

Grace shrugged. 'Not really sure. A fight over drugs? I think they arrested someone.'

She strode into the change rooms as if she belonged there, and they lost interest in her. A shower was running. The air was humid, scented with an unpleasant mix of shampoo and cleaning fluids. A strip of lockers. Cubicles. Wall hooks. And, on a chipped wooden bench, a white T-shirt, a pair of crumpled black tights and a voluminous red cotton hoodie.

Grace removed and destroyed her sim card, hung her denim jacket on a hook and pulled on the red hoodie. Then, with Adam's pack on one shoulder, she strode out, across the foyer and through the main doors. She could hear sirens.

At three that afternoon, Grace test-drove the old, sun-faded red Volvo station wagon that had been parked on the nature strip near Woodside Auctions with a *For Sale* sign in the window ever since the day she'd bought the Whiteley etching. 'Thought I'd never get rid of the blarmy thing,' the elderly owner said, as he accepted her $4,500.

Grace had a story for him—otherwise there was a chance he'd link her to the day's big news story. 'I start nursing next week,' she said, counting hundred-dollar notes into his hand. 'Take me forever on the bus.'

He twinkled at her. Patted the roof. 'This old girl won't let you down,' he said. 'Full service history.'

She let him see her drive north-east, as if deeper into the hills. When she was out of his sight, she cut across to the M1, intending to lose herself in the city. An increased police presence changed her mind; it didn't seem coordinated, just edgy, but she thought there'd be roadblocks. They might even be keeping an eye on anyone heading down to Murray Bridge on their way to Melbourne. When she got to Aldgate, she bought a sim card and some hair dye, and paid for two nights in an Airbnb.

She spent the evening switching between the TV set and her phone, and by midnight she had a vague grasp of what had happened that afternoon. Police from an organised-crime taskforce had intercepted a man named Ivan Varga and two accomplices in the act of committing a violent crime in the small Adelaide Hills town of Battendorf. Shots were fired. Varga died at the scene and his accomplices were arrested. Another man, as yet unnamed, who'd been sitting in a parked car had been taken to the Flinders Medical Centre with a gunshot wound. Police wanted to hear from anyone who had witnessed the shooting or could supply dashcam footage.

The same video clips were repeated for a few hours. Grace even saw the young probationer who'd let her leave the scene. And then a new clip: late afternoon but still daylight, the strip of parking spots outside Officeworks. Police tape fluttering in the wind; numbered tags next to shell casings; crime-scene officers in forensic suits and overshoes; tired, crumpled-looking detectives with lanyards and clipboards.

And Des Liddington, the old Barossa cop. She spotted him in the background, a dumpy figure holding hands with a dumpy woman, talking to a couple of detectives. Then, their elongated shadows striping the SecureCo carpark, Liddington and the woman crossed to the storage yard. Peered in together. Peered up together, their calm, pouchy faces taking in the CCTV cameras above the gate.

The news cut to a breathless reporter standing in front of the emergency department of the Flinders Medical Centre. Grace turned up the volume: the still unnamed gunshot victim was under police guard. Expected to make a full recovery.

She switched off, thinking about Liddington. His doggedness. The way he'd stared at the SecureCo CCTV cameras. He knows I went in there, she thought. She didn't know *how* he knew; but he'd found her and was beginning to put everything together. Perhaps he'd already talked to Erin. Or the bank. Or the woman in the coffee shop—who might have seen her get into Adam's Holden. Or he'd been monitoring her for a few days. Or he'd fastened a tracker to the ute. Or the woman with him—his wife?—had followed them in a separate vehicle.

The next day, Grace reached the city without incident and bought a hi-vis jacket and a set of nurse's scrubs from a dismal little CBD laneway shop called WorkWear near Victoria Square. As she checked herself out in the change-room mirror, she began to think that maybe her story wasn't about the perpetual moving on. Mostly her story was this: dressing as someone else, becoming someone else. Hand-me-downs when she was six years old, a nurse's outfit today.

Who was she?

Back to the Airbnb for her second night, and then, at 6 a.m. on her last day in South Australia, she was smiling efficiently at the policeman seated in the corridor outside Adam's hospital room, bustling past him with the words, 'Bedpan duty!'

The guy laughed. He looked half-asleep. 'Sooner you than me, love.'

Adam was awake, pale, bandaged, and he looked at her so searchingly that she felt sad for him. 'How are we this fine morning?' she called out loud enough for the guard to hear.

Adam croaked, 'Okay.'

His name, according to the clipboard at the end of the bed, was Louis Denton. Fussing about the bed, she murmured, 'Who was Ivan Varga? Why did he shoot you?'

Adam flopped back on his pillow. His thin, pale face was dismal. 'Something I got mixed up with on behalf of someone else.'

Grace felt the heaviness of a tide turning. She knew she shouldn't blame herself for how things had turned out for him, but would things have been different—wiser—if they'd stuck together?

'I've got your watch—and some cash.'

He was alarmed. 'You can't give it to me here. Too

many questions. They'll confiscate it.'

'I know that,' Grace said. She glanced at the doorway: voices and movement. The place was fully awake. 'Will you be okay?'

She saw a change in his face, a new expression settling, that of a man who'd figured out something central in his life. 'I'll need to lie low for a bit,' he said. 'But my prints aren't on file anywhere as far as I know, and my ID is pretty solid—for now, anyway. I told them I thought I was being carjacked, or it was a case of mistaken identity.'

'CCTV,' she said.

He understood. 'I told them you were a hitchhiker I picked up in Murray Bridge on my way here from Sydney. Your phone died, so you asked me to drop you at the nearest Officeworks.'

'How secure is your numberplate?'

'Yeah, well, they've got me there.'

She shot another quick glance at the door. 'Will you be in here long?'

He raised one shoulder. 'I was lucky. As soon as I saw the gun, I wound my window up and jerked away. The bullet got deflected across my chest and down into the side of my hip.'

Grace visualised it, the scorching pathway. Now more voices filled the corridor and she went around the bed again, making tucking-in motions as she murmured feverishly, 'I'll send you everything when you tell me it's safe. Nina Fenwick, on Facebook.'

Fenwick Street. The foster home where it all started.

His smile, when it came, bestowed upon him a layer of beauty.

52

GRACE FILLED THE tank of her Volvo and drove through the day, stopping only for petrol and food. She took a long, dog-leg route to Melbourne, first down to Mount Gambier, then east along the coast of Victoria. Her head was swimming with tiredness, everything grated, by the time she found herself battling peak-hour traffic in West Brunswick.

Finding a parking spot on a tight street of crouching terraces, she shrugged into the hi-vis jacket, pulled a blue Mount Gambier souvenir cap low over her face, and walked through to Lygon Street. She should sleep—but where?—and yet she also needed to walk for a while; her aching body demanded it. And she might already be too late.

The driver's licence and other papers she'd found in Brodie Hendren's wallet took her to a squat five-storey block of glass and concrete. She circled it, noting only two ways in, both electronic: a large door on Lygon Street, leading to a bank of tenants' post-boxes and a pair of lifts in a small lobby, and a side-street metal shutter barring access to the underground carpark. She was going to be captured on camera whatever she did, but figured she was less likely to encounter anyone if she came in via the carpark. Aiming Hendren's key fob at a wall sensor, she waited, and presently the shutter door lurched into action, folding upwards.

She ducked her head and was in, down a ramp and into a cavernous space. Too silent, too dimly lit, the empty parking spots too fraught. And too much concrete, grey, stained and roughly cast, the air too thick with engine exhausts. A confusion of corners and pillars, so that it took her a couple of minutes to locate the lift doors, hunched inside a sour little alcove. She slipped her hands into flesh-coloured latex gloves, pressed the up button and waited a moment for the lift to arrive.

A minute later, the door slid open at the top floor and she stepped out into a narrow corridor. Face averted, she strode to a T-junction at the end—walking as if she owned the joint but feeling breathless.

She'd been doing this kind of thing all her life, but today the walls were closing in.

Turning left, she realised she was going the wrong way and doubled back; took the corridor on the right. Found Hendren's door. Knocked sharply, waited, knocked again, even though her senses told her clearly that no one was in the flat. Now the key fob. The lock disengaged. Stepping into stale air and muted traffic noise, she couldn't help but think of Landau Street, with its fresh air and bird calls, and how she could never go back to any of it.

She made a preliminary scout-around. Immediately found three netsukes on a bookshelf. One look told her they were good copies, moulded plastic, worth about twenty bucks each. Hendren's way of safeguarding the real pieces?

She searched more methodically now. Curious to note that Hendren owned two vacuum cleaners, one a cordless stick, the other an upright, she took both apart and found the valuable netsuke figurines where she might have hidden them, each tucked into a sandwich bag in an unemptied clump of grey fluff in the upright machine's dust bag. She unwrapped them one by one. Wood and ivory. Old. She tucked them into the backpack.

The flat's epicentre seemed to be a large room furnished with a filing cabinet, a wall cupboard and four computer monitors on an L-shaped desk. She left-clicked each mouse: each machine whirred into life—Hendren hadn't shut them down. Three went straight to the log-in page; the fourth to a split screen showing four rooms of a house or a flat. A woman sat on a sofa in one panel, her foot propped on a coffee table. She was painting her nails.

A live feed, Grace realised. Under the monitor was a well-thumbed spiral notebook—the only paperwork anywhere on the big desk. A name had been scrawled on the cover: *Brie Haven*. On the first inside page was the woman's name again, along with an address in Kew and her birth date, phone number and email address. On succeeding pages, a log of her movements—toilet, shower, dressing, breakfasting, leaving, returning, changing, pouring a drink, rolling and smoking a joint, dinner, watching TV, using a vibrator.

Grace photographed the page of contact information, then kept searching. She doubted that an IT guy like Hendren would stick a Post-It full of passwords to the door of his fridge, but he hadn't bothered to conceal anything else. Folders of concentration-camp photographs in his filing cabinet. Glassine bags of SS badges, rings and uniform buttons in a desk drawer. An old army trunk containing a Luftwaffe pilot's cap, a dagger in a scabbard, an overcoat bearing the yellow star of David, and a pair of Zyklon B gas canisters.

All Grace wanted to do was leave. She could hardly bear to check the wall cupboard. Here she found glassine envelopes containing locks of hair, and a shallow cardboard box of documents: a crayon drawing in a manila folder marked *I Milat*, a handwritten poem titled 'Division H Jailhouse Blues' and signed Chopper, and a birth certificate in the name of Derek Percy.

That left the bedroom and the main living area. Plenty

of Hendren's clothes, bills and receipts, none of it useful, but she did find Erin's Thea Proctor woodcut above the TV set and, in a bedside cupboard, two cheap Chinese Android phones, two old iPhones and half-a-dozen sim cards. She bagged them with the netsukes and the spiral notebook and left the building.

Brie Haven lived in an old-style flat in a block of four on a leafy street in Kew. First slipping the notebook into the mail slot marked *B H*, Grace then drove to a shopping street in nearby Hawthorn, where she installed one of Hendren's sim cards and called Haven's number.

A cautious voice said, 'Hello?'

'I just put something in your letterbox. Are you at home?'

'Pardon? Who is this?'

'Never mind. Are you at home?'

'Ummm...Yes.'

'Check your letterbox,' Grace said. 'Call me back when you're ready.'

She waited, watching early-evening pedestrians in all of their shapes and sizes wandering in and out of the shops or hurrying home from work. She felt a swell of desolation. Was she doing more harm than good, letting a woman know she'd had a role in a sick man's fantasy?

Haven called back in distress. 'Who are you? Where did this come from?'

'Do you have a pen and paper?'

Silence, as if Haven wanted to argue with her. Then the sounds of a phone being set aside, and footsteps, clothes rustling, a drawer closing. Finally, a voice. 'Okay.'

'The notebook was kept by a man named Brodie Hendren.'

'That weirdo? I haven't had anything to do with him since last May.'

'He's in hospital in Adelaide, under police guard. He can't hurt you, he's incapacitated, but you might want to take legal action against him.'

'For stalking me?'

'Well, worse than that. Look at the notebook again. He installed cameras all through your place.'

Another silence, Grace visualising Haven on her sofa, looking around fearfully.

Haven stuttered, 'I don't...I mean...'

Grace broke in, reciting Hendren's address. 'It's a flat. All the evidence you'll need against him is there, but you should get onto it before he sends anyone in to clear the place out.'

'Yeah, but how—'

'Tell the police. Right away. And they should confer with the South Australia police, who, up until now, haven't known where he lives. They'll want to search his place, believe me. It's full of interesting stuff.'

Haven began to say, 'Okay,' but Grace cut the call, removed and snapped the sim card, got out of her car and dropped the pieces into a rubbish bin.

Mid-evening found her seated at the table of a rental caravan in Berwick with a new sim card installed, setting up a Facebook account in the name of Nina Fenwick. Then she did some research into Edo period netsukes similar to those she'd found in Brodie Hendren's flat. As far as she could tell, they were worth a total of at least $250,000. Erin would know where and how to sell them.

She posted the first netsuke, along with the Thea Proctor, in Bairnsdale and the second in Canberra a month later, together with a handwritten note: 'Please consider Tracey Dinakis and her refuge.'

The third, the boar, was hers for now.

And so the weeks passed. Lonely, missing the life she'd left behind, Grace slept in caravan parks, small-town pubs and in national-park campgrounds, on a foam mattress in the rear of her station wagon. Monitoring the news every day, she learned that the firearm used to shoot Adam had been tied to two murders, and that a cache of valuables stolen from a property in the Barossa Valley had been discovered in a storage depot in the Adelaide Hills.

Then a story about Adam. Police were keen to know the whereabouts of a man named Louis Denton, who had escaped custody during treatment at the Flinders Medical Centre.

She reached Brisbane eventually, scouted around, and found a collector who paid her $82,000 for her boar. By now the Volvo was losing oil badly, its gearbox was slipping and a wheel bearing had become alarmingly noisy, so she traded it in for a hybrid Toyota.

And then, two weeks later, the word *Neet,* via Facebook Messenger.

She replied: *I'll always remember life at number 4*.

His response: *Especially since we lived at number 13.*

Satisfied, she wrote, *We must catch up when I'm next in your neck of the woods.*

Nothing until the next day, when he texted her a mail-drop address in Perth. By now she was in Noosa. She found a stationery store, wrapped the Jaeger-LeCoultre watch and twenty grand in cash inside bubble wrap and sent it by express post. Three days later, Adam texted her a thumbs-up emoji and an x.

Something final about just one kiss.

Grace felt sad, philosophical...glad. She deleted the Facebook account and destroyed the sim card.

She wondered, as she drove on, if she'd always live this solitary, foursquare pattern. Steal something, sell it, stow the proceeds somewhere safe. Take a break, then do it all over again. As if a new life hadn't come within her grasp recently. A normal life, even if informed by her *ab*normal life—the knowledge, the confidence; the ways she walked and talked.

Maybe one day, if her old life retreated, she'd feel able to call herself Nina, a name that had lurked in her subconscious since she was very young. Before the orphanage and foster homes of western Sydney. Perhaps it was her birth name? Or her mother's name; her grandmother's. Not that she could remember a woman's embrace from that time, fragrant, indifferent or unwelcoming. If Nina was her birth name, it had been lost in the paperwork; lived only in her mind.

Up the eastern seaboard Grace went: a passenger in the life of a woman who mixed and matched sim cards and IDs, leaving traces as impermanent as footprints in the sand. Hitching a ride, in the expectation that one day, somewhere, she'd be doing the driving. Whoever she was.